Advance praise for Linda Lenhoff and
LIFE À LA MODE

"In her zesty literary debut, Linda Lenhoff serves up a warm slice of twentysomething life laced with a satisfying blend of sugar and spice, saucy dialogue, and a sprinkling of sharply drawn secondary characters. Readers are sure to relish *Life à la Mode* and will likely be left craving seconds."

—Wendy Markham, author of *Slightly Single*

"The satisfaction of a great slice of pie without any of the calories. *Life à la Mode* is sweet, rich, and tasty. Read and enjoy!"

—Lynne Hinton, bestselling author of *Friendship Cake*, *Hope Springs* and *Forever Friends*

Life à la Mode

Linda Lenhoff

KENSINGTON BOOKS
http://www.kensingtonbooks.com

STRAPLESS BOOKS are published by

Kensington Publishing Corp.
850 Third Avenue
New York, NY 10022

ISBN 0-7582-0493-0

First Kensington Trade Paperback Printing: September 2003
10 9 8 7 6 5 4 3 2 1

Printed in the United States of America

To Michael and Casey Everitt
for making my life à la mode

Thanks à la Mode

I am grateful to my writing teachers who read with open hearts: thank you Dennis Palumbo, Stephen Cooper, and the spirit of Lynn Luria-Sukenick. Special thanks to my MFA thesis advisor, Jerry Bumpus, for all of his motivating support and his many kind words.

Thank you to my friends and readers of the early drafts for every comment written in the margins, especially Kim Everett, Renée Swindle, Jennifer Ball, and Beverly Ball. Special thank-yous to Jinny Chun, Cindy Lambert, Lynn Sassenrath, and Jill Yesko for years of friendship, cups of tea, and talk about writing, and to Christina Pitcher for all those things plus copy editing in times of need.

A very special thank-you to Sally Hill McMillan, my agent, for embracing this book and its characters and finding a home for them, just as promised, for which she has my eternal gratitude and years of lavender to come. Thank you to my editor, John Scognamiglio, for making this book his own and asking all the really hard questions.

My fondest thanks and hellos to everyone who worked in the production editing and art departments at Alan R. Liss Publishers way back when, especially Rick Mumma and Angioline Loredo, for making the place so sweet to look back on.

And finally, thank you to Michael and Casey Everitt for daily doses of encouragement, love, and popcorn, and for being my family.

Chapter 1

I Love a Rat

When it's been raining nonstop like this, I sometimes find myself walking around my studio apartment, following imaginary diagonal pathways until I come right up against an off-white wall. Then I'll turn and discover a new path, until eventually I get to a window, with the sound of rain on the glass just like the tapping of fingernails on a desk. I scan the street for something unfamiliar, but it's all the same outside—even the purple and red flags on top of the restaurant across the street still hang there, sad and dripping wet. The rain is beginning to seep into my windowsills in dark, sooty streaks. As if five days of rain weren't bad enough, now I'm going to have to clean.

I've finished with my exercise for today, which involves going downstairs to get the mail. Really, I do try to breathe in and out properly, lifting my knees high as I journey up the four flights. The stack of mail is about six inches high, which I can stretch to last several hours, if the requests for donations are really detailed. Not to mention time spent figuring out which parts of the junk mail are recyclable. This is how I fill a Saturday morning.

I've been trying to sew new curtains for my apartment, blue and white ones. Actually, "new" curtains isn't quite right, since I don't have old curtains, just not-so-cheerful white shades. I'm using my mother's old Singer, and it probably would work very well if I knew anything about sewing. I think it's the thunder, though, that keeps making it sew off course.

When the phone rings, I count to five, so as not to seem overanxious, before grabbing it and saying hello.

"Good morning, Holly dear. Busy?" It's my mother.

"Hello—Mom—no," I say, like a mantra. I pull the fabric out from under the machine's needle. It's sewn to itself in a couple of places.

"Well, I called to ask you to join your sister and me for lunch today," she says, and I think I hear nail-filing in the background. "My treat," she adds, as if waving a Baby Ruth over my head. Come to think of it, I'd really like a Baby Ruth right now.

I turn to my stack of mail and start opening. It's good to have something to distract you when you're talking to your mother. So you don't say any of the less positive things you may have thought of in thirty years. Not that our relationship is bad, but sometimes I feel it's best to keep part of my brain occupied while dealing with family.

"I thought I'd just stay in and do some things around the house," I tell her, not exactly lying.

"Well, I'm sure your apartment could use a little tidying. What's that ripping sound?"

"Oh, I'm opening about a week's worth of junk mail," I say. "Looks like I may have qualified for about two hundred and fifty million dollars in prize sweepstakes."

"That would be nice, dear. Then you could buy a new dress, for special occasions like lunch with your mother and sister."

Now I think I hear her shaking a bottle of nail polish,

that little ball inside hitting the glass. My mother refuses to allow anyone else to do her nails. I refuse to stop biting mine.

"Yes, well," I start, "you'll have to settle for the old, shabbier me. At least until Ed McMahon calls."

"I really think you should come to lunch," she says, "so that you can listen to your sister brag about her engagement. If we don't listen to her, she'll bother total strangers with it, you know." She's right, of course.

"I don't know," I say, "I had to listen to the other five engagement stories. Let her tell it to strangers. That's what subways are for."

I examine a large padded envelope in my stack of mail, shaking it, hopeful it will be something wonderful I ordered from a catalog and have forgotten about. Something paid for. Inside, I find a corkscrew, no note, no receipt.

"By the way, Mom, you haven't sent me any kitchen utensils lately, have you?"

"No, why, is there something you need?" My mother can be so sweet at times.

"No," I say, "I just came across something that seemed sort of out of place."

"In your kitchen, what a surprise," she teases. "Anyway, I also called to include you in our dinner plans for tonight."

"Dinner, gee, I—"

"Ronny and I are going to that new little French place near you in the Village, and we just happen to have reservations for three. Very hard to get, chance of a lifetime!"

My mother has recently begun dating, or at least dining with, a very tall gray-haired man who insists that I call him Ronny. Ronny sounds to me like a name for a three-year-old. Still, it's good to see Mom dating—and eating—these days. My father left three years ago to go live in Texas with Sophie, his third cousin twice removed, or something like that. They started chatting at the family reunion and have been together ever since. None of us likes to talk about it.

I excuse myself from dinner, though. Ronny, I know, likes to stab his fish with a fork, hold it up, and yell "Caught ya!" Seems he likes to fish.

"Sorry, Mom, busy tonight." An out-and-out lie.

"Oh? Do you have a date? Not that it's any of my business, but it is Saturday night, you know. Date night for millions of young people. Or so I've heard."

"I think that's just a nasty rumor promoted by women's magazines and toothpaste companies," I tell her. "I'm fairly sure that most of us are far too busy to date on Saturday nights, what with all those magazines and toothpaste ads to look at."

"So you'll be by yourself. Eating cold leftovers by the TV, no doubt."

Actually, I'm out of leftovers. "No, no," I say, "I'm going to have a good hot meal. Here, I'm taking some food out of the freezer right now."

In a sudden desire for honesty, I move into my small kitchen and open the freezer, which is frozen over by a solid block of ice. A noise escapes from me.

"What was that?" Mom asks. "I'm afraid to think what may be in that freezer of yours. You shouldn't eat anything over five years old, you know, dear." I think I hear my mother giggle.

Quick thinker that I am, I grab my newfound corkscrew and start hacking away at the ice. After all, there could be ice cream in there.

"So is there more, Mom? Or would you just like me to leave the phone by my ear and you can pester me awhile?"

"Well, I wanted to remind you to be nice to your sister when you see her, like at lunch, if you'd agree to come."

"Did you call the waiter and ask him to be nice too? How about the maître d'?"

"My next two calls," Mom says.

I take a big swing and knock off a piece of ice. Unfortunately, I think I've hit Freon, too.

"What's that hissing sound, dear?" My mother once heard my watch ticking when I was seated three people away from her at a Mets game. She asked me if I couldn't muffle it somehow.

"Hissing?" I say. "Must be a bad connection. The rain. Thanks for all the invitations, Mom."

"What are mothers for? Bye, dear," she says finally. "Wear a coat."

I stuff the freezer door shut, and a chunk of ice falls onto my socks.

After sewing my curtains to my bathrobe, I decide to go to lunch. I'm sure my mother expected no less.

It's a neighborhood place not far from my apartment, and when I walk in I'm thrilled by the smell of hot soups and stews coming from the kitchen. A young woman with well-applied lipstick leads me to a table where my sister, Janie, waits, flipping through a *Brides* magazine. I really love my sister who, at twenty-six to my almost thirty-one, is just under five years younger than I. She sits there with her dark blonde hair curling politely but not obnoxiously, in that way little sisters with perfect hair often seem to do. My own hair, brown and baby-fine, refuses to curl in any way, polite or otherwise, although on this rainy day, each strand feels as if it's headed in a different direction. Still, seeing her, I'm reminded again that I often very much want to pull on the left side of her hair and drag her around the room in that affectionate yet commanding way I had as a child.

Janie looks up. "Holly, I'm engaged!" she says, waving a sparkling left hand in my face. It's a large ring, even by Janie's standards. And she has standards, because she really has been engaged five times before. I think she has a long-standing subscription to *Brides*.

My sister holds an important position in a gallery downtown where the artwork is made of glass. Large, ambiguously formed glass sculptures that all seem dangerously breakable to me. I'll admit I do admire the way Janie flies around the gallery on high heels. At openings she's always telling me to mingle, but she doesn't seem to realize I'm really just afraid to move.

"Congratulations again," I say.

"Now listen," Janie starts, "I know I'm early. I realize that, so don't start in about my always being early. I'm not always early, I'm just early today."

"I'm glad that's settled," I say. "Where's Mom?"

"*She's* late."

I notice my mother coming in behind the heavily lip-sticked girl, who is now staring at her well-polished nails as she leads Mom in. Even the lipstick girl doesn't have to watch where she's walking, which makes me wonder about my sense of balance. But before I can think too much about it, I get a look at my mother's outfit as she takes off her coat. She's wearing a little sailor suit, a cottony white blouse with a blue bow tie, a blue short split skirt. Mom brushes kisses against both of us. I catch Janie's eye, and Janie makes a "hmmm" sound and writes something down in her daybook, the one I gave her as an engagement present several times back.

"Sorry I'm late," Mom says, smoothing out a napkin, then smoothing back her unmussed hair, which is a natural-looking shade of light brown somewhere between Janie's dark blonde and my brown, "enhanced" she always tells us by her hairdresser. "There's just so much to do these days. Have you ordered? You really could have gone ahead and ordered."

Janie and I seem to both be staring at the blue bow.

"You both look very nice," Mom says.

"You look, ah, nice, too," I try.

"Sporty," Janie comes up with.

"I thought we all agreed today was going to be casual?" Mom asks, although it feels a little more like a dare.

"You're right," I say, giving in, "and you really look—"

"Casual," Janie says, "perfectly casual. Nothing wrong with that."

I pick up a menu that isn't quite large enough to hide behind. I knew there was a reason I usually avoided this restaurant. I'm hoping no one will comment on my appearance, which consists mostly of very old black leggings I wear all weekend long, even though they often pick up all sorts of fuzz, although I'm not sure from what. On top I wear an equally old sweater that I think is fuzzy on purpose, and since it's a dark gray, it hides all types of smudges really well. Janie sits dressed in a better class of casual wear, a light blue sweater with tiny flowers on it, and light creaseless pants that I'm sure I'd get dirty in the first minute. Hers look surprisingly clean. I watch as my mother orders the marshmallow and cranberry soufflé, and Janie orders the Surprise Seafood Stew. I order a plain green salad and bowl of vegetable soup, then notice them staring at me.

"That's all right, dear," my mother says, "we're family. We won't make fun of the food you eat. Only the way you eat it."

Mom and Janie share a laugh as I wonder why it is that Janie, the younger sibling around here, isn't the one getting teased. I try to boost myself by remembering that Janie has no sense of humor. Right now, she's showing Mom the ring.

"You certainly have a nice collection," Mom says to Janie, who does not believe in returning engagement rings. I guess you could call it teasing if Janie didn't take it so seriously.

"Well," Janie says boldly, "what shall we talk about?"

"How about men?" my sailor-suited mother offers.

"Maybe we should try something safer," I suggest. "How about the weather. Has anyone noticed it's been raining for about three weeks straight?"

"I don't want to talk about the weather," Janie says. "It's so depressing."

"Ronny finds the rain romantic," Mom says. "He told me it's as if it's just he and I alone together, with the rain protecting us from the world."

"Wow," Janie says. "He said that?"

"Two or three times," Mom says. "You know, he forgets."

"Well, now—" I try changing topics, unsuccessfully.

"Actually, Ronny and I are going to take a little trip."

"How exciting!" Janie says, always interested in potential new honeymoon ideas. "Where to?"

"We're going on a four-month African safari," Mom says excitedly.

"Four months," I almost yell, "isn't that a little extreme?"

"It sounds fabulous," Janie says, jotting something in her daybook again.

"It is," Mom says. "We'll be seeing over forty different kinds of wild animals up close."

"How close?" I want to know. Well, maybe I don't.

"We'll be sleeping in tents with mosquito nets over our cots, cooking in the wild, discovering nature in her truest sense," Mom continues. "At least, that's what the brochure says."

"I'll have to plan a long engagement, then, so you'll be back in time to help with the plans," Janie says.

"Oh yes, dear, the long engagements are always nicest." Mom rolls her eyes at me as Janie continues making notes.

Our food arrives, and my plain salad is covered with pink flowers. I'm not too sure what to do about this.

"Did you know," Mom asks us, "that there are about two hundred kinds of biting insects in Africa?"

* * *

I walk back to my apartment through every muddy puddle, just to hear the splosh, and settle in for a long afternoon filled with thunder and lightning, which can be annoying because it ruins the TV reception. I spend much of the day working on my curtains and watching golf. It's nice to think that somewhere it's sunny and there are large numbers of men in short-sleeved shirts. I get a big kick out of watching those men wade through the sand traps, like little kids trying to walk on the beach. Finally, I take a hot shower and imagine being in the tropics somewhere, where the rain is warm and misty.

To accompany my new mood, I put on an old *South Pacific* soundtrack I used to listen to as a child, and I pull out last week's travel section, where I'm invited to See Mexico's Many Worlds, Travel the Kona Coast, and Visit the Picturesque Paradise of Puerto Vallarta. I look around my apartment and suddenly see it as a white sandy beach, the uneven pieces of fabric all over the place as beach towels spread on the sand, my cup of orange tea a fruity drink with an umbrella. An ad in the paper insists that I "Enter Now" for a chance to win a $1,000 pearl necklace, and I grab a pen, ready to fill in my winning entry, sure that a pearl necklace is the proper accessory for an evening on the cool sand.

I hear a knock at the door. Someone delivering my pearl necklace, no doubt. Actually, it's Josh, to whom I used to be married. Yes, I married a man named Josh. The dark hair's a little curlier around his ears, but the face is generally the same. I used to take care of those curls personally. No doubt, Mrs. Mazzalo, my downstairs neighbor, let Josh into the building, as she's fond of chatting with all members of my extended family, even Josh. Not that I've ever mentioned the details of how we're not exactly related anymore.

"Hiya, Holly," Josh says, bouncing his head from one side to the other, trying hard not to look wet. "Rain getting you down?"

I swear, just then, there's a huge clap of thunder. Swear to God.

"Your timing seems to be improving," I say.

I let him in. He's stopped by a few times before, since the divorce. The rainy season seems to bring him out a little more often, I've noticed, kind of the way it does with worms. Although that may sound a little harsh. We've been divorced now for four years, after having been married an equal but longer-seeming time, and at what most people shook their heads at and called "such a young age," which for us was twenty-two, not that math is my strong suit. Still, there's no talking to college sweethearts who met sharing a table at the campus coffeehouse and felt that this was more meaningful than all the other meetings going on at all the other tables. I can still remember that thick coffee smell combined with the scent of canvas-covered textbooks, and that air of accomplishment you get from sitting next to someone with just the right shade of brown hair, not to mention matching brown eyes. Oddly enough, Janie was the one who tried the hardest to talk me out of matrimony, not that I can explain this in light of her love for all things bridal.

Josh pulls out a picnic basket he's been hiding behind his back.

"Thought I'd bring a little sunshine indoors," Josh says. Honest, he says stuff like this.

"Well, that's very thoughtful of you," I say. "Corny, but thoughtful."

Josh starts unpacking little boxes that smell of the delectable spices you can only get from take-out.

Josh holds up a bottle of wine. "How's this look?" he asks.

"Very timely." Experience reminds me that Josh has great taste in wine, if only fair taste in clothes. His dull gray jeans are frayed at the bottom and fading in the seat in an almost endearing way. I just know his socks have holes in them. And his glasses are covered with spots.

"You wouldn't happen to have anything to open this up with?"

I give him a look and go to the kitchen for the new corkscrew that so mysteriously arrived only this morning. With no note. This is new, a technique bordering on the romantic coming from Josh. Josh planning ahead. Josh was never the type to plan romantic dinners or outings, preferring what he called spontaneity and what I came to feel was just a lack of effort. It's not that he wasn't romantic in his way, or, say, that he didn't surprise me with presents, it's just that he didn't like to give that much thought to them. Like the time he found a heart-shaped leaf on the ground at the last minute and handed it to me when I mentioned it was Valentine's Day. It's not that it wasn't a beautiful leaf, and I did press it, and I'll admit I still have it. And I did appreciate the gesture, plus the ability to spot a heart-shaped leaf just when you need one. It's just that Josh really believed it was more romantic this way—the less thought, the better. I guess I stopped seeing the romanticism in it. So this planning ahead catches me by surprise. I hand him the corkscrew and wonder how I could have missed his handwriting on the package.

"Would this do?"

"Now, that'll come in handy," he says, looking it over. "Gee, where'd you get that?"

"I can't imagine," I say. "It arrived unexpectedly."

"Good things often do," Josh actually says. He moves the furniture around to make a picnic site.

"We need a blanket to keep the ants away," Josh says.

"You underestimate my ants' determination," I say, but I reach for one of my drape fabrics anyway. It's washable, I figure. And it looks kind of cute on the floor like that.

"You knew I was coming," Josh says.

I pull a dust ball off the floor. "I've been cleaning all day."

We begin picking at hot pieces of chicken and cobs of corn. Josh reaches for my travel section.

"Planning a vacation?"

"No, just dreaming about someplace warm, with a beach and no rain," I say.

"We took a vacation at the beach once, remember?"

I don't. "Where?"

"On Long Island, you remember."

"Josh, we went in October. It was freezing." He couldn't get away before then, as he was desperately trying to finish yet another research paper. Another late research paper.

"You had that cute little red swimsuit," Josh says, reminiscing.

"Yeah, but I could only wear it for about ten minutes, and only while standing directly in front of the heater. We should have gone someplace warm, Josh."

"But we had the whole beach to ourselves, and the room was always warm. Always very warm," he says. "You just forget."

Maybe I do. "I remember missing our train."

"And staying an extra day!" Josh says. "And getting our kite stuck in the telephone wires."

"That was awful," I say.

"No, it was great." He seems convinced about this.

"It did rain every single day," I tell him, and I'm sure of this.

"Yeah," Josh says, "lots of rainbows."

I don't answer him for a minute. "Let's not talk about rain anymore."

So we don't. Instead, we turn on one of those Lifestyles

of the Rich shows, not the original show, but a copy of it that features people who aren't quite so rich anymore. We leave the sound on low, and watch tan women water-ski in a land far, far away, to the tropical music still playing on my stereo. Let's just say it's an evening of multimedia events, with no more talk about the weather, which becomes increasingly fair and mild, a tingling low-pressure zone, at least indoors.

When I wake up the next morning, I'm on my couch, wrapped in layers of blue-and-white fabric. Josh has gone, having left behind a plastic flower in the now-empty wine bottle. I do wonder where he found such a thing, where he hid it in his clothing, which I thought I'd gone through fairly thoroughly. I wonder if a real flower would have suggested something more serious, or only more transitory. Maybe I should consider what all this means, exactly what the consequences are of being caressed through the night by a badly dressed mathematician, especially one I used to be married to. He has dropped by a handful of times over these years, but this is the first time he's caused a weather disturbance, let's say. And not an unpleasant one. And maybe one I'm ready to continue. Still, is it a starting point, a turning point, or one of those other points that are supposed to be so meaningful in life, the kind of things that family, friends, and therapists push you toward or warn you against, often at the same time? None of these thoughts stays in my mind for long, I'm afraid. I'm sure I should be much more concerned, but instead I go to one window and raise my shade, and streams of sunlight come blasting through, finally. I stand there a moment, letting the sun warm me through the pieces of fabric, which may someday cover the windows. Then again, maybe they've already served their purpose just fine.

Chapter 2

Screaming at Your Seat-Back Tray

It's no secret that my dad took off from a family reunion with Sophie, a distant cousin we can't quite seem to connect to the family.

"You're old Aunt Ethel's little girl, right?" my father asked her at the picnic reunion.

"No . . ." she said with a laugh, then tasted the side of her wineglass with her tongue.

"You're related to that guy, what's his name?" I turned to my dad for help. "Used to swallow pennies for the kids?"

"Bertie!" my dad said.

"Noooo, getting warmer," Sophie indicated, twisting her purple bubblelike beads round and round in her hand and occasionally bringing one up to her lips as if to bite it, or maybe kiss it.

Getting warmer was pretty much as specific as Sophie got—I still don't know how she's our cousin, but she swears she is. I don't entirely believe her, but I wonder why anyone would insist upon an association with our family if she didn't need to. She and my dad played the guessing game for hours, then seemed to disappear from the party. These are not happy memories.

* * *

For my father's fifty-fifth birthday, he has sent me a round-trip ticket to Houston, in hopes I'll break down and visit for the weekend. I've seen him since the picnic, of course, on his quick visits back to New York, but I feel a strain with him, something pulling at me that says, Hey, here's a man who has run off, who has not exited the scene gracefully. I'm often torn between wondering how friendly I should be and wondering what kind of person I am that I would bother wondering such a thing. I think the two worries end up canceling each other out, and probably I behave around him pretty much the way I always have. I hope this, anyway.

My sister, Janie, also received an invitation to visit, but she returned her ticket Federal Express, sending a polite yet deceitful note about not being able to get off work.

"Besides," Janie told me over the phone, "I have an appointment to look at bridal gowns that day. They're very exclusive."

"I'm thinking of going," I said.

"I also have loyalty and a sense of moral righteousness," my little sister said.

That's why you've been engaged six times, I thought but did not say.

Better not to have married any of the previous five, I know Janie thinks, than to have divorced, which she has some kind of fervent religious aversion to, not that we have any particular religion. She holds Dad responsible for our parents' divorce—clearly, he had a lot to do with it. Oddly though, she seems to blame me for my own divorce, not Josh, although she always seemed unsure about Josh. She always seemed to stand a bit too far away from him in conversations, as if he smelled a little musty. And his forgetfulness, or the way he just didn't seem to try, as I came to see it, that got to all of us, after a while, until I couldn't take anymore. Not that it was easy to leave, and it made me wonder about how my father could have left my mother, as he had so many more years invested, but it also made me a little less willing to judge my dad, somehow. A little less willing than Janie, at least. I can imagine what Janie would think about my spending the night with Josh—although it's been over a week since that event, with no sign of Josh. I can just see Janie wriggling up her nose at the thought, then shaking her head back and forth quickly, trying to clear the image from her mind much the way you clear an unpromising picture from an Etch-a-Sketch.

"Would you question my undying love and affection if I take a trip, hypothetically speaking, to see my father?" I long-windedly ask my mother, in her apartment, where she's lining up empty suitcases for her extended trip to Africa. She's pulled out her eighth bag.

She thinks for a moment.

"Would you question my good taste if I were to tell you that Ronny and I spent several days together in a mud bath in a very exclusive resort upstate?" my mother counters.

"Um," I respond ambivalently. I'm pretty sure I don't want to hear the details of this.

"It was fabulous. Took years off my upper arms," she says, pulling back her sleeves to show me her fairly tight upper arms.

"About Dad?" I venture.

My mother looks at me, then takes hold of my short sleeves to peek at my own upper arms, which aren't half bad for someone who considers pouring a glass of water as weight-lifting. Really, they make those water bottles so heavy. She nods at my arms, impressed.

"You don't have to tell me everything you do, dear. That's why God gave us therapists. I still love you for free."

In other words, I have her permission. My mother's never been one of those "Tell me everything" moms. I'm sure there's plenty about this mud-bath experience she's not telling me, which she feels might somehow be more than I can handle. We all have our little secrets, most of which are only important to the bearers, things that delight us to think about but don't do well in translation to others.

And there's one or two things we could all stand to forget, hurts and betrayals, my father's disappearance with a blonde cousin, my older brother's death on my college graduation day. Actually, he only went into a coma that day, following his motorcycle accident, but he died the next. It was all so mixed up with the joy we all felt about graduation, which evaporated instantly, then the feelings about my brother, who'd skipped college and was trying to go his own way with computer programming, and was just starting to get some great work. My brother, John, older than me by four and a half years—just enough to keep us from being close, I always felt—was popular with his friends but always a little distant with us, with me and especially Janie. I could tell he cared, especially about my mother, but he still didn't seem to offer much advice, or pal around with me nearly as much as I would have liked. I always thought we would grow into that relationship, so it hit me hard when he died so suddenly. I was lucky to have Josh in my life, I remember feeling at the time. And maybe my parents weren't getting along all that well even then. I roll these things over in my mind, in some little part of it I like to think of as just above my right ear, the historical part of the brain, where logic doesn't stand a chance. But these aren't things we much talk about, my mother and I, except (as she says) with therapists every once in a while, and, on occasion, with total strangers.

*   *   *

And with Maria. My best friend for longer than I can quite believe, Maria knows all my details, including that I once removed a mole from my foot all by myself. Although I won't go into exactly how I did it. Maria and I met in college biology class freshman year, where on the first day, I managed to let my test tube fall to the ground. For such a small container, it made quite a piercing noise. When the youngish TA asked who did that, Maria, to my left, immediately dumped hers to the ground in a show of support.

"Uh-oh," she said, but not in a concerned way at all.

Maria shrugged off my worries.

"Forget it," she said. "They buy them by the hundreds, plus I saw the teacher drop a whole case yesterday. You have to admit, it made a great percussive sound, though." She has come to my aid dozens of times since then.

As with most who know me, Maria's also fully aware that I'm not one much for flying, which most people I know are pretty sick of hearing about. Maria is the only one who will still come with me to airports. Maria grew up with five brothers on Staten Island and as far as I know, she isn't afraid of anything. She does, however, have a problem with shower stalls.

"Never set foot in someone else's shower," Maria swears. "You can't see what's in there. You can't know everything."

She's lost a few boyfriends to this rule; I guess they took it personally. Although several of the guys of hers I met probably wouldn't have noticed if Maria bathed at their apartment, let alone bathed at all. I've mentioned this to her.

"They have other priorities," she's said.

So Maria drives me to Newark, one of her favorite airports, in her nineteen-seventy-something Dodge Dart, formerly her grandmother's. Dressed in her huge black raincoat, Maria has on what she calls her "dress hair." Although she's blessed with a lovely bunch of independent-minded hair anyway—I'm from the thin (and thinning) brown straight hair school, myself—Maria teases the hell out of hers and changes color regularly. Right now it's long and kind of frosted, the way women used to lighten hair in the sixties. My hair tends toward a fairly respectable chestnut color, and when I have temporarily changed colors, I've always gone for shades like walnut or maple, although I'm a little disturbed by all the tree imagery. Maria's colors are always called something like Cranberry Cocktail Craze or Beam-Me-Up Brawn, and I don't believe she's ever disturbed by the potential imagery. She has also puffed her hair up and out. There's really a lot of hair there.

"Look at that cute little man with the three eyes," she says, directing me toward Gate 5.

"That's not an eye, it's a huge bruise," I say, but she won't hear of it.

"Naw, wait till it heals. I think it makes him more interesting, don't you think?"

She's just kidding me now, trying to get my attention off my flight or at least away from biting my nails. It's one of the few things I'm very good at concentrating on, as is rubbing my upper front tooth with my thumbnail, or what's left of my thumbnail. As my mother has said, these are not attractive qualities.

Maria picks up her oversized black tote and starts removing items carefully placed in zip-lock bags.

"Here are your treats!" she says.

"That flight attendant looks like my mother," I say. "That's a really bad sign, isn't it? What if she's on my flight?"

"Then you just ignore her and insist you're old enough to pour your own beverage."

She's remarkable, though, this flight attendant. In less than a minute and a half, I've seen her rearrange her scarf, comb her hair, and button her jacket all while walking at top speed and pulling one of those suitcase trolleys behind her. I'm in awe.

I tear myself away and turn to Maria's Baggie items. The first bag holds little colorful pills, all separately wrapped in smaller Baggies.

"Where'd you get all of these?" I ask with an innocent look.

Maria gives me a straight face. "Your doctor highly recommended them." Maria works as a respected junior pharmacist on the lower East Side, in a store that sells lots of hot-water bottles and pink boxes of candy. The place has dimmed artificial lighting that always makes me feel sleepy, as if it were time for an afternoon nap. Her favorite clients—and the ones who love her best—are all over seventy. I've never seen anyone in the place, besides us, who wasn't over seventy.

"These orange ones are for motion sickness. Take half now." She hands it to me, so I follow my pharmacist's instructions. Maria only gives me over-the-counter medicine, or at least I think she does. She just likes to look suspicious.

"The green ones are for really bad motion sickness, if it comes to that, like if you feel your head is spinning at a different velocity than your body, or in a different direction. But they might put you to sleep. Feel free, during battles with turbulence, to share them with seatmates who won't shut up, if you know what I mean."

I nod. Maria's not careless with this stuff. She just doesn't believe in stigmas: "You're an adult. You need it, you take it. You don't need it, you don't take it," she's said. "If somebody criticizes you for it, you have to remember their lives must be awfully devoid of any meaningfulness for them to be focusing on your little tiny pills. Pity them." I've heard her say this regularly.

"Take the white ones if you get a headache or stomachache," she continues, "and only, only take the yellow ones if you start clawing at the seat or screaming at your seat-back tray, hear me?"

I nod again. I know the yellow ones.

"Or if the plane really does start to crash," she says with her sweetest pharmacist look.

Maria also equips me with two "movie" magazines and a *Teen Beat*, because, she says, the boys are really cute. She hands me a bag stuffed with a bialy loaded with raspberry jam. For the finale, she places in my hands a pink box of candy.

"If you don't eat it, you can give it to Sophie. It's really trashy candy," she says, smiling modestly.

Maria and I share an affection for really trashy candy. The kind you can take a bite of and throw away without feeling guilty. The kind you can squeeze with your fingers just to feel that gentle tug of caramel. It's usually an unspoken fact between us, our appreciation of sugary nougats and the cheesy satin boxes they come in, so this gift means a lot to me. Maria gets up and takes a little camera out of one of her many pockets. She snaps a picture of me holding my pink box of candy, my face very, very pale. I smile anyway.

But the plane ride goes just fine—no need for chocolate or drugs. My method for falling asleep on a plane works for me again: First, I'm usually so exhausted from worrying that I get sleepy once I'm belted in and moving, like a child in a car seat. Also, I try to watch the movie without listening to the sound, which has some sort of hypnotic effect on me, although Maria always says, "It's just boredom." My seatmate— a young man with a pink-and-green-striped tie (I wonder if he really could have picked it out himself)—settles in with a computer magazine. I only hear him mutter, now and then, words that sound like a secret code, or the kind of single-syllable thing that might escape your mouth if you were surprised by a slap in the face.

I don't miss out much on the movie, which features two

actors who died unexpectedly this last year. I remember thinking, before falling asleep, that this might not be a good omen for flying. But I'm wrong. We arrive in Houston on time and all in one piece. I guess I always expect part of the plane to break off or something. I expect it to look slightly black and blue when we land, after fighting its way through those winds. But no, it's still shiny with little red stripes, as if it's been through a lot less than I have.

Because when I catch sight of myself in the airport mirror, I see that my hair is flattened against my head on the right side and I have a long red line on my left cheek. My face has a bluish cast that oddly complements the pink box of candy I'm holding, or at least I think so. I walk out to the waiting area slowly, trying to rub some more normal color into my face. When my father raises a cowboy hat to wave at me, I raise my arm, still gripping my box of candy. I'm pretty sure I look like the ghost of daughters past.

My father scoops me up with his cowboy hat, which he uses to hug me with. Our hugs have always seemed a little tentative, a little anxious to me, as if my father were asking himself, Is this hug too hard? Is this hug too soft?—worries Goldilocks's own father may have had. But this is more of a Houston hug, I guess, a little tighter and bolder. I see families all around me hugging and patting relatives hard on the back—I escape without such a beating, fortunately.

My father, Doug, seems to be doing well in Houston. At fifty-five this weekend, he's a shade tanner than I remember him in New York, and maybe this brings out what must be recent gray hair around the back of his collar and over his ears. I'm a bit jealous, since my own hair started to show signs of gray when I was twenty-two, at the movies with Josh. I remember Josh leaning over as if to kiss me, but instead pulling out a gray hair from the left side of my bangs. Funny, I can't remember the movie. I guess you could admire a man who can both find and remove your one gray hair in a darkened movie theater. But maybe "admire" isn't the right word.

But my father looks well, which is a comfort, since you start to think all sorts of things when your parents reach a certain age, what with all those articles on prostates and sun exposure. He's dressed in a blue shirt and brown pants; only the cowboy hat says Houston. I notice, though, that he seems to be speaking with a bit of a drawl.

"Holly, Holly," he says, his special greeting that always touches me somewhere with a spark of heat, even if he is only saying my name twice.

"How was the flight?" he continues. "Did you get a movie? Dinner? Any turbulence to speak of?"

"It was fine," I say. "I slept, mostly, which always makes economy class a lot more comfortable. Until you wake up, at least."

My father and I share a laugh—an oddly similar one, too—as Sophie appears, an almost exact duplicate of my memory of her, except this time all in pink: pink silk blouse tucked into a pink silk long skirt above pink ankle socks and pink Ked-like sneakers. I can't think what to say, but I do know what to do. I hand her the box of pink candy.

"Candy! For me!" Sophie says, almost bowing to the box. Could it be we share a fascination for trashy candy, or does she think this is the expensive kind?

"What a sweet girl," she calls me, although I don't think Sophie's more than ten or fifteen years my senior, not that I'm not trying to think about things like that right now. "Isn't that nice, Dud?" she asks my father.

"Sophie's little pet nickname for me," my father says proudly.

Sophie pulls out a treat for me from behind her back and hands me a gardenia corsage. I admit to having a small fear of gardenias, or the smell of them, that stems from some experience in childhood that I can't quite place. I can only recall a small dachshund-type dog snapping at my heels and that pungent smell of gardenia, then pedaling my bike very fast. This may have something to do with my dislike of exercise, too, it occurs to me. Sophie pins the flower on my jacket, a bit too close to my chin. I feel a little like someone's grandmother on Mother's Day, except that I feel a little ill.

"Thanks," I say, grateful that my mother drilled us on "please" and "thank-you" so much that it's second nature.

"Welcome to Houston," my father says, throwing both arms into the air.

My father shares Sophie's large house that she inherited from a previous marriage.

"But I've completely redecorated since then," she assures me.

It's a nice enough suburban house, which doesn't mean you'd want to live there if you saw it, although I suspect Sophie might think you would. She takes me on a tour, explaining that each room has as its theme one of her favorite flowers—rose, mum, iris, lily, and pine, although I don't think of pine as a flower. As a special touch, Sophie seems to have each room sprayed with the scent of its namesake. I'll be staying in the lightly fragrant hyacinth room, and I'm thankful not to be staying in rose. I wonder if I'll have an allergic reaction to Sophie's house.

I find my father in what's known as his office, even though he's retired from his engineering work. Sophie calls this the pine room. The green and brown make for a pretty traditionally masculine study, but the room is filled with ducks. Duck portraits on the wall, decoys lined on the shelves, a matching mallard stapler and penholder kit. His phone quacks, too.

"I didn't know you were fond of ducks," I mention, seated in his office on a green corduroy chair with a blue duck-embroidered throw blanket.

Dad shrugs. "Oh, well, you can't have too many ducks." We have a moment alone together—Sophie has gone out to the hair salon for what she called "a quick fix"—and I want to ask him if he's happy here. If the ducks make the difference, if Sophie does, if the overheated weather and abundance of Dodge Caravans on the road have made him happy, if they're all part of the puzzle we call Dad. But as always, and for reasons I've never quite understood, I find it hard making even simple conversation. Mostly we just sort of listen to the ticking of the duck-billed clock on the wall.

"Janie's doing okay?" my father asks.

"Oh, sure," I say. "Janie's always on top of things. Kind of amazing."

"Yes, she is," Dad says. "But you're doing well, too?"

"Work's going well," I say. I don't feel like getting into my private life much with my dad, not that there's much to get into. The evening spent with Josh crosses my mind, but it doesn't seem like the kind of thing you drop into a casual conversation with your father.

"Good, good," Dad says, fingering a magazine. The article he's on seems to be called "Golf and the Man." The clock ticks. Finally I excuse myself to go wash up. I think this is what they always say in old movies, "Guess I'll wash up," although such words have several unpleasant connotations to me. As I'm leaving Dad's study, he picks up a little duck-head wine cork and hands it to me with a wink.

"You keep this one," he says.

My weekend in Houston goes by in a warm, slow-motion blur. Sophie takes me shopping, where she tries on a bright yellow poncho-like outfit she concludes is "unbecoming" to her figure.

"Why bother to have a figure at all," she says cryptically, placing the poncho back on the hanger.

She buys two eyelet-trimmed blouses and a big orange baubly necklace, which she spotted from across the room with a "Now, there's something." I had to move fast to keep up with her. She's also purchased, despite my protests, a large red, white, and blue scarf for me.

"A girl can't have too many scarves," she says, which reminds me of my dad's phrasing about not having too many ducks. I guess my dad and Sophie have been together long enough for their dictions to merge. I find this an unsettling thought for a daughter, and I also wonder what it means for my mother's diction. Is it still like my father's former speech, or has she taken on the words and phrases that are Ronny?

For the birthday dinner, the three of us huddle around a small table at a barbecue place that features cows mooing cheerfully in the background, and the occasional yee-haw of someone who may or may not be a real cowboy. I order the seafood special out of respect for the cow sounds around me. Dad and Sophie shake their heads at me slightly, I think, then order two huge steaks. Sophie says she and my father will get together with friends after I'm gone for further celebrations, but claims they didn't want to subject me to these people they call "boisterous." Another daughter might be insulted, but I'm pleased enough, or maybe I'm just distracted by all the mooing and yelping.

During dinner, Sophie directs most of the conversation, broaching such subjects as walking shoes (both she and my father like to walk around the neighborhood, although they seem to disagree about how many of those little bumps you want on the bottom of your sneakers—the old "you can't have too many" doesn't seem to apply here), the advantages and disadvantages of teeth bleaching, and something about the dietary fallacies of raisins that I can't quite grasp. Sophie asks me if I belong to a health club, and despite my saying no, she tells us all about hers, an exotic-sounding place with seventy private Jacuzzis. Mostly my dad smiles at me a lot, offering me tastes of all his food, despite my plate of truly jumbo-size shrimp masked by a thick layer of batter.

"Taste of baked potato?" Dad offers.

"No thanks, I have to be fair to my shrimp," I say, although I don't know what I mean, really. I'd like to break off the batter from the shrimp and hide it somewhere, like under a baked potato, but I have rice instead, which is useless for my purposes. Actually, I like the batter quite a bit.

All this leads us up to birthday cake, something we can all agree on. My father blows out the birthday candle on a huge piece of chocolate cake, the kind the management knows is enough for a table of three or four—maybe five or six if someone dislikes chocolate. After making his silent wish, he smiles and takes hold of my hand, and Sophie's, but doesn't say anything. Dad just smiles and almost shakes our hands up and down slowly, as if conducting his own symphony.

This is pretty much all of the conversation I get to have with my father, and although we've covered subjects like ducks and dentistry, we haven't broached the tough ones, the ones that the space between New York and Houston tries to hide but doesn't really. I want to ask him if he thinks my visit has brought us closer together or just emphasized what's between us, or maybe both. I think of our relationship and picture one of those auto club maps where they draw a big purple line for you, New York at one end, Houston at the other, between them a jagged, turning line, a path that seems impossibly long but still crossable. I'm not sure what to make of the weekend, but it reminds me of the way I felt about Josh's last visit, that it signaled something, rough crossing ahead, or maybe something more positive. I keep feeling like perhaps these moments in my life are snapping their fingers at me, trying to tell me something, but in a foreign language I can't understand. It's getting a little frustrating.

"Thanks for the trip," I say ignoring all the real issues banging on the walls in my head, desperate to escape. I write them off as a simple headache.

The next day, Sophie and my father stand at Gate 4, seeing me off. The plane looks smaller than the last one, with a dull gray finish. I could swear the first one shined.

"You're welcome anytime," my father says as we exchange brief hugs. He's forgotten his cowboy hat, or maybe that's just for show after all. I look to Sophie.

"Oh, of course," Sophie adds, handing me two packs of sugarless gum, the kind that oozes something when you chew it. That kind of gum makes me feel a little woozy, because I really don't want unknown substances oozing into my mouth when I bite down on something. She also gives me two *Texas Home Decorating* magazines for the flight, where I can read up on the latest in home fabrics and the true meaning of ranch-style homes.

"The article on designing your own barbecue pit is adorable," Sophie says, confirming what I knew, that she's already read these issues. I thank her.

"Ya'll come back now," both my father and Sophie say, but jokingly.

"You have to say that here," my father says with a shake of his head, pointing to a sign over the gate that reads the exact same thing, with three exclamation points.

Back on my plane, with no seatmate this time, no one to think about or offer my juicy gum to, I thumb through the decorating magazines. A checkerboard tablecloth brings a down-home feel to any family room, I learn. Bathrooms done in periwinkle and orange are taking over the state, even in the best homes. And it seems that ducks are out, one article insists, pheasants are in. I can't help but notice that Sophie has placed a big checkmark next to this article, but I'm not sure who she really intended the checkmark for.

Chapter 3

Listen While You Work

"**D**on't underestimate Janie," Maria says of my sister, much the way she might advise me to finish all of my medication.

"Beneath that obsession with all things bridal," Maria continues, "lies a deeply serious woman."

"A deeply troubled woman, you mean," I say, not sure I'm willing to really consider the psychological significance of Janie's six engagements.

"Troubled, maybe," Maria says, "but I've seen her run that art gallery, I've seen her sell five-figure glass bubbles without breaking a sweat."

"I sweat just looking at the things," I say. "I'm always afraid my arms will fly out while I'm talking and I'll take down a sculpture." All the sculptures are molded out of glass, at the McAnderson Gallery, where Janie's the assistant manager.

"Never make sweeping gestures in a glass gallery."

"But Janie gestures," I consider.

"Yes, she does, with confidence," Maria says. "Sometimes I just stand outside the gallery and watch her."

"Has she seen you?"

"Sure. Sometimes I go in. Sometimes I just stand out-

side. We wave. We have some kind of understanding."
Maria nods as she speaks, all this being very normal to her.

I admire this understanding. Some days I think there's
nothing I'd like better than to watch my little sister at work,
complimenting a sculptor using all the right jargon, managing an opening night champagne reception without getting
even the slightest pimple. Some days, my little sister amazes
me.

"Where should we throw a shower for her this time?"
Maria asks.

I jot down bridal shower ideas while eating lunch at my
desk. We don't exactly have a lunchroom here at Science
Press, Inc., where I'm one of twenty-four or so production
editors. We mostly eat in our cubicles, which turns the
whole room that we share—divided by those modular walls
that only come up to your chin—into a big picnic site,
minus the smoke from the barbecue. It's probably also the
quietest picnic site in history, since we tend to keep to ourselves. I suppose if you close your eyes, you can imagine the
turning of *The New York Times'* pages as the sound of walking through crisp autumn leaves, that the smell of egg salad
and root beer really waft from the family picnicking next to
you, about to play volleyball. Daydreaming during lunch is
one of our fringe benefits.

Most of the production editors wear Walkman-type
headsets, and a lot of us listen to the same rock station.
When they had their last call-in contest—they gave away a
Camaro—I heard plenty of us dialing at the same time. We
even compared lists of recent songs played, since we try to
be an equal-opportunity editing room. That contest involved naming all the songs they'd played during the noon
hour for the last three weeks that had the words "But I love

you" in them. A simple "I love you" wouldn't count. As editors, we of course knew the value of a good conjunction. Still, we do work hard sometimes, but radio contests help fill in what's missing in our lives.

I start scribbling a list of previous bridal showers we've thrown for Janie.

(1) The Chinese Food Shower: Write Your Own Fortune Cookie. Janie liked this one. I think she still has all the fortunes we wrote, probably tucked away with her old engagement rings. Maria wrote: "She who is wisest does not take advice from cookies." I think I wrote: "No such thing as unreturnable gift—can always give to sister." Something like that. I never found out what my mother wrote, but I remember it made Janie blush.

(2) The New Lipstick Swap Shower. Everyone brought one or more of those lipsticks you get when you buy the shade you really need (Your Gift With Purchase!) that never work for you. Janie questioned my taste with this idea, but I got a great shade of burgundy. My mother grabbed all the peach tones, but then, she brought us all a little face scrub.

(3) The Harbor Cruise Shower. Janie felt a little queasy with this one. She insisted I wasn't responsible, though. Maria kept saying she saw a shark in the Hudson, but it turned out to be sludge. "Probably the man-eating kind," Maria said.

(4) The Food Fight Shower. Okay, it didn't start out as this. Janie says I ruined a new white silk blouse. I still say my mother started it.

"I only tossed a roll," Mom always says. "It was a gesture of affection."

"But it was the first gesture," I remind her.

"That's right," she'll say. "Always blame the mother."

(5) The Dog Show Shower. Some of the women had an allergic reaction, but Janie enjoyed comparing each dog to

her then-fiancé Jerry, as did we all. In the end, she said the gray schnauzer was the most like him, but she refused to explain why.

"I'm sure we don't want to know her exact criteria," I told Maria.

"Frankly," Maria said, "I think he takes after the Pekinese, especially around the little pink hair bow."

"Not an attractive animal," my mother whispered to Maria and me, before moving toward the boxers.

I end my list writing Shower Six? trying to imagine what comes next. New York Marathon Shower? Flea-Market-Find Shower? Blood Drive Shower?

A round, pinkish face appears just above the partition in front of me at my desk. It's Tom, whose baby-boyish features always make me smile. I want to reach out and tickle his cheek, almost, but this would be inappropriate behavior between production editors, I fear. Tom's the perfect officemate—almost always silent. I've heard his phone ring, but I seldom hear his voice after it, and he's really only sitting a cheap fake wall away. Once, though, I think I heard him humming. I've noticed that hanging on his inside wall, Tom's got one of those little surgical masks, although I don't know why, and I've never seen him wear it. It may be the kind construction workers use to avoid breathing too much asbestos, which worries me.

Tom always politely hands me my mail, which often accidentally lands on his desk for some reason, and he never seems to try to peek through the envelopes' transparent windows.

"Hi," I greet him, restraining my right hand that almost reaches for his face.

Tom nods hello in what I've come to accept as a quietly friendly motion and then hands me something, before his moonish face descends behind the wall. It's an invitation, like you might receive to a party, with tiny horses and rabbits printed in blue and yellow. Inside, he's written, "Won't you join me for lunch?" This seems to me an awfully complicated way to go out to lunch with your officemate, but it's also pretty original. Besides, as I said, few of us ever even go out to lunch. I do know that when my boss, Monique, wants to eat out with one of us, she usually throws a wadded-up piece of construction paper at our heads. She's known as a good shot.

I knock on the wall, and the moon rises.

"Sure, deli?" I ask in code, meaning the place across the street. It's really called The Jelly Deli, which is far too silly to say in professional surroundings.

Tom nods again, the agreement nod. Like the hello nod, but with a slight blink of the eyes. I have not actually stopped to think about why I know the details of Tom's nods quite so well.

I'm at home that evening watching war coverage on the news, although I've turned the sound down a bit so I can't really tell what war they're covering. They may even switch wars in the middle. Sometimes I just make myself watch this stuff, maybe to make myself feel guiltier for not donating to all the charitable causes that solicit me week after week. Maybe I watch this stuff to appreciate how well my own life is going, but this never really works. I'm not sure what the purpose of watching war coverage really is.

When Maria comes over, she looks at the TV, turns the sound up for a moment, then slams the power button off, temporarily halting my fascination with numbers of bodies missing.

"What are you watching!" Maria calls out in disgust. "You probably watch that stuff while eating, don't you?"

"It makes me think about how lucky I am," I say, "how few worries I've got."

"It's sick."

"Yeah," I say, "but I don't eat as much if that's on."

"No talk about dieting!" Maria scolds. It's one of her rules. Maria doesn't think much of diets. They're like religion, I know she feels, too many commandments and low in nutritional value.

Maria likes to spend time at my apartment since it's bigger than her own. After all, my studio apartment has a separate kitchen, for which, as Maria says, I get Extra Points. Extra points for having a tiny kitchen, extra points for not cutting someone off while making a left-hand turn, extra points for not swearing at someone who cuts you off, or (for even more points) swearing at them in a highly creative way. Still, my apartment never seems quite finished, what with the attempted blue drapes now stashed in a corner, a half-attempt at a collage for my mother behind the TV table, and the obligatory guitar with one broken string that I haven't touched since college but can't part with in another corner. I've had this place since college, when I shared the minimal living room/bedroom with two other girls desperate to live here in the Village. And then I shared it with Josh, who always seemed a little too big for the place and so seemed to spend most of his time at his university office, which of course was even smaller than my living room. Still, although the place is small, relatively untidy, and not particularly flashy, it's me. It's home.

"I called you at twelve to ask if you knew the answer to the noontime trivia question," Maria says. She listens to the same radio station. "Were you just being secretive?"

"I went out to lunch."

"Why, what's wrong?" Maria asks.

"Nothing. My cube-mate Tom and I went to Jelly Deli."

"It's *The* Jelly Deli, don't forget," Maria informs. "They get really pissy if you leave off the The. Do I know Tom?"

"No one really does," I say. As always, Tom was quiet as can be at lunch. Mostly I talked about the seven books I'm working on, the authors who call me, how nice it will be when winter ends, the kind of thing you'd talk about with your grandmother. Tom mostly continued his expert nods, with the occasional smile in between. Over his chicken soup, Tom's face took on a soft peachy color. I tell Maria all this.

"Did he say anything meaningful?" Maria asks. "What planet he's from, what pharmacy he frequents, whether he makes more or less than you? Or maybe something about how when he hears you type your Fed Ex labels, his heart surges with exciting yet life-threatening momentum?"

I shake my head. "He said he likes the office, especially the color scheme." I hadn't realized the office had much of a color scheme, but Tom pointed out the calming mix of gray and blue. That's about as personal as our discussion got.

"So it was just lunch," Maria says, her voice trailing off at the end. I guess she hoped for more. I'm not sure what I'd hoped for, but I don't feel disappointed, exactly.

"It was just chicken salad," I say. "Little more than chicken salad ever happens to me."

My chicken salad is front-page news.

Nina, my closest production-editor friend at work, comes up to me the next morning, moments before lunchtime. She steps into my cubicle and sits down on my milking stool that I keep handy for such visits, a gift from Josh in my previous life. It's an antique, which basically means it wobbles. When Nina sits down, we both remove our headphones. She looks around.

"You went out to lunch yesterday," Nina says softly.

Nina is my favorite production editor. In her early twenties and just starting out, Nina tends to look nervous and worried. She's the kind of blonde girl you're not jealous of in the least, the kind of blonde who doesn't flaunt it, but wears it with a natural sloppiness, without giving it much thought, the way the rest of us throw a bag over our shoulder before leaving the house. Plus, when Nina smiles, her smiles come out big, with what seems like an extraordinary number of small white teeth.

"It was just lunch," I say. "Chicken salad. With Tom." I point next door.

"Shh," she says, then peeks over the wall into Tom's cubicle before sitting down again. "Oh, he's not there."

"I think he jogs sometimes," I say.

"Runs."

"Runs?"

"Runs, not jogs," Nina says. "Jogging is bad for you."

"Are there different shoes for the two?" I ask her. She seems on top of this.

"Yes. You can't even buy jogging shoes anymore."

I wonder what has happened to all the unsold jogging shoes, but I don't ask about it.

"You could have brought lunch back yesterday," she says.

"It was just to talk."

"Oh, well," Nina says quietly. "It's true, nobody really talks in here. But you could have sat in the refrigerator room."

Someone once nicknamed our lunchroom the refrigerator room, although some call it the frost room. Not only is it cold, most of it is taken up by the huge double-door refrigerator. Otherwise the room only has one old ice cream parlor table, two cold iron chairs, and the coffeemaker, so it's not much of a lunchroom for eating in, only for cooling off your lunch. We all do go in there to talk, when we feel like it. It's okay to chat quietly in your cubicle, like we're doing now, also. No one can hear you through their headsets, anyway.

"I thought maybe you two were talking about leaving," Nina says. "You know, job hunting."

"Why would you think that?"

"I don't know. I hear things. Or sometimes I think I hear these things." Nina's talking about the rumor mill, I think, rather than voices in her head.

I wave away Nina's worries. "It was just lunch," I say again, swatting her with a file folder. "I love my job," I tell her, and I guess I do.

"I know, I know," she says, picking at an index fingernail. "Is this a big thing? My going out to lunch? I mean, are people talking about it?"

"No, no. People just saw you and wondered. Plus, you weren't here when I came by to ask about the noontime trivia question."

I can imagine the rumor mill at work over my simple chicken salad. I wonder if we'd gone somewhere for something extravagant, something rich like lobster bisque, if it would have changed the tone of the gossip, heightened the worry. It seems two production editors socializing makes people fear the worst.

My sister, Janie, calls my office at lunchtime to say that the owner of the art gallery she manages, Melody McAnderson, wants to throw her an engagement party at the gallery. It's not the first time.

"I realize there's a difference between an engagement party and a shower," Janie says, "but I suppose we could pass on the shower this time."

The way she says "this time" makes me wonder if there will be a "next time." Still, I'm a little disappointed. For all my complaining, I guess I've enjoyed all the bridal showers we've had for Janie. I'm sure my disappointment shows in my voice, even though all I can say is "Oh."

"It's just that Jackson thinks I have enough household items," Janie says. "He disapproves of too many juicers."

Jackson is, of course, this round's fiancé, number six, a young lawyer in a firm downtown. He rents a house up in a cool place each summer, a place his family has visited for fifty years, he always claims. The only thing my family has done for fifty years is argue. Actually, we may have done that for centuries.

"And his feelings about lingerie?" I ask.

"He's more open-minded there."

Something about Jackson bothers my mother, but she's never said what. When I ask her about him, she'll say, "How could you improve on Jackson?" but something in her tone indicates maybe a mate needs some room for improvement. Maria's response was simpler, if more critical: "Have you ever seen him wear the same tie twice?"

"Well," I say, "maybe we can still all get together, some kind of shower, besides the party." I know Maria will be disappointed, too. She likes dressing up for the showers, and thoroughly enjoys wearing one of the Hi My Name Is Maria! nametags she always brings along.

"Of course we can," Janie says, as if to a child.

After she hangs up I sigh and stare at my blue pen, wondering how to make it through another round of Janie's engagements. I doodle rooster faces over my list of possible bridal showers, as rooster faces are the only type of doodle I've really mastered. Sometimes the roosters appear to be singing, or at least they look that way to me. Tom's face has appeared above me, over my wall, and looks at me with an unspoken question I can't quite pinpoint. I smile, but not very convincingly.

Tom gently sails a tiny paper dove my way, then disappears. The origami bird lands in front of me, its wings expertly sculpted by sharp scissors. I admire the craftsmanship, not to mention the timing. At moments like these, I suspect that Tom doesn't listen to a headset.

Chapter 4

Janie's Answer

Janie's the first to figure out how we can get together after all, offering an untried bridal shower idea. Normally, I'd be in favor of anything new, but I suspect this isn't that good an idea. Still, here we all are in a car—my mother, Janie, myself, and Maria—on our bridal-shower road trip. This may not have the civic responsibility of the blood drive shower, not to mention that lightheaded feeling of good will, but, as Maria pointed out, we can still stop for cookies and juice. Maria begged to come along.

"There were so many boys around, growing up," Maria explained of her five big brothers, "I want to see women bond."

I want to see this myself, though I doubt an '89 Toyota is really the place. "A car trip can only be trouble," I said.

"My middle name is trouble," my mother said bravely, "but I get to sit in front."

I can't remember being in a car with my mother and sister since adolescent days. I can picture Janie decked out in a junior cheerleading outfit. And shouldn't I be in the front seat, battling a wave of car sickness as I study from heavy history textbooks, memorizing facts I'll really only use in trivia games or to win valuable cash and prizes from radio contests? But no, here we are in my mother's pleasant sedan, even though Maria did offer to drive us in her Dart. Maria's really excited about the trip and has packed lightly and worn casual, easy-to-tend hair, pulled back haphazardly in a ponytail. It's the perfect kid-in-the-backseat look.

Maria's own mother, she's told me, was busy with the five boys while Maria grew up. "She'd say things like, 'I have to go talk with one of your brother's teachers about the tetherball he ate,'" Maria has said. "'You're the girl, so you'd better be no trouble. I'll keep your clothes clean, but that's all the attention I can spare.'" Maria wants to see how a circle of girls, of women, works, how the attention gets divided up.

Janie drives first, because, she says, "I'm a very clearheaded driver." Plus she's attentive, polite, and apparently, clever, as she's talked her way out of five speeding tickets that we know of.

"Maybe we'll get to see how she does it," Maria whispers to me in the backseat. Maria refuses to admit how many speeding tickets she's gotten but has said she's shooting for her own private record, and, besides, the police are always interested in seeing how anyone can get a Dodge Dart to speed.

My mother sits in the front passenger seat with neatly folded maps of New York, New Jersey, and Pennsylvania, our destination, where we plan to "admire but respect the Amish way," as Janie has said. It seems to me that having reached thirty without ever having to gawk at Amish people is something to be proud of, but my mother insists I'm missing out. Maria agreed with her and told me that observing strangers in black would teach me something about myself.

"This is so cool," Maria says now. "If we were in a car

with my family, someone would have been left by the road-side by now."

I think about all the things in my apartment I could be doing this weekend—making drapes, washing clothes, ironing the bedspread, figuring out my age in exact number of days—when I'm interrupted by my mother's voice.

"Should we play car games, or are we all too old?"

"Old is a concept I refuse to allow into my mind," Janie says.

"I still don't want to play car games," I say.

"You're no fun, Holly," my mother and Janie echo.

"And," I say, "just because we're a group of women together doesn't mean we have to sing."

"Or discuss periods," Maria adds.

"Or breasts," Mom says.

"That's men who always discuss breasts," Maria says.

"Or men," I say.

"Or diets."

"Or makeup."

"Or sales."

We arrive at a moment of silence.

"I know," Mom says. "Let's discuss politics. Let's say you have a chance to spend the evening of your choice with the president."

"The president of your choice?" I ask.

"Whichever one is tallest, and still living, of course," Mom says. "It's all okay with the First Lady and the Secret Service and all those talk show hosts who get so involved in things today. So, would you go?"

"This is silly," Janie says.

"Is it just dinner?" Maria asks, "or do I get to wear something that zips in front?"

"It depends if you voted for him," I say.

"I'd like to see how a president behaves with a TV remote control," Janie says. "You can tell a lot about a man if you put something electronic in his hands. Does he seem confused? Can he work the pause button? Does he ask your advice or just bang it on the table when it seems not to work?"

We all consider this a moment.

"So you'd go out with him?" Maria asks Janie.

"Of course not," Janie says. "I'm engaged."

"It's hypothetical," I say to Janie, then wonder if I really mean the date or the engagement.

"What if you could go out with him and help him make an important decision that affects women in cars everywhere?" my mother asks Janie.

"And wear something zippered," Maria adds.

Janie thinks a moment. "I don't want to play this game anymore. Look, there's a police officer."

Janie hits the gas and Maria and I grab on to our respective door handles. We approach a policeman on a motorcycle, waiting by the side of the highway for speeders just like us. He looks up, gets a glimpse of white Toyota, and waves to Janie. She waves back. We're halfway there.

We go out to dinner in a place that could either be an authentic Amish hideaway or a tourist trap, I can't really tell. But the blue-and-white checked tablecloths look inviting and familiar, the baskets with pinecones used for centerpieces make everything smell like Christmas. This seems like a family kind of place, where they wouldn't get upset if you spilled a glass of milk when you're a kid, or maybe even when you're an adult. My mother thinks the Amish-style caps on the waitresses are a good idea, as they keep those unwanted stray hairs out of your food. Her comment impels Janie to grab her little notebook and write in it. We all struggle to see what she's writing, but when she sees us, she's on guard.

"No, no, no," she says, sneaking the book into her lap. Our dinners arrive, perfectly arranged treats of simple but well-seasoned foods, the kind of chicken, fish, and potatoes that come with gravy but no surprises. Maria and I swipe pieces of each other's dinners, as we're not shy. Janie looks on, displeased.

"I'm not sure the Amish would approve," she says.

Maria and I look at her, then at each other, and then trade plates entirely. Janie's face registers complete horror. She turns to my mother for support, but Mom spears one of Janie's green beans. The group dynamic has somehow managed to work out not in Janie's favor.

"Eat your dinner, dear," Mom tells her. Maria and I both grab one of Janie's beans. Mom giggles.

"Now, girls," Mom says to Maria and me, "she is the guest of honor."

"She's right," I say. Maria and I give Janie some of our peas and carrots. One of the carrots bounces off Janie's plate and lands on the carpet near another table. Janie looks a little woozy.

"Now it's starting to look like dinner with my family," Maria says.

Janie excuses herself. While she heads off for the ladies' room, my mother and I toss a coin over room arrangements for the night. I lose, so I get Janie. My mother does not try to hide her relief.

"She has so many face creams," my mother explains. "I find it intimidating."

Maria says she really wanted to room with my mother, anyway.

"Allison can ask me all those mothery questions about boys that my family has given up on," Maria says.

"Don't worry, dear," my mother comforts Maria, "I promise to thoroughly invade your privacy." Maria smiles gratefully.

To make up for the teasing Janie's so unused to, we let her eat her key lime pie all by herself. I do notice her looking at my ice-cream-topped pecan crunch pie with admiration, but I know she'd never accept a bite. We all keep our spoons to ourselves.

I try to think of this as an opportunity to get to know my little sister better, to observe some of the twists and turns we call Janie's mind. Our room is country before country was cool, with an old-fashioned broom in one corner that smells lightly of nutmeg. I assume that we don't have to use it. Our matching bedspreads have pine trees and hunting dogs on them, and our brass night lamps buzz slightly, the sound of friendly country insects. As a child I would never let Janie share my room because she used to talk in her sleep to storybook characters. I once distinctly heard her tell Cinderella to ask for some nice lace-up boots instead. I hope Janie's outgrown all this.

Janie sleeps in a long pink T-shirt with a Scottie dog on it, her blondish hair neatly combed into a pink Pony-oh. For bedtime reading, she takes out *The Joy of Sex*, which she reads boldly. I find I want to ask her questions, but I don't know where to start. I wonder if she would have read this if she'd roomed with my mother. I wonder what my mother would have found to say about it. I wonder if my mother has her own copy, but this again isn't something I want to know. For a moment, I'm pretty convinced I'm the only one in the family without a copy. When Janie sees me looking, she says only, "It's the new edition," which makes me wonder what has changed. Has sex been updated? Does my little sister know something they invented after I thought I knew it all? Finally, Janie puts down the book. Time for girl talk, I think, that gossip that gets really good the more tired you get. But Janie just looks at me. So I have to start.

"I didn't know there was a new edition," I say, cautiously.

"It's really just the artwork that's changed I think," Janie says. "But I like to keep up."

Actually, Maria and I have spent plenty of time speculating on Janie's sex life. With six fiancés, you just have to wonder certain things. Janie herself has never confided in me about sexual matters, never come to me with questions. But then, she has the books. There is, of course, the very odd chance that the proper Janie is still a virgin, but we don't really think so. Still, now seems like a good time to pry.

"And Jackson," I say, "has he looked at the new edition?" Clearly, none of my business.

Janie seems unfazed. "We like to read parts out loud to one another. Sometimes, we make up little quizzes."

I nod. This is what I get for asking questions.

"Once," Janie says, lowering her voice, "he made me a connect the dots."

"Oh, that was thoughtful."

"He's not much of an artist, though."

I search my mind for a reply. "Still, it's nice to have things you can do together."

"It's essential," Janie says.

I'm at a loss. I try to imagine for a moment myself with the man of my dreams, turning the pages of *The Joy of Sex* together. I can't quite get the picture right, as the man begins looking a little like Josh, then turns blurrily into more of a semblance of my officemate Tom. The book itself begins to read more like the *TV Guide*, and the people in my imagination look a little frustrated, as if they can't find anything on. I listen to the lamps buzz and wish I were with Maria. I heard her and my mother whispering something about Truth or Dare as they walked off to their room.

Janie sits up straighter. "I worry about Mom," she says, flattening her book on her lap.

"I think Mom's doing well," I say. "She's got Ronny, and

that lengthy trip they're planning, but she seems pleased with it."

"But what happens to Mom if I get married?" Janie asks.

"To Mom? She'd be happy. What else?"

"Oh, Holly, you're hopeless at reality," Janie says, though not meanly. "It would change the whole family dynamic." Janie begins turning through her book again, smoothing the pages.

I think Janie's wrong, at least about Mom's being affected by Janie's intended wedding, if that's what she's talking about. I try to figure out what she means by our family dynamic, which certainly has undergone changes before, as when my dad left us for Sophie. I'm usually the one who's pretty averse to change, in the family, in the weather, anywhere. But as far as Janie ever getting married, ever following through on one of her engagements, I think change would be a positive thing.

"I'm not sure I follow," I say.

"I just don't know" is all Janie will say, before picking up her book and delving back into sexual technique. I guess this ends our getting reacquainted conversation, our sister-to-sister exchange. I feel confused, as if maybe I didn't hear Janie right, as if I answered a question she didn't ask, or maybe she never asked the question at all. I feel a little as if I've misplaced something, under the sheets or on the bed-side table, or just somewhere a few inches from my body. I do want to understand Janie, to help her get past whatever this is that might be holding her back, but she seems engrossed. I guess she's turned to experts for advice. I wonder if there's a chapter on sexual relationships in the era of dys-functional families. It is the new edition, after all.

I try to straighten out my old gray ripped T-shirt, which I think used to be Josh's, or maybe he stole it from me before I stole it from him. I turn off my night lamp and close my eyes, wishing at least that I'd brought my own book, a book of fables, maybe, something with a happy, even if improbable, ending.

We all meet for breakfast in our inn's dining room filled with more pinecones, which begin to remind me of Christmases that didn't go so well. Janie has been chattering away to me about wedding plans since she woke up, so I may have imagined last night entirely. She tells me about bridal veils, about how fashion today questions whether you even need one. I question this myself.

My mother and Maria come in, and I catch a bit of their conversation.

"I just never find those sleeveless shirts attractive on men," my mother says to Maria, then turns to us.

"Hello, dears," she greets us. "Sleep well?"

"Eight hours in dreamland," my punctual sister says. My own dreamland seems kind of vague now, but I know I had a dream where I was the guest of honor, as at a shower, and everyone gave me sex manuals. My dream mother gave me a videotape of some sort, then passed it to the dreamlike Maria and Janie, who nodded approvingly. One woman, a cross between someone I met in high school and my dental hygienist, gave me four blue-and-white-checked balloons, which everyone oohed over, but I wasn't sure if the gift was of a sexual nature. I'm probably the only one in the dream who didn't know.

"We talked all night," Maria says. "And your mom Frenchbraided my hair." Maria looks like a Catholic schoolgirl this morning, despite her conversation about sleeveless-shirted men.

"Don't you love road trips?" Maria says, deeply inhaling the pinecone smells of the room.

* * *

During breakfast, my mother brings out a shower present for Janie, even though Janie doesn't expect anything. Sometime after the third shower or so, Janie asked that no one give her gifts, most of which she had been returning to people, unlike her practice with engagement rings. Sure, some people wouldn't take back their gifts, but I wasn't usually one of those. After a few showers, I just always wrapped up the same juicer and gave it to her over again, then got it back. I still have it, wrapped and tied with a yellow bow, under the sink on a shelf behind the blender. Maybe I'll drop it by her place, sometime.

But my mother disapproves of not giving gifts, as if not to do so tempts fate somehow. She's bought this herself but put Maria's and my name on it, as if we were the children we seem to have reverted to this weekend.

"Happy engagement," Mom says. "May it be a fruitful one." She winks at me, and Maria giggles.

"Now, you know you're not supposed to do this," Janie says.

"Oh, yes, dear," Mom says. "I remember hearing that a few times. Open it."

Janie unwraps a small square shape to find a framed painting that nearly fits into her two hands. The watercolor of trees and flowers—in this family we're all suckers for a soppy landscape—looks much like a picnic area near where we grew up. I can almost see the picnic bench hidden behind the trees. Janie, I know, especially enjoyed family picnics, usually held at these parks. The rest of us always tried to suspend any and all arguments in progress for such picnics, and it felt as though we did it for Janie's benefit, although probably for our own as well. I always wanted Janie to have a blissful, if oblivious, childhood—I guess because I was older and she was that well-behaved and pretty kind of child who made you want to do things for her. I guess I also turned the attention I might have given my brother, if he'd wanted it, to Janie. Janie holds the painting, truly touched. "It looks like home," she says quietly, then thanks us all. A waitress headed for our table with two pitchers of coffee takes one look at our group and turns sharply away.

"Now, girls," my mother says, "no one likes a cold waffle," managing to break the silence and remind us to eat at the same time.

We spend the rest of the day ducking the unexpected downpours of rain, which seem to quiet us today. The sound of water hitting the ground serves as our language as we tour the sights and listen to guides. We move quietly and respectfully through mists of drizzle that fill the time between showers. When I first felt the drops on my hair, I felt reassured, relieved. I've gotten through rain before. It continues to subdue us on our return trip home, where we listen to my mother's old tapes, complemented by the back-and-forth beat of the windshield wipers. We all seem soothed, if not completely hypnotized.

At the end of our trip, after my mother drops me off, I parade down to the corner through a tamer, more citified rain, then I buy a bag of oranges. I'm looking forward to unwrapping that yellow-ribboned box hidden in my kitchen. A juicer is a terrible thing to waste, and I feel the need to be alone with something tangy.

Chapter 5

Giraffe Feet

The photographs in one medical book I'm working on are so disgusting, so painful looking, that all the editors cringe when they walk by and see them lying on my desk. Still, people keep sneaking in to take a peek anyway. We publish a variety of scientific research, and my grandest book, with twenty-two color plates, is called *Detailed Strategies in the War on Ovarian Cancer*. I've noticed that many of the new medical texts have taken on military-sounding titles like this. The photos show jellylike, soft blobs—the kind of pictures that make you grab your sides with sympathy pains. My supervisor, Monique, a no-nonsense woman from the Philippines, never flinches at such photos, though. Monique, in her forties we think—no one would dare ask her—likes to come by my desk and flip through the book's pages.

"Awful," Monique says, studying a photo closely.

"Terrible," she says at the next one, grimacing. Sometimes she uses a magnifying glass, inspecting whatever it is that fascinates her about these photos. She goes on this way for a while, taking in each page, then shakes her head. She'll usually pat me on the arm, say something like "ugh," and walk off.

I can't stand the pictures anymore, coming across one that's just been sized and that someone left on my desk, or checking through the book and trying to blur my eyes so I won't see them, but getting a look at too much pinkish stuff anyway. I decide to go into the art department for some kraft paper. I cut it up and tape the brown paper over each photo, which gives the manuscript something of an *X*-rated look. The next time Monique comes by, she flips through the pages and sees the papered-over pictures. Although she looks a little disappointed, she says, "Good for you, Holly."

I notice that people have stopped lurking around my desk so much.

Right now I'm working on a much more pleasant whale book—with pictures of live happy whales gliding through chilly waters. Monique calls this book "Orca," as she has a nickname for all my books. I'm imagining the whales diving into the dark waters, bumping one another gently, and making those crooning sounds they make, when I hear a tapping on my modular wall in front of me. I tap back. A small paper lobster comes floating over the wall. Intricately folded, it sails almost as well as its predecessor, the paper bird, did, which seems a little funny for a lobster. I realize I haven't heard much from Tom since our lunch, not that I heard that much from him at lunch. He tends to sneak into his cubicle, then sneak away, occasionally nodding at people, but quiet. Even his nods have a practiced silence.

Tom has neatly printed on the side of the lobster the words "Won't you join me for dinner, a week from Tuesday?" I'm impressed by Tom's obvious mastery of origami and his ability to plan way ahead. I decide to tease him.

I stand up and look directly over the partition, locking my chin over the top. "Thanks for the lobster," I say. His desk has an assortment of colored paper stacked in one corner, along with five or six sharpened pencils next to it. I hold up the lobster as if I haven't seen the invitation part. I don't even know why I'm doing this. It's Monday. I'm happy to be back in my safe cubicle with my crooning whale pictures. I feel a tug of obnoxiousness coming on.

Tom looks at a loss. He points to the message on the lobster with one of his sharp pencils, so I turn the lobster over. "Oh," I say, then "what's this word?" I point with my finger. There's no way you couldn't read such neat printing.

"Dinner," Tom says softly.

I realize that in my desire to be so clever, I've left myself no out, no polite way to refuse. What will we talk about, that is, what will I talk about over dinner, which usually takes longer than lunch? Will something like candlelight change the way Tom nods, somehow filling the conversational gaps? All this flashes through my mind as I stand there looking at the paper lobster. Then again, it's such an original sort of invitation. I'd hate to discourage such innovation. Or maybe it's something more, some secret desire I've had that I can't quite recognize, maybe because my chin aches, posed on the wall as I am.

"Sure," I say, then unhook my chin. Oh, well. I've never met a man who makes paper lobsters before.

My mother is down to two large bags and two carry-ons. "I thought you could have only one carry-on," I say.

"A common misperception," my mother says. "Always check with your airline first." We're examining her display of bulging luggage for her extended trip to Africa with Ronny. All of the luggage should fit easily on her unbreakable plastic trolley, she claims, although it'll make for an awfully heavy trolley.

"I'm not relying on Ronny to carry my luggage," she says. "I'm an independent woman."

"Good," I say.

"Not that he can't help," Mom says, removing an anorak

from one bag and replacing it in a carry-on, then taking it out of the carry-on and somehow fitting it into another full case. She stands back and we admire her collection of bags, which look balanced but heavy. Mom leaves for Africa the day after the engagement party.

"It's funny to think you can fit four months of your life into four bags," Mom says. "And a trolley cart."

"Four months," I echo her. "Are you sure about this?"

"Your mother the adventuress," she says. Mom adds one final can of bug spray to her smaller carry-on, then pats the bag twice, as if it has been extra good.

"How many biting insects do you suppose there'll be at Janie's engagement party?" I ask her.

She raises her eyebrows, as if there's no way of telling.

One thing I do like about the McAnderson Gallery, where Janie works as the assistant manager, is the feeling you get from the lights: a sense of magic. The two-room gallery, always gushing with cool air, has overhead spotlights that make the colors in each glass sculpture seem to dance. A hidden spotlight here, a sudden flash of light there fill the room with sparkling glass baubles and, accompanying them, little particles of something fairylike—it can't just be dust—that spiral from ceiling to floor. I always expect a wizard in a pointed cap to come out from his hiding place, tap me on the shoulder, point to a shining crystal ball, and ask me if I'd like to see how he does it all. But that, of course, would spoil the magic.

Still, this is a crowded place to put a party, but then, I'm a little fearful of a crowded glass gallery. I'm a little fearful standing by myself in a glass gallery. I'm also just not comfortable at parties, especially when you have to stand, and especially if there's someone standing behind you. I tend to turn around and around in a circle, trying to see everyone. Tonight, the other guests don't act as though they feel restricted by the sculptures, or if they do, they hide it well. With the spotlights and magic dust particles floating all around me, I feel as if I'm moving in slow motion. A kind of soft, tinkling music plays behind the crowd's murmur, music that may not fire up guests for an out-and-out bash but that perfectly accompanies my anxiety-induced snail-like pace.

Maria, my fairy godmother, magically places a glass of champagne in my hand.

"It'll keep one hand busy, at least," she says, knowing that old adage about idle hands. "Have you met Henry?"

She knows I haven't and all of my worries fade away to allow my curiosity to take over.

"Henry, this is Holly Philips, my oldest friend and sister-of-the-bride in perpetuity," Maria says.

Maria's new boyfriend's name is, she swears, Henry Wadsworth James, and all she's told me about him so far is that he works with the Transit Authority and that he looks great in bright orange.

"He gets his hands really dirty," Maria has said to me proudly. She's not being condescending—she really does admire anyone who works hard, especially if there's dirt involved. She has extra affection for really greasy dirt.

I check out his hands first, which have a pinkish clean layer to them. This gives me a warm feeling for Henry right from the start. He's muscular and dark blondish and very cute, about thirty, our age, or maybe even younger. He greets me cheerfully, if a little shyly.

"You have a very interesting name," I tell him, between sips of much-needed champagne.

"I think," he says, "my parents had very high expectations for me. I probably fall short of most of them," he says quietly, lifting his left shoulder up to meet his ear.

"So you don't write?" I ask.

"No, I get nauseous just writing checks for the electric bill," he says, rolling his eyes.

"Ah, good," I say. "One of the few people in any room not writing a novel."

"That's me."

"Henry has other positive qualities, too," Maria assures me. "He can tell you what stop to get off at anywhere in the tri-state area." Henry smiles, embarrassed. "He has a mind like a map. Like several maps."

"I just always seem to know which way is north," Henry says, glancing over his right shoulder, which I guess if I thought about it long enough I'd figure out is north. I tend to get confused going up and down the stairs.

"It's kind of a curse, sometimes," Henry adds.

We're interrupted by a voice that seems too loud for a room with delicate glass figures.

"Hello, Holly, how have you been, having a good time?" Jackson, Janie's young lawyer-with-a-future fiancé, extends his hand to shake mine. It's not a firm handshake, but more the way you'd ask a dog for its paw. I half expect him to say "Shake?"

"Jackson, isn't that a new tie?" Maria teases him. We once wagered on how many ties Jackson owned, but Janie said she got tired of counting after two hundred, so we never got a final count.

"Why, yes, I found this in Boston last month," Jackson says, "dead of winter, no one out shopping. The owner of the store and I discussed gun control, as I recall."

We're stymied for a reply. Henry looks a little frightened. None of us seems to want to ask where Jackson stands on the issue, or whether the tie is real silk.

"This is Henry," I say. They exchange paws. Jackson seems to notice Henry's tieless apparel with an expression that says he might never have considered the possibility of such an outfit. It's not an entirely displeased look he's got, more one of surprise. Henry looks at his own hand as if he's checking to see if something has rubbed off on him.

"I think I left my tie somewhere," Henry says almost sadly.

"The last time I saw it was when you tied me to the bedpost, I think," Maria says.

Jackson excuses himself quickly, after which Maria and Henry giggle quietly.

"I'm so sorry," Henry says to me. "She's just joking." He's broken out in a blush from his dark blonde–covered forehead down to his neck. He knows he's all red, and ducks his head behind Maria.

"Henry's okay," Maria says, patting him on the head. "And he really does own only one tie."

"And I really don't know where it is," he says, still hiding behind Maria's hair, done especially large in Janie's honor tonight.

I get a bear hug from Ronny, my mother's sixty-fivish boyfriend and one of the most enthusiastic creatures on the planet. Ronny's hugs are the real thing—he never treats us like fragile goods, more like big sturdy barrels he's grabbed hold of and lifted for some reason. I always feel slightly dazed afterward.

My mother wears a nice mauve suit with an animal print scarf around her neck. She's got it tied just right, a feat I can never accomplish. Usually I just wind a scarf around and around my neck until I reach the tips, but it ends up coming all undone an hour later and falling in the middle of the street. Still, it gives me something to play with. Ronny wears an animal print pocket square in his suit to match my mother's scarf.

"I guess you're ready for Africa," I say, pointing to the print.

Ronny throws an arm around my mother, which she absorbs without faltering too much.

"I've got seventy rolls of film," Ronny says.

"But I've got the camera," Mom says, and they laugh.

"Your mother, such a kidder," Ronny says. "I've waited my whole life for something like this. Don't you wait that long, Holly."

"I'll try not to," I say.

"Not that I'd trade Allison here," he says curling his arm out for my mother again.

"Not even to be twenty?" my mom asks him.

"Oh, twenty, you can have that," Ronny says. "Who remembers twenty, anyway? Why, here's our little bride-to-be."

Janie approaches in a perfect white suit.

"Always the bride-to-be," my mother whispers to me, "never the bride."

Janie hugs each of us in turn, although Ronny's hug seems to crumple her for a moment. She recovers with a shake of the head.

"Now, then," Janie says. "Are we all having a good time?"

"Yes, dear," my mother says. "We've been admiring the art. Some of these things would look lovely with a few pieces of candy in them."

"Oh, we're especially pleased with this exhibit," Janie says of the bowl-like and rounded sculptures that stand on high bases every few feet around the room. Some look too thin to touch, as if a piece might break off into your hands. Others have a weightiness, a seriousness. You might need help carrying these out of the gallery. We're huddled in a small circle between three of them, spotlights shining around us as if to keep us in our place.

Jackson, the groom-to-be, comes up to stand next to

Janie. For a moment, he looks as if he might shake her hand. Instead, they join hands routinely.

"Doesn't she look just like you'd hope?" Jackson asks us of Janie.

"Don't we all?" my mother replies. I think she's trying not to let sarcasm get the best of her. Not that Jackson and Janie would notice.

"Too bad my folks couldn't make it," Jackson says. "You know, they had a fundraiser, AIDS, very important, Mother in charge, couldn't be changed."

"Will they fit the wedding in?" my mother asks sweetly.

"Oh, the wedding, they wouldn't miss it, of course. You'll love them, everyone does," Jackson rattles.

"I just love weddings," Ronny bursts out and grabs Jackson for a good-old hug. Jackson's feet leave the floor as he continues to hold one of Janie's hands. Janie seems to be trying to balance him somehow. I look to see my mother enjoying this moment immensely.

Melody McAnderson, the gallery owner and Janie's heroine, leads us in a toast to the happy couple. Some days I wake up and wish I were someone else, someone like Melody McAnderson, a woman in her late thirties who not only owns a profitable, artistic business but who looks great wearing flashy earth-tone resort wear–type clothes. She's one of my idols, despite that I'd really never dress this way. My style is much more the baggy trousers and soft shirts or turtlenecks look I wear to work every day, plus my beloved black leggings and tickly sweaters on weekends. Tonight I've thrown my black jacket over a soft white shirt and the one long black skirt I wear for special occasions—usually engagement parties for Janie. The jacket always makes me feel more dressed up, even though I wear it most of the time, although not usually indoors. It's not the earthy but elegant look Melody McAnderson pulls off, but maybe it's all in her attitude. I do worry that Janie and I seem to share a fascination with Melody McAnderson, but then, some women just deserve your admiration. When Melody calls for our attention, everyone in the room turns to her, under her spell.

Maria and Henry have come up beside me to gaze at Melody McAnderson as well.

"Great hair," Maria says.

I don't really pay attention so much to Melody's toasting words as to the casual way she holds a champagne glass, gently, with just two fingers. I try to imitate her, balancing my own glass in a thumb and third-finger grasp, and I begin to feel more elegant, more successful. It dangles nicely. I show Henry, but I'm not sure he understands what I'm doing. Glasses clink as the toast ends, a symphony of tinkling.

My mother and Ronny leave not long after the toast, to rest up for their journey tomorrow. I can't think of a way to leave gracefully, so I'm stuck listening to Jackson tell us about a boat he's thinking of buying that's especially sleek. Or maybe he's talking about a horse. My champagne glass dangles from my unmanicured fingers, and every so often someone seems to refill it. A waiter approaches and offers me some fingertip-size sushi—the kind without fish—so I take a piece and balance it in my left hand, the right hand occupied by looking dignified with its glass. I'm feeling sophisticated, cosmopolitan, at ease. Maria leans over to whisper to me.

"Where'd Janie find Jackson, anyway? At one of those male auctions?"

I laugh, which causes me to lose the grip on my glass for a second. I regain the glass, but somehow lose my own balance and step backward a few steps into a pedestal. The sushi goes flying, and my arm swipes a blue-green bowl that heads for the floor in slow motion, or maybe it just seems that way to me. The bubbles in it seem to be swimming slowly through the dust-particle air, the slender bowl turning round and round as if the glass were being blown all over again, as it heads for the pinkish-gray floor of the McAnderson Gallery. In these few seconds I'm reminded of a carpet cleaning commercial I've seen where something like this happens, but this seems more real, if oddly more distant. Instinctively, I reach out to save the bowl, but I hear Janie's commandment.

"No!"

Janie calls out as if to a small child about to dive into a drained swimming pool. That child is me. Her yell has managed to collect everyone's attention, and it does make me withdraw my free hand. The bowl lands with a surprisingly muffled thud, not the crash I'm expecting, but it breaks apart anyway.

"Whoops," Maria says.

Janie's here in a flash, scolding. "Never, never reach out for a falling glass object," she tells me, not that the whole room isn't listening. "You can severely injure yourself."

"I'm sorry," I say, both for reaching out and for bumping into valuables, and for being here in general.

"Nonsense, it's insured," Janie says with a wave of her hand, and immediately a waiter appears with a dust broom and small vacuum to clear away all traces of shattered art.

"I think I have to be going now," I tell Janie, who tells me not to be silly.

Maria puts an arm around me. "It looked like a doggie dish, anyway," Maria tries to console me.

"You get extra points if you can take out that huge glass artichoke thing by the counter," Maria says.

"I'd pay to see that splatter," Henry agrees.

I'm still grasping the champagne glass I'd truly like to get rid of at this point, as I'm sure it will hinder my slinking from the room. I look to Henry, who reaches out and takes the glass, then hands it to someone passing by. It might have been a waiter, but I don't think so.

"Come with us to this diner we know," Henry suggests.

"Right," Maria says, "we've found this great place. Every hour or so the chef and head waitress arm wrestle. Sometimes you can place bets."

"Nothing major," Henry says. "Mostly you can just bet desserts."

"It's casual," Maria says.

I say no, thanks, as they lead me through the door.

"I think I'll just go home and soak in the bathtub overnight," I say. "That'll make for a new me."

Maria and Henry still try to get me to come along. "They have cherry pie, à la mode," Henry says, a hurt expression on his face, as if he just knocked over the doggie dish instead of me. Finally, they put me in a taxi, the tempting words "à la mode" still in the air.

In the taxi's backseat, I scoot way over to the side as if I've been a bad child forced to sit in the corner. I find that there's a rich smell coming from the taxi, maybe from the front seat, not of air freshener or heater fumes, but of something comforting and familiar, hot cocoa maybe. Or spicier. Hot cocoa with nutmeg. I give the driver the address without thinking about it much, that smell luring me. I know for certain that I don't want to sit in the bathtub all night or watch people arm wrestle for cherry pie. I want to go someplace with familiar scents and sounds, someplace where I don't have to impress or please or keep myself from breaking anything.

Josh's face greets me at his door.

"Hiya, Holly," he says reliably, throwing the door open wide.

*   *   *

My ex-husband's plaid couch has worn-out arms but over-stuffed cushions, and I seem to dissolve into it as I try to explain my evening. I hold a puffy throw pillow tightly to the top of my head, but not for any particular reason. Josh is dressed tonight in a washed-out red work shirt with his faded gray jeans—his whole body cries out with the warmth and comfort of soft denim. I haven't seen him since our overnight expedition in my couchbed a few weeks back, which seems like a dream now, or maybe something I read in a novel and imagined happened to me. Something written in a style with succinct yet pleasing adjectives.

Josh places an electric fan on the table directly in front of me and turns it on high.

"It's a theory I'm testing," he says. "See if the blast of air doesn't make you feel better."

I sit there with air pounding into my face, wondering if it's blowing the bad thoughts from my mind or just making it difficult to think straight at all. Josh watches from a nearby chair.

"Is it working?" he asks.

"I think I'm getting a chill," I say.

"I'll get you something hot," Josh says. "I'll serve it in something childproof," he teases.

I turn the fan down to low, and let the buzz lull me in Josh's quiet apartment. He's got stacks of papers, science-y journals and notebook paper filled with equations scattered around the room, and a few spider plants that litter the carpet with dried leaves.

"Are these plants or experiments?" I ask, as he brings me some chamomile tea in a large plastic cup.

Josh looks at his plants a moment. "I thought they were doing fairly well," he says.

"Oh, they are," I agree. "When we were married, I never saw you water a plant. These look great, in comparison."

"Yeah, I have a research assistant who takes pity on them

and comes over to water them sometimes. Hey," he says excitedly, "did I tell you they're publishing my book?"

"That's good news, Josh. Wow, you have good news." I try to think of the last time I greeted Josh with good news, then realize I'm just feeling sorry for myself. Still.

Josh reaches over and turns the fan back on high. "I think you need more time," he says, as a blast hits me.

We sit for a moment sipping tea. Josh guiltily pinches a few dead leaves from his plants. I watch as he strokes the good leaves in approval. It's an almost hypnotizing gesture, methodical, soothing. I try to let all the things I want to tell him about Janie, the gallery, my mother's trip, and my own doubts flow from my mind with the surge of wind. The thoughts escape and ride the flow, which is directed over my shoulder and toward Josh's kitchen sink. I close my eyes and imagine the thoughts landing in the sink, dissolving in drops of old coffee, flowing down the drain. I realize that Josh hasn't asked me why I'm here, what exactly made me come here. I think it's not a question that would occur to him, although it may be one I should ask myself. Instead I let it flow over my shoulder with the rest of my thoughts, freed from my mind by an electrically induced breeze.

Josh comes over with a trimmed plant.

"This one isn't bad," Josh says, sitting next to me and shielding the plant with his hand from the cool air. "Do you want it?"

I put the plant next to me on the couch, admiring its green-and-yellow brightness. I'll take it home with me tomorrow and give it a place of honor, on top of the fridge, maybe. Or in the bathroom, behind the door, where it can wait to surprise me every day with its slender leaves. For tonight, we'll both stay right where we are.

* * *

In the morning I return to my apartment to find a herd of little paper giraffes lining my front doorstop. At first I think it's a joke, a good-bye from my mother headed for Africa and bigger and better giraffes. Then I pick up one and see the craftsmanship, the even folds and smooth corners to each giraffe, from largest to smallest. I picture Tom's face, rising against the grayish blue of the office walls, nodding hello at me, and realize he's the only one I know who would be capable of making such perfect giraffe feet.

Chapter 6

This Room Is Mine

I decide all of the sudden to paint the trim on all my window-sills and baseboards over the weekend. They were sort of pink-ish before, faded to a shy flesh tone. I want to be bold and go for a deep blue, even though the man at the paint store was just dying to mix a bright greenish color he called Atlantis.

"Makes you think of mermaids, doesn't it?" the paint store guy asked me as he showed me a sample of sea green.

I don't want to think of mermaids, and besides, I think he's got his myths mixed up. Still, he made me a nice batch of blue anyway. It's a rich blue, a blue the color of the ocean and sky in an environmentally correct world. It's the blue of possibility, a blue that says I am in command, I am taking charge of my baseboards.

I start with sanding, because I want to do this right and I like the sweeping sounds sandpaper makes against the wood. The sound is just packed with cause and effect. I turn on my radio to Saturday morning jazz and sand along with the bass player, indulging my creative needs for the week. Someone taps lightly at my door, which at first I mistake for the percussion section.

On second knock I rise to find Janie standing behind the door, wearing my mother's blue-and-white sailor suit and an expression of near misery on her face.

"Are you selling cookies?" I point to her outfit and ask. Janie straightens her bow. "Mom gave it to me. Everything else is at the laundry, so it was either this or fishnet leggings someone gave me at a shower once and wouldn't take back."

"Please come in, before anyone else sees you," I tease her. I kind of wish she were someone selling cookies. I'd buy some Thin Mints right now.

Janie mopes across the threshold, and it occurs to me that she's not just depressed over her outfit.

"Are you painting?" she asks, a little alarmed.

"I'm just painting the trim," I say.

"That seems manageable," Janie says, aware that I still have some unfinished projects lying around the house. Newly painted trim would look nice with the unfinished drapes, if they were finished, I'll bet.

"It's over," she says, slumping across my couch.

"It is?" I ask, thinking first that it's something about my painting job here, then realizing what she probably means.

"I broke off my engagement."

"Oh, I'm sorry," I say.

"Don't you want to know what he did?" Janie asks.

I'd like to consider the question longer, but I say, "Okay," and sit down on a chair. The light jazz has turned into a classic blues tune, something about defeated love, which I figure isn't good for Janie's mood, so I turn it down.

Janie sits up straight, pure Janie again. "Well, he went to my boss, you know Melody, and he insisted that she give me a raise, since I'm left in charge much of the time."

"Why would he do that?" I ask. And, "How much of a raise?" I think but don't ask. I've long suspected that my little sister may be making more money than I do, but I don't want my suspicions confirmed.

"I don't know what he was thinking. He didn't even know exactly how much I made."

I'm pleased, in a way, that Janie won't marry Jackson, pleased that I won't have to smile at him at family events or ever have to meet his parents, pleased that I can stop wondering if his way of speaking is grammatically correct. Still, Janie's my sister, and part of me wants to put her in a swingset and push her back and forth until she feels better. The sailor suit only adds to the mood.

"Would you like a juice?" I ask.

"Yes, please," she says like the little sister she'll always be.

I get her some fresh-squeezed orange juice from the juicer I've appropriated, her former shower gift.

"He was obsessed with money," Janie says. "And always working. Like Dad." Janie takes a sip. "Don't you wonder why we surround ourselves with men like that, men who hide behind stacks of paper and don't pay us nearly enough attention? It all started with Dad, you know."

Janie's suggestion, although it sounds slightly like something she might have found in one of those "Foolish Women"–type books, makes me feel a little defensive. I refuse to stop and think why I feel defensive, although I'm certain one of her books could tell me.

"Dad's not working anymore," I tell her. "He's retired. He has ducks now."

"Ducklings?" Janie brightens a little.

"No, wooden ones," I admit. "Decoys."

Janie thinks a moment. "Isn't that just as bad?"

Newly invigorated by juice, which has long been a cure-all in our family, Janie gets ready to leave.

"I'm going shopping now," she informs me.

"You should never shop when all of your clothes are in the laundry," I say. "It's like food shopping on an empty stomach, you'll come home with too many impulse items. That's why we all have so many ponytail holders."

"Oh, Holly," Janie says with a laugh. She comes up to me and gives me a hug. We're not much of a huggy family, except for my mother's boyfriend Ronny, but I realize this is a moment between sisters. It's not like I never wanted to hug Janie, just that I always felt I might muss something.

"You're so lucky, you never have these problems," Janie says. Maybe she doesn't mean to offend, but I'm still surprised. While I haven't been engaged six times, I like to think I have as many problems with men as the next girl.

"I saw Josh," I say, the words slipping through my mouth, like "I do so have problems!" My intonation also makes it clear that I did a lot more than just "see" Josh.

"Why?"

That's the one little word I usually refuse to think about. Why did I go to see Josh, or allow him to stay over that time? Why sleep with Josh at all? Because I know where he is? Because there's no first-time nervousness? Because I don't have to explain everything about myself over again? I picture the questions in my mind along with one of those Scantron-style answer sheets. A blank one, yet to be filled in.

"Familiarity?" I ask. It's just a guess, really. I also remember reading that on multiple-choice exams, you're not supposed to guess. It can be held against you.

"That's too easy," Janie says. She sits down again. "It's like working out. If it's too easy, it doesn't do anything for you."

My baby sister is lecturing me on love, or maybe sex, or maybe just aerobics. Life gets strange when the girl you remember as always throwing up in the backseat on car trips starts advising you on sexual matters. It's even stranger when what she says may be true. I can't think of a reply.

"Well, off to Bloomingdale's," Janie says with a leap.

"Like that?" I always find salespeople refuse to take me seriously unless I'm all dressed up, and even then they tend to ignore me.

"It's Saturday, they'll never notice this," Janie says of the sailor suit. "Besides, they'll still take my credit card, even if I'm naked."

"Maybe I should try going there naked next time," I say, "so someone will rush over and help me."

"Oh, Holly," Janie says, "you and your confidence."

"You think I lack confidence?"

"Others might. I know better," she says mysteriously with a wave. Then she's gone.

While I had planned to sand everything first, I decide just to get started painting the window trim after a few swipes at it with sandpaper. I find something hypnotic, something soothing about the back-and-forth motion of painting, the repetitiveness, the smooth look of fresh paint against wood. I begin to make sweeping motions with my paintbrush, slowly moving my right hand along, as if conducting a band. I sing that old song "Down in the Valley" as I paint, although I'm not sure why that song comes to mind. I don't sing at all well, but this doesn't stop me. I especially enjoy singing the lower parts, and I've managed to put myself into a lulling trance. I guess I'm one of those people who don't need drugs. Just the odd job around the house and camp songs will do it.

A much louder knock on the door this time cuts into my song, making me shriek and get a little blue paint on the wall. I grab a cloth to work on the spot. Someone knocks again. I pull the door open aggressively, and Jackson, Janie's latest ex-fiancé, takes a step back. I've scared him.

"Hello, Holly, good, glad to find you at home," Jackson says in his usual run-on manner.

"Jackson, hi."

We just stand there. I wonder for a second what he's doing here, and whether he heard me singing the low parts. They're the most potentially embarrassing.

"Janie's not here," I say.

"Oh, no, sure. I thought we might talk, though, if you've got time, of course," Jackson suggests.

"Oh," I say. It hadn't occurred to me that Jackson might ever want to talk to me, one-on-one. I've never had the urge to talk to him this way, really. Not that I can't think of a few questions. I invite him in.

"Are you painting?" he asks. I wonder why people say such things when it's pretty clear you're painting. What else could an open can of paint, unfinished trim and a stray spot of blue paint on the wall mean?

I decide the question is rhetorical and don't answer it. Jackson sits down on my couch just where Janie sat before. Maybe I was wrong about them. They might have been just the right match. Or perhaps I'm building too much into a coincidence. Still, I'm intrigued: None of Janie's former fiancés has ever come to see me before.

"Janie's left me, thrown me over, dumped me, left me for dead," Jackson says. Really he's beside himself.

"I wouldn't say left you for dead," I offer.

"I want her back," Jackson says.

"Why?" It's the first thing out of my mouth and maybe not so nice, but I realize I'd really like to know.

He looks at me with big eyes.

"Oh, you're taking her side, I see. Of course you would, I understand, I don't mean to try to divide your loyalties."

"Well, good," I say. "That's a relief." I'm just talking without thinking now, since I don't really follow Jackson and the place is alive with paint fumes. I wonder if they have any effect on Jackson.

"She's meant so much to me, you see. I've never been engaged before."

"But Janie has," I say, wondering if I'm dividing my loyalties.

"Oh, I know that," Jackson admits.

"And it's never bothered you? Even a little, even in the back of your mind?" I'm starting to sound like a therapist, or a talk-show host.

"No, no. As long as she was marrying me, I didn't care how many others she didn't marry. Everything would have been perfect."

"It's never perfect," I say. "Janie isn't perfect."

Jackson tilts his head and looks at me, doglike and a bit pathetic. He hasn't considered that my younger sandy-blonde-haired independent but marriage-minded sister could be anything less than perfect. Clearly, he hasn't seen her in the sailor suit. Although actually, she didn't look half bad in it.

Jackson lets out a long breath. Relaxed here on the couch— or more like disintegrated than relaxed—Jackson takes on an almost attractive, if a little pitiful, quality. When you let the air out of him, he begins to seem more normal.

"I've blown it," he says, and with perfect, simple grammar, I notice.

"It might be best to move on," I say gently. "Janie never changes her mind about these things. Honest."

"Maybe," he says, almost like a suggestion, only he stops there.

Jackson tilts his head way back and loosens his tie. Yes, he's wearing a tie on Saturday, although it's crumpled around the edges. He holds his head back as if trying to stop a nosebleed.

"Would you like a juice?" I ask him.

"I never liked juice," Jackson says sadly, as if admitting

this might have been his downfall with Janie. He looks lost in a zombie state. "Can I help you paint?" he asks.

"Don't you have something you should be doing?"

"I was supposed to play squash at three," Jackson says. I don't even know what squash is, which I'd say, but I don't feel like having him explain it to me. I guess I like that I'm the kind of person who doesn't know what squash is.

"But I canceled," he says. "Now I just have a therapist appointment at two-thirty." Jackson looks at his watch, then lets his arm fall to the couch. Poor guy.

"Therapist?" I ask. "As in, well, therapy?"

He nods.

"I didn't know you saw a therapist."

"I do now," Jackson says with a sigh.

It's not like me to engage in one of my household tasks with someone on the premises, I guess because I get such a thrill out of doing it myself. And I'm sure I'd get a real sense of fulfillment if I were ever to finish anything. Still, I tell Jackson he can sand the baseboards. This seems to inflate him a little.

"I'll be very careful," he says, although I don't see what harm he could do with sandpaper.

"Don't you want to take off your tie?" I suggest.

Jackson gives me a look of surprise, then of daring even, and he rips off his tie and holds it up like a prized, just-caught fish. Jackson smiles, for the first time today. Maybe it's the first time I've ever seen him smile, and I can't help but laugh in approval. Jackson walks over to my opened window, careful not to mess the trim, and throws his tie out to the world. He doesn't stick around to watch it sail to the ground, but instead turns his attention to the sandpaper, examining both sides carefully, as if trying to decide which to use.

*   *   *

Later that night I listen to call-in radio, which always seems especially sad on Saturday nights. I like the voices, though, I have to admit. The first caller wants advice about a love affair that happened nearly ten years ago, and the talk-show host gently tries to suggest that the caller move on with her life. The next caller disagrees, insisting that these things have a way of staying with us, that we have to resolve them. I refuse to take sides, certain that I can understand both viewpoints, that neither is completely right or wrong. To accompany the voices, I put on a Bach concerto I'm fond of. I discovered a while back that I can play my cassette deck at the same time as the FM, a feature I might have paid extra for, if I'd had to. Probably the stereo's just broken. I find the combination of low voices and violins kind of like having someone lean over and chat softly with me at a concert.

I'm on the last baseboard in the living room, the second coat of deep blue paint. As I finish it, I find I want to sit back and absorb the fresh color into my mind, but I can't lean back or I'll smear the paint. Instead, I sit on my couchbed in the middle of the room, inhaling the cold breeze through my open window. I'm wearing four layers, but the cold is worth it—the smell of a chilly Saturday night mixes perfectly with the now-irresistible fresh-paint scent, not to mention the faint musk of accomplishment. I close my eyes and pull a hat down over my ears. *This room is mine*, I whisper to the voices on the radio. *This room is mine*, the violins play softly, echoing our voices.

Chapter 7

Tuesday Approaches

The new diner that Maria favors these days is simply called Pie, and above its front door hangs a large neon sign of a pie minus one slice. The neon blinks on and off, and as you enter or leave the diner, you can hear it buzzing with killer-bee intensity. Inside they have those mirrored display cabinets that show off the pies. The center showcase features five golden-brown pies, all missing that one front slice and oozing with inviting berries. A sign over the counter reads "Try Life à la Mode!"

Maria and I meet over warm slices of cherry pie with vanilla ice cream, although she insists I return sometime to try what they call Skip-to-My-Lou pie. She won't tell me what's in it.

"They had a contest to see if anyone could figure out the exact ingredients, but no one could," Maria says.

"So that means you'll never know what you're eating?"

"You have to admire that in a pie," Maria says.

I'm glad we've stuck with the cherry. Maria's boyfriend, Henry, will join us later, on a break from his job with the subway, since there's a stop on the corner.

I tell Maria about my weekend.

"It's the first time any of my sister's ex-fiancés has come to me for help," I say. "Not that I could offer much help."

"I'll have to speak to Janie," Maria says. "I love to hear how she dumps them. Did you know she never uses the same line twice?"

I didn't know this. My sister has told me little about the process she uses to extricate herself from her engagements. But then again, I'm always embarrassed to ask, and it's not like I'd actually use the techniques myself.

"She says she likes to develop an appropriate, individualized speech to give any boyfriend or fiancé," Maria says of Janie, "to help him on his way to future relationships. She'd make a great personnel director."

"As long as she didn't start dating the employees," I say.

"Imagine Jackson coming to see you. Did he look all sad and puppy-doggish yet appropriately accented with a tie?"

"Pretty much," I say. "He looked like he'd come from a blood-letting session."

"And did you take pity on him and try to seduce him?"

"Me? No, of course not."

"You didn't even consider it?" Maria asks.

"No. I did offer him juice."

"See, and you think you're not a good person," Maria says.

"Is Jackson seducible, theoretically speaking?" I ask. "I mean, is he seduction material?"

"It's a good question," Maria ponders. "He's male and human in a general sense, which is the starting ground."

"He sanded my baseboards."

"That's a prerequisite for seduction in several Third World countries," Maria says. "Besides, I like a man who works with his hands."

"He wasn't all that good at it, though," I admit.

Maria makes a sighing noise and we scoop up pie. Henry comes in, beaming in an orange zip-up jumpsuit. Maria takes one of his hands.

"You've washed," she says, trying to hide her disappointment.

"I'll get dirty again, don't worry," Henry says.

"It's okay. You have a nice smudge on your face," she tells him.

Henry orders the Skip-to-My-Lou pie with Oh-My-Darling ice cream.

"Someone guessed what was in the ice cream," Maria says, "but they've sworn not to tell."

A bell rings and a man in an old-fashioned chef's hat comes out from the kitchen. He and a waitress who's about forty-five, with a name patch on her blouse that says "Oh, Miss," begin to arm wrestle at the front counter. Another waitress yells out, "Place your bets!"

"That's Belle wrestling Simon," Maria says.

"I've seen Belle throw a fight," Henry whispers.

"It's true. But Simon's no match for her," Maria says. We all watch attentively as Belle takes her time, then slams Simon's arm to the counter. Cheers go up from the crowd, and pie changes hands. Belle offers Simon a Coke on her before he returns to the kitchen. I look back to see Maria and Henry holding hands.

"This is our place," Maria says, looking to Henry. He nods.

Tuesday approaches. I try to dress normally for work, picking out a clean black turtleneck—I have a few that are less than clean—and trousers. Actually, the pants have a spot on them just above my heel, but this isn't worth getting them cleaned yet. This is my standard workday editing gear, although we can wear whatever we want at Science Press. By Fridays, most people seem to throw on an old flannel shirt. Sometimes we buy coffee for the person with the shirt closest to disintegrating. But for Tuesday, the turtleneck will do, not to mention that tonight I'm having dinner with my officemate Tom, per his written origami invitation. A disintegrating flannel shirt might give the wrong impression.

On my desk I have a list of the songs my radio station has played at every half-hour point between nine and five over the past two weeks. Lots of the others at work do, too, and we're not above comparing notes. The prize of five thousand dollars seems worthwhile. Most of us won't bother with a contest under five hundred dollars, although I do sometimes. One of our art directors won a new Walkman that way, and she seemed pleased.

In between writing down the half-hour songs, I continue to work on my projects, and I admit to thoroughly enjoying my job. Most people don't know that a production editor is different from a regular editor, that we're technically farther down the food chain, especially in terms of how many lunches Science Press allows us on them. Production editors buy their own. It's not as if the acquisition editors or senior editors are better people than we are, they just get paid more. My work involves talking to authors to keep them happy about their books-in-progress, gathering work from the art department (and keeping the art department happy on their books-in-progress), and generally keeping track of each stage of each book. I love all the intricate interaction. Twice a week, my supervisor, Monique, comes by my desk for an official visit to check my progress.

"How's 'The Cyst'?" she asks, using her code name for the ovarian cancer book. She has a nickname for each project.

"It's responding nicely to final paste-up," I say.

She checks through each book on her list. "This is dull," she says. "How's your boyfriend?" she asks me belligerently. "Tell me something good."

"I'm unattached," I say. "Same as last week."

"Yeah, but one day you'll surprise me, huh?"

We don't know much about Monique's personal life. My editor friend Nina once saw Monique walking down Thirtieth Street with an older man, in his fifties or sixties. Monique was slapping some dust off the arm of his raincoat. "She was laughing while she did it," Nina told me. "Really enjoying it."

"How's *your* boyfriend?" I ask Monique.

"You don't want to know," she tells me. Monique hands me a folder with a new book project in it.

"Because you've been so good," she says dryly.

I love getting a new book, and I start to look at it right away.

"Take your time," Monique says. "Don't get overheated."

My new project contains research from a symposium held in Norway, which looks good at first because it could mean transcontinental phone calls to men named Per. Everyone will be envious. But then I see the title, and I'm a little disappointed, because the research is on moles—not the animal kind, the kind on your skin.

"Moles?" I turn back to Monique. "This is the best you can do?"

"You've never seen moles like these babies," Monique says. We place the close-up photos across my desk to examine them, Monique's favorite part of the job. They're numbered, so we can't get them out of order, which allows us to rearrange them in our own "most frightening" ranking.

"Scary," I say.

"My cousin had one like this." Monique points out an unattractive splotch.

"Eew. How'd it turn out?"

Monique shakes her head and sighs. "Ugh, look at this one," she says, and gives it first-place ranking. "Looks like something you'd see on the floor of the subway. Something you wouldn't dare to step in." She pats my arm and rises to leave.

"Enjoy," she says.

I spend the afternoon organizing my mole book. It seems that one of the photographs is missing after all, so I'll get to alert the author in Norway. I check under my desk a few times to make certain we didn't drop the photo while we were ranking them, but then I realize it was never logged in. If it were a truly disgusting photo, I might wonder for a moment if Monique had sent it in for a copy. She keeps a private collection of the most terrifying artwork published by Science Press, which she shows at parties, although not everyone gets a look.

Between pictures I think about Norway, a cold land to the north that I might never visit, where I imagine people wearing large furry hats and coats. A place where the air smells crisp and clean, with the faraway smells of stews cooking over wood-burning stoves. I imagine trudging through the snow for a loaf of thick bread and some salmon, wearing thick sturdy shoes that magically do not ever give me blisters.

At five o'clock, Tom peeks over the wall at me. He's been eerily quiet today. I passed him once in the hallway, but all he did was nod and keep moving. It must be nervousness: Tuesday night has arrived. Date night.

"I got a new book," I tell him. He nods, impressed. "Moles. See?"

I hold up a photo with a mole shaped like a duck, although Monique thought it looked more like the *Titanic*.

Tom takes hold of it for a look.

"Bad color on that one," he says, handing it back over the partition.

"You bet," I say. At least Tom's not squeamish.

Monique passes us on her way out of the office. I say good-bye and Tom waves at her.

"Yeah, yeah," she says, happily miserable, I think.

Tom says he'd like to cook dinner for us, claiming he dislikes restaurants. I'm not fond of restaurants either, since I never know where to put my feet, or my purse. Sometimes I put my purse under my feet, which solves things until I cross my legs and kick the purse across the floor. That's just one of my problems with restaurants.

We take the train to Carroll Gardens, where Tom lives. We share a few uncomfortable moments there when the train stops dead in the middle of a tunnel. No one tells us why. It stops and starts a few times, not getting very far, but jolting us enough to make us look really stupid trying to hold on to the pole.

Tom just shrugs at the train's convulsions. "This is often the best part," he says. "Tell me more about moles."

"Oh, I don't just edit moles," I answer. We've never talked about our projects together. Mostly we've just traded variations on the word "Hi." "I also work on larger mammals, rashes, and internal disorders," I say. "I don't really have a specialty."

"I do," he says. "I get the books with the most equations. The typesetters counted them up once. They sent the proofs back to me with a red ribbon. Higher math," Tom says.

"Nina's books all start with the word 'epidermal,'" I tell him.

"I guess we're lucky, then," Tom says, as we arrive at his stop.

Tom has the garden apartment, and when we step inside, he flicks two sets of switches. On come a series of little white lights strung together, like you might find at Christmastime. He's hung the lights around the center of the room, surrounding a small table covered with a red-and-white-checkered tablecloth and, I notice enviously, a set of matching silverware. A table for two.

"It's lovely," I say, and it is. "All that's missing are waiters singing arias."

"I can't afford them," Tom says. "Union wages." He puts on a tape of Vivaldi. "You can take your shoes off if you want."

"Wow, my favorite kind of restaurant," I say, putting my shoes in a corner. I decide to explore the place after Tom makes a series of hand gestures that I think mean "Make yourself at home." He disappears into his kitchen, only halfway out of my view. This isn't a large apartment, although it's twice the size of mine.

"You must entertain often," I say, admiring his wineglasses. They're hand-blown green goblet-size things, and Tom has four that match.

Tom pokes his head out of the kitchen and looks at me, then shakes his head no.

This means he's probably gone to a lot of trouble just for me, or he's extremely adept at hanging lights. I run my hands across a desk made out of a deep-colored wood with small black knots. There's a matching bookshelf off to the side. Both pieces give off a cozy scent, as if they came from your grandmother's country house, if she happened to have had one.

"Your furniture is wonderful," I say, noticing a coffee table of what I think is called cherry wood, or at least that has the color of fresh-picked cherries, not the jarred kind. "Where did you get stuff like this?"

Tom appears carrying a salad bowl in one hand and an oil and vinegar set in another, not to mention a tall pepper mill tucked under his arm. He places them on the table gracefully.

"Stuff?" he asks.

I'm momentarily speechless by his waiter skills, but I turn back to the furniture and gesture, like a game show hostess.

"I made those," Tom says.

"Wow," I say again, although I regret it almost instantly.

It's a word I've been trying to eradicate from my vocabulary, mostly because it makes me sound like I'm twelve.

"It's beautiful," I say, although I feel like I've said this before. He pulls out a chair for me. After I sit down, he lights the two red candlesticks at the center of the table, then sits also. I wonder if he's made the chairs, which are pillowless, the kind you might find in a library, yet comfortable enough to rest upon with a classic for several hours.

"So you make your own furniture," I say, wanting more information.

"My neighbor lets me have space in his garage to work in. It's just something I do," Tom says. He leaps up unexpectedly from the table and runs to the kitchen. I wait to see if he'll explain this behavior. He's gone several minutes.

"Everything okay in there?" I finally ask.

"The clams seem a little pensive," Tom says, then returns from the kitchen with a bottle of wine.

"Notice the fine vintage," he says.

I examine the Italian label. "I can't find the year."

"There isn't one. I think they made this last week," Tom says.

"Well, it must have taken at least a few days to get over here, so it's aged some," I say.

"The pasta should be ready soon." Tom spoons salad onto our plates professionally. Not one of the cherry tomatoes goes astray.

"I hope you don't have a problem with clams," he says.

"Somebody in our office is working on a book on clams," I tell him. "I asked Monique if I could have it, but all she said was something like, 'Mollusks, you're better off not knowing.'"

"She watches out for us, in her way," Tom says. He nods awhile.

We seem to have run out of shoptalk. I decide not to initiate conversation for a bit, see if I can force Tom to talk more. After about ten seconds of silence, I change my mind. Ten seconds can seem like a very long time.

"This is great salad," I say. Tom looks down at his, as if to check, then smiles. He pushes an unwanted olive over to the side of his plate. Although I've already had a few olives from my own salad, I think about reaching out for his. I don't, though, because you never know what might happen when you put your fingers in someone else's food.

"How long have you lived here?" I try.

"A couple years," he says. "I had a roommate, at first, but the neighbors asked him to leave. Noises," he says cryptically.

"You have persuasive neighbors?"

"It's a family area," Tom says. "Large families. They've been very supportive."

Tom brings in our pasta dinner. I didn't see him put it together, so I can't swear he didn't have it delivered at his back door. But I don't really think he has a back door. The meal doesn't at all resemble the spaghetti dinners I've thrown together since college, which consist of undercooked pasta, defrosted peas, and that sugary sauce that's often on special. Tom's, though, is the kind of food they photograph.

"That's beautiful," I say. "You could market that."

"It's just linguine with clams," he says, but I think he's pleased.

Surrounding the pasta, Tom has created a bed of small, cutout paper clamshells that match our place mats, which are larger, more absorbent paper clamshells. It all has that handmade look to it, not the crummy kindergartner-with-a-scissors look, but the take-your-time, master-craftsperson look.

As we eat, the candles cast a reddish glow over the small table, which I imagine must be another of Tom's handmade items. I admire his hands, the makers of all these homey touches—I expect them to look beat up, pounded by the erring hammer or grazed by the occasional power tool with a mind of its own. But no, his hands are just hands, regular size, not especially large or dinged up. Like what I figure a magician's hands would be like, capable of hiding all sorts of surprises. And in his own apartment, Tom's face has lost some of its boyish roundness, easing into a relaxed, more mature oval.

We both fall into talk about the office again, comfortable ground for us, discussing the building, the art department with its collection of tiny dinosaurs, the elevator that breaks down once a week. The mailroom has a pool about when the elevator will break down next, and it turns out Tom won fifty dollars once. After dinner and dessert—cannolis made fresh and given to Tom by the neighbors—Tom rides back with me on the subway to make sure I get home safely.

"I have an old car I could drive you in," Tom explains, "but it's locked in the neighbor's garage. I don't want to wake them starting it. It's not a quiet process."

Tom walks me to my door from the subway, and I await that moment of awkwardness, that moment when it's just you and him and a door you can sometimes lean on, sometimes escape through. Sometimes the door just brings up more questions, as to how many of you should walk through it, but maybe I'm dwelling too much on an innocent piece of architecture. Tom, seeming suddenly not at all awkward, takes my hand and shakes it professionally, coworkers that we are. And yet there's something not at all professional about it, something warmer about the touch of his hand, the shake-shake gesture and then a pause, all in slow motion it seems to me. Would one coworker normally pause during a handshake with another as Tom does, gently turning my hand over onto its side to rest in his for just a moment, causing me to step back to rest upon my door? I'm left to wonder as Tom leaves with a little nod that's almost a bow. I listen to him walk softly down the steps and feel a warmth in my right hand as I consider our evening. I realize I've never met a man who makes paper clamshell place mats before.

Chapter 8

Aromatherapy

Maria drives me in her old Dodge Dart to a spa north of the city, just beyond the New Jersey line.

"Who goes to a spa in New Jersey?" I ask her.

"We do, because we're young, adventurous women and the passes are free," Maria answers.

One of Maria's best customers at the pharmacy, an elderly, raspy-voiced woman known to all as Pearl, has given Maria two weekend passes to the MaryAnn Spa. Maria gets lots of gifts from such women, who claim she's the only one who will listen to their health problems. She probably is.

So we've left our usual weekend full of dirty laundry behind and packed our swimsuits, leotards, and shower flip-flops (Maria insisted) for a weekend of working out and relaxing, although more of the latter if I have my way. I've read about these spas in women's magazines. I know they have special oils and herbal mixtures they massage into you, extracts and fruitlike concoctions you can soak in that persuade you to forget your quest for the meaning of life and just breathe deeply instead. Allow your pores a rest from the pressures of everyday life, the articles always tell me, forget about how black soot manages to get into your windowsill after a rainstorm when you're several floors up from the ground. Free your mind from those worries about never being able to get your change out of your wallet quickly enough. The articles have me convinced, I admit. I'm looking forward to soaking in something strawberry for a few hours.

"Actually," it occurs to me, "I've never heard of the MaryAnn Spa."

"It could be so exclusive no one's allowed to write about it. It could be the answer to all of your problems. MaryAnn could change our lives," Maria says, steering the Dart with one hand.

I love being in the pristine Dart, passed down to Maria from her late grandmother. The Dart still has firmly padded seats, even after all these years. Beige vinyl upholstery, matching dashboard, push-button radio. The Dart is a throwback to our childhoods, even though I never rode in one as a kid. Still, I can imagine playing with those push buttons, driving my own grandmother to distraction. We are riding through New York in our own histories, heading for New Jersey.

Maria wants details on my dinner with Tom. She even wants to know exactly what spices went into the linguine. I'm never good at identifying individual spices.

"Green with a hint of red," I say. "I can't be more specific."

"Too bad. You can tell a lot about a guy by his choice of spice. Oregano versus sage, for example. The difference is enormous."

"Fresh versus that dried stuff in the little plastic bottles, you mean?"

"Oh, if he used fresh?" Maria lets out a whistle of approval, even though we'll never be sure. I think Tom would have used the fresh, though.

"You know," Maria informs me, "lunch at The Jelly Deli is one thing, dinner in a garden apartment with spices? Well, that's a whole different level of involvement."

"Maybe," I say.

"No witnesses," Maria says, nodding solemnly.

"I don't know," I say. "I mean, he went to a lot of trouble, but it was still just dinner."

"You said it was salad, dinner, and dessert," Maria specifies.

"Yes, we had all three," I admit. "And rolls."

"Bakery or Grand Union?"

"It's possible neighbors baked them specifically for the occasion."

"Then you'd better figure out your feelings for this guy, take it from me," Maria says.

I haven't exactly followed her logic, but I suspect she's right.

I can just see Tom's face softening before his flickering candles, but I can't really make out how I feel about that face. I do remember admiring that he had one of those little brass candlesnuffers that leave behind a trail of smoke when you snuff the candles. I also remember the smooth feel of his wood table beneath my hand, Tom's grinding fresh pepper over my salad without causing either of us to sneeze, and the way he gave me the biggest cannoli. I don't know what to make of such thoughts, although I have a whole weekend to Ping-Pong them around in my mind. Or try to just leave them alone. As Maria hunts for a radio station with her push buttons, I think of my late-night call-in radio shows, what the pros would say about homemade place mats and little white lights strung around a homemade dinner table.

"Remember the three Ls, from high school?" Maria asks me. "You know, Like, Lust, and Love? Things were so simple then, when you could decide that you liked him, but didn't lust after him, or you lusted after him, but didn't really love him. Then there's the worst, when you love him but don't really like him."

"Or no one else does."

"Oh, I'm a case study in that one," Maria says.

"I like Tom," I say, following Maria's formula, "but I can't attest to the other *L*s."

"Can you rule them out for the future?"

I think a moment. "I'm just not sure. I do lust after his coffee table." At least his coffee table, I think.

Maria shrugs. "I've started relationships on less," she says. Then her pharmacist voice takes over. "But I wouldn't advise it."

We arrive at the MaryAnn Spa, a series of pink buildings connected by overpasses. With its two-story structures and neatly trimmed but not flowering hedges, it looks a little like a junior college. In the center of the complex, surrounded by a circular driveway, stands a sculpture of a woman with her hands on her hips. She's not a particularly thin woman, I notice.

We're greeted at the front desk by a not-quite-so-large real woman whose T-shirt says "MaryAnn" across her chest. Her hairdo is even puffier than Maria's tends to be. Maria's eyes light up.

"It's her," Maria says. "MaryAnn!"

I look around to see that the other employees wear similar "MaryAnn" T-shirts, all in pastels.

"They're all her," I say.

"Do you suppose MaryAnn is a conglomerate?" Maria asks.

"Maybe there's just a little MaryAnn in all of us," I suggest.

Maria nods and walks over to the middle of the room. "MaryAnn?" she calls out quietly. The three employees nearby all turn to look at her, but no one exactly responds.

She returns to my side. "Just testing," Maria says.

A MaryAnn replicant shows us to our connecting rooms and points out our daily schedules on the beds. She leaves us to discover spa life for ourselves with the simple instructions: "Don't overdo it now, girls."

I look around my room, which is more Ramada Inn than I'd hoped. I admit I'd imagined something luxurious, or at least frilly. The room is a severe peach tone, although I'd never considered peach a severe color before. Peach Aztec bedspread with matching shams, a sheer peach set of drapes, peach wall-to-wall carpet. It's almost blinding. The MaryAnn Spa seems to take its pastels seriously.

We leave the door open between our rooms.

"I don't have a Jacuzzi," Maria calls out from her room.

"I don't have a bathtub," I counter.

Maria heads into my room.

"It's a stall shower," I say.

Maria scrunches up her face and takes a good look. "It's a very clean one, you have to admit," she says. "And you've got your flip-flops."

I nod.

Maria looks back at the peach interior. "My room is more what you'd call honeydew," she says. "Nice to wake up to, but a little hard to take after a few drinks, I'll bet."

I nod again.

"I have a feeling," Maria says, "we haven't really discovered the best parts yet."

We're in time for "Saturday Morning Aerobics with Sal," our schedules tell us, so we slip into our binding leotards and tights. Well, mine bind, anyway.

"I haven't done aerobics in a year and a half," I confide to Maria before we enter the Femme Aerobics Lounge, "unless you count that time I was late and ran twenty blocks to meet my mother."

"Not to worry," she says, taking one look at the room. In the ideal feminist world we try to live in, where we're all sisters, you might say that this room consists of our mothers and grandmothers. We're the youngest women in the room by far, and that includes Sal, what they used to call a full-figured woman in a really binding leotard.

"I like her whistle," Maria says.

I'm actually feeling a little encouraged, since this may mean I won't have to work out so hard. The women smile and wave us into an uncrowded area. No one has ever smiled at me at aerobics before. And no one in New York has ever cleared a space for me, anywhere. Somehow, I fit right in.

The friendliest of the women around us, Jeanette, has short, well-kept gray hair and an impressive trimness—she must be in her early sixties. I envy her easygoing haircut. Short hair, I've always felt, would make me look like an unhappy donkey.

"That's my mom, Gloria, although everyone calls her Gran," Jeanette tells us, pointing out her mother in a chair over by the side. Gran's far into her eighties and yelling for things to get started already. Gran sports what can only be described as a blue-and-gray punk haircut.

"I'll bet she'd do the aerobics," Jeanette says, "if I'd let her."

We exercise to records I'm sure my mother would recognize, artists I've heard somewhere, maybe on those commercials on TV late at night, lifelong collections of hits from the fifties. Or maybe the forties. Music to get close to that special someone by. Those commercials always feature a fireplace, or a tall, grassy field with two unidentifiable people holding hands. Or maybe this is the Polka Songs We Love collection. Either way, the music is familiar and safe, the aerobics simple but still pleasing, kind of like doing the hokey-pokey and turning yourself around.

After the workout, Maria says, "Let's do it again," but I'm ready for lunch. We head to the Cafe la Cuisine, for our first encounter with the light spa cuisine we've heard so much about. A lot of the signs around here seem to be misusing French, but I don't say anything.

Gran and Maria have moved ahead of me, so I speed up to catch them.

"A boy down on St. Marks cuts it," I hear Gran tell Maria, who nods at Gran's shorn blue head.

"It makes a statement," Maria tells her, and Gran smiles.

Lunch takes us a bit by surprise. None of the others seems bothered about sitting around in our leotards, although none of us has exactly broken a sweat. The Cafe la Cuisine continues in the pastel-in-a-blender color scheme, mixing my peach with Maria's honeydew, and toping it off with tangerine-and-wintergreen tablecloths. A lopsided green plant—it looks like it's in the same plant family as the hedges outside—serves as a centerpiece, as someone has tied pink satin bows to it here and there. The real surprise, though, is the food.

"I didn't know a chili burger was considered spa cuisine," Maria says, looking at a neighbor's lunch.

"And such a big one," I whisper.

"Oh, it's not like those fancy-schmancy spas," Jeanette tells us, "where they serve you a raw onion ring for a meal, with a little parsley on the side."

Gran agrees. "They don't expect you'll need to eat the garnish here," she says.

A waitress serves Maria and me our Très Bien chicken sandwiches with what looks to me like Thousand Island dressing, which my mother always calls Thousand Calorie dressing. I must admit I'm pleased, and my gratitude escapes me in the two simple words I say to Maria: "French fries!"

"Please," Maria says, "pommes frittes. I knew you'd like it here."

The day goes by in a pleasant and not very strenuous way, which includes horseback riding along tree-lined groves just beyond the pink stables of the MaryAnn Spa.

"I think they're just ponies," Maria says, but I like mine, a gray horse named Darcy with a periwinkle ribbon in her hair. Darcy clops along at a pace that will in no way interfere with my digestion of the Très Bien chicken and fries, not to mention the apricot torte I split with Maria. Maria's black horse, Jocko, holds his head up tall and shakes it every time Maria pats him, which she can't seem to resist doing.

"Jocko's ticklish," Maria says, and Jocko shakes again with pleasure. I can't help but take a mental step back and admire this picture. Here we are, riding along a glade in New Jersey on ticklish ponies, another of life's surprises.

After pony rides and showers, Maria and I peruse the gift shop for MaryAnn memorabilia. We settle on MaryAnn Spa visors in our pastel shades of peach and honeydew, although Maria is tempted by the colorful display of flip-flops.

"You have to admire a place with this much variety in shower shoes," Maria says. She finally selects a couple of pairs, his-and-hers in an un-MaryAnn-like neon orange.

"For Henry," Maria says. "They're perfect."

At dinner we join a table of women who try to encourage us to order Boeuf à la MaryAnn. We decline the heavy meat covered with a dark sauce and choose instead the baked salmon, even though it doesn't have a cute name. We try to make amends to our tablemates by ordering the MaryAnn Mais Oui dessert, even though it turns out to be a giant Oreo-like cookie stuffed with pale mint ice cream, no doubt color coordinated to match the decor of Cafe la Cuisine. Maria holds up a spoon of the stuff, comparing it to our tablecloth.

"MaryAnn must have approved," she says.

While we're far from exhausted by our day, we still feel we deserve a nice long soak in the indoor mineral baths. I feel my anticipation rising in hopes of the aromatherapies I've heard so much about, the sparkling baths of pleasure that have spoken to me from the pages of too many women's magazines. We arrive at the baths to find it's clothing optional, but most of us stick with our swimsuits.

"You girls need to live a little," Gran tells us, naked and at one with the minerals around her.

The mineral bath looks a little like a Jacuzzi, but one sniff of these minerals tells me we're not in paradise anymore. In fact, if we were children, we'd probably hold our noses before getting in. We'd probably run away, or at the very least, make fun of the odor. Since we're all adults, we pretend not to notice. Although I'm disappointed, I try to make the best of it, since otherwise I'll end up acting like a spoiled baby, which I try never to do in front of strangers. Some behavior seems only appropriate for family. I erase from my mind my hopes for a foamy strawberry bath and settle instead into a land of unknown minerals that smell a little like the airport.

Maria shrugs. "It's good for your pores."

Besides Jeanette and her mom, Gran, our soaking companions include two sixtyish women who've pin-curled their hair before getting into the water, Shirl and Clara Louise. Clara Louise passes around lip balm.

"Why don't you girls tell us about your love lives," Gran says. You'd think the hot water might make her sleepy, but no.

"Yeah," Clara Louise says, patting her hair, "and none of that stuff about just having a career."

"Well," Maria starts. "There's this one guy, Henry."

"Is it serious?" Jeanette asks.

"Don't interrupt," Gran instructs.

"I have this philosophy, I guess you'd call it," Maria says. "I'm not desperately looking for someone. I don't go out and fall all over men, but sometimes one appears who makes an impression. Henry has his good points."

"Such as," Jeanette says.

"Well, Henry's basically a happy person, which is hard to find these days. Plus he has a good attention span."

The ladies in the tub nod. Gran pats Maria on the shoulder.

Clara Louise takes out her lip balm again. "How's the sex?"

"Well, as you've probably heard, sex is complicated these days," Maria says in her pharmacist voice. "But I don't personally have any complaints."

Gran leans over to Maria. "I like the sound of this Henry," she says.

"Okay, Holly," Jeanette turns to me, "you're up."

I consider pretending that the water has put me to sleep, but I've no doubt Gran would splash me mercilessly to wake me. I've figured out that Maria and I are the evening's entertainment, although we could all be inside watching a *G*-rated Dudley Moore movie that invades no one's privacy.

Maria comes to my rescue, sort of. "Holly has an interesting officemate and an ex-husband."

"Thanks a lot," I whisper to her.

"Ooh," Clara Louise says, "I like the idea of two."

"What's the deal with the officemate?" Gran asks. "Let's break it down."

Not a bad suggestion, really. "He's nice," I say.

"Nice is good," Jeanette says.

"Please," Gran says, "you can have nice. Sexy? Nurturing? Muscular?"

I try to think if any of these adjectives fits for Tom, or if I somehow want them to. "He makes a nice clam sauce," I say after thinking a moment.

"You can't go wrong with a nice clam sauce," Shirl says. The women all nod, even Maria. Even me.

"And the ex-husband?" Gran asks.

It's a relationship I generally avoid analyzing, despite the protests of some people I know—Janie, my mother, Maria, a therapist I visited briefly who seemed to sneeze every time I mentioned my mother. All of them have asked what's going on with Josh, my ex-husband of several years now. He once brought me roses to celebrate our divorce, having honestly confused it with our original anniversary date, having seemingly forgotten we were divorced. For some reason, I wasn't offended. Then there's our new sometime sleepover arrangement to worry about. Or as Maria calls it, The Return of the Sex Thing. Something in the mineral bath opens my mind to taking a look at the situation again. It must be the heat, or maybe something petroleum-based.

"We were married very young," I say. "I think we both needed to be out on our own, after a while. Or maybe just I did."

"A girl needs time on her own," Shirl says.

"Shhh," Gran says.

"Now we see each other sometimes, without the pressure of wondering if it's going to last or not, I guess."

"You still see him?" Jeanette asks, amazed.

"You still sleep with him?" Gran asks, then turns to Jeanette. "No sense in being shy."

"A couple of times now," I say. "I've known him so long, you know?" I think about Josh and me doing laundry together in our college dorm, somehow finding it sexy that our shirts were all turning the same color gray together. I remember us at our small wedding in my mother's backyard next to a dogwood tree my father had planted, despite Janie's attempts to have us married at a large inn by a huge waterfall, which even my mother had to admit might be a little too misty.

"Is there a future?" Jeanette wants to know.

"I'd always thought no, not necessarily. But there might be. We don't talk about it, and I'm not sure I really want to right now. Although I know we'll have to, sometime." I start to think about sitting down with Josh for that "serious" talk, getting all sweaty like you do when you discuss life's major issues. I dislike such serious conversations—at least the few I had with Josh, which led us, eventually, to divorce, since, well, Josh is Josh, and he couldn't really change the things about him that bothered me then. I'm not sure if he could change them now, either. Could Josh be more reliable? Could Josh remember my mother's birthday? My birthday? Should it matter so much to me, or does it all add up to someone who takes me for granted?

"I don't have to worry about it all now," I tell them.

"Good girl," Gran says. "Independent minded."

"Good girl," Maria whispers to me, but I give her a look.

"I don't know," Shirl says. "If I ever got up the nerve to leave my husband of thirty-seven years," she thinks a moment, lays back into the warm water, "I doubt I'd ever want to see him again."

We think about this awhile.

At night back in my room, I check the schedule for the rest of our spa activities the next day. We get massaged at nine, then have what they call a light breakfast. I'm hoping for hash browns at this point. After that comes swimming and sauna, with the option of a synchronized water aerobics class. I know Gran will be right out front in her bright red bathing cap. "Chlorine does funny things to blue dye," she told us, referring to her punk hair. In the afternoon we'll have "Beauty and Hair Tips with Josephine." Maria's looking forward to meeting someone named Josephine and playing with eye shadow. Maria's also told me that she wants to show all the women the proper way to tease their hair. I didn't know there was a proper way, I told Maria, to which she responded, "It's true. It's an acquired skill, and it can be taught."

In bed I lie down on the peach bedspread. I think there's a peach-scented air freshener in here, also, but I haven't been able to find it. I close my eyes for a moment and pretend I'm soaking in a peachy mineral bath at just the right temperature, my mind floating in peachy clouds of thoughts. It'll have to do, after our stinky mineral bath. For some reason I remember that I brought my mail with me, having grabbed it from my mailbox right before we left. I interrupt my meditation to get it from my purse. Among numerous flyers, I find a postcard from my mother and a note from my father. My mother has shortened her African trip from its original four-month plan to a more manageable two weeks. She'll be home next Wednesday. I can't decide whether her decision to come home soon is based on logic or something less pleasant, something like torrential rains. The card shows two baby elephants at play who seem to be annoying their mother elephant no end. I wonder just what sort of meaning Mom meant to convey. She does mention that she's remained bug-bite free and she's proud of it.

The note from my father is even more of a mystery. I open up one of those Hallmark "Thinking of You" cards and can easily imagine his girlfriend, Sophie, lending him something like this from her stationery drawer. She's the kind of woman who has a stationery drawer. Inside the card, my father has written the following:

> *I'm so glad we got to see you down here. Hope all is going well in the big city for you. Take care now. Looking forward to seeing you sometime again soon.*
>
> > *Love,*
> > *Dad*

It occurs to me that in my thirty years here on planet Earth, I've never gotten a note from my father. My mother signed all the birthday cards and report cards, notes to school about ear infections and all of that. I recognize his handwriting from work I used to see on his desk, but I can't remember anything ever addressed to me before. I turn the card over a few times. It's a little baffling. Maybe it has no special meaning at all, maybe he was just "thinking of me." I can see Dad in his duck-filled room, trying to write me a message with a duck-headed ballpoint pen, a message that says he's thinking of me. I must be starting to fall asleep, as the image of my father turns into Josh, and I can see him in his comfy apartment patting the fronds of his spider plant. He may even be cooing at it a little, although this seems like odd behavior for a mathematician. But it's my daydream. As I turn over to my right side the image turns into Tom, or it turns more Tom-like, with him sitting amongst his white lights strung around his table, carefully folding thick paper into strange animals, a parade of little predators. I slip further into the peach bed, and try to work my way back into a peach state of mind. My body tingles from minerals and hokey-pokeys, which really isn't a bad way to feel at all.

Chapter 9

A Kiss on the Cheek May Be Quite Continental

I'm fiddling with a postcard I bought on the way to work. The front shows an orange-striped kitten with its paw balanced just above a bowl of spaghetti. On the back, I write, "Thanks for dinner!" but that's all I can think of. I did try to thank Tom personally in the office hallway, but he slipped away in the middle, somewhere between "thank" and "you." I think this card is a polite gesture that won't say too much, since I'm not at all sure what I want to say to Tom, although I do mean the thank-you part. Both of us seem a little unsure as to where we stand right now, although we've only had one lunch and one dinner. We seem to have crossed over some unspoken production editor line, I suspect. I think I don't especially want to encourage Tom, but I'm not certain I want him completely discouraged. I just don't know.

I'm planning to sneak the card onto his desk later. Until then, I put on my headset and start to check the proofreading for one of my books that's been moving right along, a book on intestinal blockages that my boss, Monique, nicknamed "The Tummy." Sometimes when Monique drops off proofs or something to do with "The Tummy," she'll place a little roll of Tums on top. It's her idea of office fun.

My friend Nina stops by and pulls up my visitor's milking stool.

"Holly, have you heard anything?" Nina asks, a serious look on her face. She's far too young for such a look.

"Nope. No one's told me," I say. "What are you talking about?"

"You know," Nina explains. "Carl said he heard from Jan that there's been talk upstairs."

Nina's cryptic statement, deciphered, shows how the production editor grapevine works, more or less. Upstairs from us sit the higher-ups, the acquiring editors, the vice-presidents, and some people who have titles I've never learned. We seem to talk about them constantly, speculating on exactly what they do, on how long they take for lunch. I don't think they usually talk about the production editors much, though. We're a whole floor beneath them.

"Changes are in the air," Nina says.

"Well, I've heard talk about remodeling," I say.

"Carl said he thought he heard something about moving."

"That would be too bad," I say, thinking how much I like walking to our dilapidated Village office, not having to take the subway. I try to be positive for Nina. "But there'd be more room."

"We could have a lunchroom," Nina says, brightening. "A real one. Maybe even a snack machine."

"See, you worry too much," I tell her.

"I know," Nina agrees. "I'm editing a book on worrying, what the wrinkles look like. It's got me all anxious."

"Go look at the clam book—it's more soothing," I say.

"It is," Nina says, then rises and leaves.

I'm a little upset at the idea of moving, but I try to ignore it. For one thing, rumors along the production editor grapevine are almost always wrong. Once they said that Science

Press was hiring a Kennedy, but it ended up that we hired a guy named Kenny for the mailroom.

After working for a few hours on "The Tummy," I slip off my headset and take my postcard over to Tom's cubicle next door. I hear voices coming from in there, so I approach slowly. When I see the source of the voices, I think I'm more surprised than I've ever been, at work at least.

"Hiya, Holly." It's Josh, my ex-husband, seated on a chair next to Tom's.

"Hello," I say, casually tucking the postcard behind me into my pants.

"Tom here's been working on my book," Josh says. Tom sort of waves his hand in the air at the mention of his name but otherwise remains quiet.

"Your book?" I ask.

"They're publishing my book. I told you that, didn't I?" Josh asks. I don't think he's told me this, exactly. He holds up some galleys with equations on them.

Tom gestures between Josh and me, somehow asking how we know one another, I think.

"Oh," Josh says, "Holly and I go way back."

Tom nods, then speaks. "Were you looking for me?"

"No," I lie. "Just passing by, wondering if you'd seen the mail cart."

"Not yet," Tom says. "Try the north corridor. I've seen it overturned there lots of times."

"Well, thanks," I say. I look from one to the other for a moment, although I'm not sure if I'm looking for similarities or differences. "See you."

I head for the ladies' room to hide and consider the laws of coincidence. Not that I'm sure coincidence has laws. Maybe properties, or fallacies, or maybe there's just no way of knowing. I find Monique in the ladies' room, leaning against a sink.

"There's a green bug in the fourth stall," she tells me. "It's got an unusual shape, plus antennae. I called the art department to come get a picture, so don't step on it yet."

"Okay, I'll save that part for you," I say.

"You've always been my favorite," Monique says without much expression.

"My ex-husband is here," I say.

"Which stall?"

"No, out there," I gesture. "Helping put his book in order."

" 'The Tummy' ?" Monique asks.

"No, something mathematical, lots of formulas," I say. "With Tom."

"Ugh," Monique says, "the 'I Can Count' book. You know what they say about men who play with numbers."

"No."

"You don't want to know," Monique says, waving her hand.

Nina comes into the bathroom.

"There's a large green bug in the fourth stall," Monique tells her, "but it might have jumped into the second or third by now. Face it, it could be anywhere."

Nina freezes by the door. "Oh," she says, searching the floor around her, paralyzed with fear.

"Might want to try the restroom upstairs," Monique says, and Nina takes off with a "Thanks."

"She's afraid of me," Monique says. "It's so sad. I'm down to only one of you who's afraid of me. I used to inspire a lot more fear." Monique shakes her head at herself in the mirror. I notice she has a really good haircut.

A woman named Denise from the art department appears with a camera and follows Monique's pointing over to the fourth stall.

"I'll go check out the ex, hmmm?" Monique says, starting out of the room. I decide to stay put awhile.

From the doorway, Monique turns back to me. "You have a kitty postcard sticking out of your pants."

I grab the postcard and slip it into my pocket as the camera's flash goes off a few times in stall four.

Several days later, the kitten postcard remains stuck to my refrigerator door with a ladybug magnet, right where I put it when I came home Monday night. After a day or two, I realized the card would never make it to Tom's desk, let alone to Tom. It's another chore I haven't followed up on, but still, the card looks cute on the refrigerator like that. Now I can see why people stick things on their fridge. The one simple decoration makes the room seem more important, although it's not a very big room. It's as if now someone lives here, someone with an interest in kittens, or maybe spaghetti, or maybe just decorations. I feel my life take on a whole new part to it, expanding, although I might be placing too much importance on a kitty postcard. But I still like the effect.

Thursday evening finds me in my living room with my mother, who has appeared somewhat unexpectedly after her African trip. She has two suitcases with her, which she places in the kitchen but doesn't mention.

"Well, how was it?" I ask. I admit I've longed for tales of elephants gone wild, escaping through villages, my mother and Ronny running behind with their cameras, snapping photos of swinging elephant tails.

"The trip was invigorating," my mother begins. "More walking than I've done in my whole life, and nearly all the walking I plan to do the rest of it, too."

"You're not tanned," I say.

"Sunscreen," my mother explains.

You can't tell she's been anywhere at all sunny. She might

have been living in the subway the last two weeks. Then again, none of us much likes the sun. I'm usually the palest in the room, and in college, somebody once nicknamed me "shark bait," although I don't think it was a term of endearment.

"Ronny shot all eight roles of his film," Mom says, "mostly of me with my back to him, admiring the natural habitat. Not my best angle."

"How is Ronny?"

"Very cheerful for a man who has slept on a folding cot for two weeks."

I almost hate to bring it up. "Wasn't the trip supposed to be longer? Not that I exactly wanted you away for four months, but what happened?"

Mom thinks a bit. "I think there comes a time in a woman's life when she agrees that the next lion she sees will be the last one. I think it's a mature decision to make."

I give her a funny look.

"It doesn't always have to be a lion, dear," she says. "Each woman has her own decision point."

There's a knock at my door.

"That's Janie," Mom says.

"Janie knew you were coming but I didn't?" I know I sound eight years old.

"You know your sister," Mom says.

I let Janie in. She's come from work in her tailored beige suit. Since I've already changed into a stained T-shirt and sweatpants, I feel a little inferior, a little disadvantaged, and also the tag in my sweatpants feels scratchy against my back. I reach around and rip it out right in front of Janie, whose eyes widen a little before she marches in.

"You look great," Janie says to our mother. "Was it wonderful?"

"Almost all of it," Mom says.

"I want to see the pictures," Janie says.

"Be careful what you wish for," my mother replies.

I fix a pitcher of orange juice and bring it to the living room. It's not the fresh-squeezed kind, but this is family, so either they don't notice or don't say anything.

"I've brought you both presents," Mom says. She disappears into the kitchen and rummages through her luggage, then brings out matching tote bags with an elephant patch and beaded necklaces.

"Those are real African beads, not the ones from Newark," Mom says.

"I can tell," Janie says appreciatively. I'd never know the difference, I'm sure, but these are nice.

"Why do you have your suitcases here?" Janie asks.

"Yes, why?" I echo. I'm glad Janie brought it up.

"Funny thing," my mother says, settling onto my couch. "It seems that they've decided to fumigate my building."

"You mean tonight?" I ask.

"I'm sure they sent notices around while I was away," Mom says.

"It's not funny little green bugs, is it?" I ask, remembering the ladies' room experience earlier this week.

"Yuck," Janie says.

"I hope never to know," my mother says.

"Well," I say, "of course you're welcome to stay here. You can have the couch bed. I have an extra mattress in the storage downstairs."

"You could stay with me," Janie says. "I don't have an extra bed, but I'd be willing to sleep on the floor." I get the feeling there's a race on, a contest, but if Janie really wants to win, I'd let her sleep on her floor. My apartment, after all, really consists of just the one room, with its tiny separate kitchen and bathroom. It's true, I have an extra bed, but still.

"I think Holly's sofabed will do," Mom says. I've won without much effort and feel a little guilty about not making more of a fuss. "I'd ask to stay with Ronny," Mom says, "but I think he could use a break. Plus he's gone out and bought more film, and he keeps taking pictures of me when I'm not looking. He has a role of me being airsick. It's getting on my nerves a bit."

"Maybe I should stay here, too!" Janie says. "It could be a slumber party."

"I'm sorry, dear," my mother says tactfully, "I'm just too tired for so much potential fun."

I'm relieved, even if Janie does seem sad. She sits on her chair sipping her juice, playing with her beads.

I am not alone. It's only the second night that my mother's been here, but I feel as if a market researcher has followed me home from the grocery store with a clipboard, questioning my every move. So far, my mother has asked what's in my concealer and where I found pitted jarred apricots. I don't know what's in my concealer. I didn't know I had concealer. It must have been a free sample. The jarred apricots I got from a grab bag at work last Bastille Day, which we always celebrate because someone upstairs is French, but we don't know who. The apricots might have gone bad, but I don't want to admit this to my mother. I don't want her to know I'm the kind of girl who keeps old fruit in the refrigerator.

It's Friday night, and Mom has mentioned that tomorrow she leaves for Ronny's, come what may with his camera.

"You don't have to leave," I tell her.

"What's that expression about guests who smell like fish?" Mom asks.

"I know it, but I can't ever get those things right," I say. "There's also one about catching flies with honey I've never understood."

"Still, most house guests begin to fester after an hour or

so, I think. I'll be gone for your big Saturday night," my mother says.

"Oh, good," I say. "I wouldn't want you inhibiting me on bondage night."

"If you like," she says, "I can send Ronny by to photograph it."

"That won't be necessary. We all wear masks. You couldn't identify who is who."

"Is it who, or whom? I can't ever get that straight," Mom says.

"The secret is," I say with editorial authority, "if you wear enough black leather, it just doesn't matter."

The doorbell rings. I admit that my popularity this week surprises me. Then again, it could be another visit from Janie.

It's Josh.

"Hiya, Holly," Josh says at the door. He's carrying a large bundle of orangish-yellow flowers, the kind that attract bumblebees, I think.

"Hi, Josh," I say. "Who gave you the flowers?"

"No, these are for you."

I debate letting him in, but then I hear my mother's voice behind me, saying, mock-innocently, "Isn't that Josh?"

Josh's smile stays on his face a moment too long. "You're not alone," he says to me, as I sweep him into the room.

"Hiya, Allison," he greets my mom. My mother, to be fair, was very fond of Josh while we were married. He's the kind of man you want to help match his socks anyway, and perhaps a mom feels such things even more strongly. Since the divorce, though, she's less thrilled with him. My mother hates dwelling on the past, especially any past where her daughters may have been hurt, she's admitted to us.

"Why, Josh, what a surprise," she says. "And you've brought flowers. Thoughtful."

Josh hands me the flowers. "We're publishing Josh's book at our office," I say.

"So this is a professional visit? Not that it's any of my business," Mom says. It's been a slow night for us. Mom's trying to have a little fun, I guess. I go into the kitchen for a vase, which I've hidden in the back of the cupboard, somewhere. Dusty, no doubt. I'm not the kind of girl who keeps a clean vase around, handy.

"Holly's publisher has been very helpful," Josh says.

"But you don't get any special treatment for knowing a lowly production editor," I say from the kitchen.

"I'm sure you're indispensable there anyway," Mom says to me.

I can't find the vase, so I leave the flowers on the sink. I don't want to miss anything in the living room. Josh hasn't sat down and looks a little relieved to see me.

"You could have stayed and had lunch with Tom and me," Josh says to me. "We went to The Jelly Deli."

"I wouldn't want to interrupt boytalk," I say.

"Oh, no," Josh says, "we talked about fractals, time-space, mathematical principles, the Knicks."

"Boytalk," I say. My mother just shrugs.

"I should be going," Josh says.

My mother and I groan loudly. "No, stay," we echo. I've decided it'd be worth it to have a little fun at Josh's expense. I feel the need to tease.

"No, I have work." Josh bows his head, embarrassed. He probably does have work, stacks of it. He and my mother say their good-byes, and I walk him out the door.

"I think it's just not my night," I say to him, quietly.

"We can talk sometime else," Josh says.

He kisses me sweetly on the cheek, and heads for the stairs. I don't think Josh has ever kissed me on the cheek before. Not even when I had a cold, or a fever, or that flu-like thing you get every year with the annoying cough that lasts two weeks, where everyone you work near avoids you the entire time. Not even then.

I close the door and just stand there a moment, my cheek warm from the kiss. A kiss on the cheek, I keep thinking, repeating it over and over, as if after saying it enough times, a truth will present itself to me. But it doesn't.

I go back inside to find my mother in the kitchen, looking sad, deep in her own mantralike thoughts. She looks at me.

"I'll help you find that vase," she says, then bends down to examine the cupboard's depths, withholding all comments about disorganization and dust.

I pass by my refrigerator again and put a hand on my still warm cheek. The kitten on the postcard watches me from just under the ladybug magnet, desperate to put its paw into some lovingly homemade pasta. Desperate to make a mess of things.

Chapter 10

You Say It's Your Birthday?

"Thirty-one will be a breeze," Maria says, since she's got a year and a half on me. I hate to admit that when I turned thirty last year, I had one of those crises all the women's magazines say you'll have. I'd figured this kind of thing only happened to people completely obsessed with their own lives, people who carry more than one cell phone at a time, say. But no, suddenly there they were, all the doubts. Would I live in my small apartment forever? Alone? Should I be making more money? Should I have more friends? Fewer friends? Would I ever buy one of those matching bedroom sets, and would I ever even have a separate bedroom? The questions flooded me, making me dizzy at work, off-balance walking home, where I'd bang into newspaper racks and fire hydrants. Little black-and-blue spots appeared up and down my legs. But then I turned thirty and the doubts eventually vanished. I celebrated by buying a new down comforter. The bruises faded.

My birthday arrives at the beginning of the year, the first stepping-stone, in a way. But number thirty-one hasn't affected me much, blowing in with the first real snowfall, which always puts everyone in the office in a good mood.

We all watch the snow flicker by our windows. We stand there quietly, as if it's the first snow we've ever seen, as if the gathering of black sludge that will form by the gutters in a few days will never bother us, as if nothing will ever bother us. The first snow feels a little like finding an unexpected present under your pillow.

One of the perks at work is that we can take birthdays off, a paid holiday, without having to make up an excuse. It's a fairly recent policy. People used to take off on their birthdays anyway, coming down with a variety of unexplainable aches and pains. I worked through my birthday a couple years back, finishing a book, and I remember Monique coming up to me, suggesting, "It's your birthday—don't you feel fluish?" But things have changed.

On the day before my birthday, the production editors gather round my cubicle to sing the worst "Happy Birthday" rendition they can. With practice, they've become amazingly bad. It's a sign of how much they care, how badly they sing for you, so I'm touched. Nina places a cupcake on my desk—I recognize it as one from The Jelly Deli, gooey-looking chocolate topped with strange blue sprinkles, so that it looks both appetizing and sort of sickening at the same time. Peer pressure forces me to blow out the candle on top, which threatens to drip on "The Tummy" anyway. Carl, another production editor, brings out a kitchen knife.

"Here, let's cut it into twenty-four, some for everyone," Carl says, approaching my cupcake menacingly. Monique pulls him out of the way.

"Children shouldn't play with knives," Monique tells him, removing the utensil from his hands. "Go to your cubicle."

After singing, the editors disperse, many putting headsets back to their ears. I look at the birthday card they've had the art department create for me. It's a lovely collage of all the books I'm doing, with cartoony sketches of whales, tummies, tumors, and a few unrecognizable splotches. Some of them may be moles.

Monique looks the card over. "No photos," she says, a little disappointed. I offer her some cupcake.

"I'm not the cupcake type," Monique says, shaking her head. "Here—"

She steps out of my cubicle, then comes back with a present, another milking stool, this one painted black and white in a cow pattern. The legs have black cow's feet at the ends. Underneath I spot signs of a big pink udder. It's both tacky and wonderful in just the right balance.

"I love it," I say. "You shouldn't have."

"Just don't ever ask me to sit on it," Monique says, leaving my cubicle.

I admire my card and start reading all the jokes people have written, some of which are legible, another sign of affection. I hear tapping on the half-wall in front of me, once again. I tap back. A large, yellow paper sunflower comes my way over the wall. It's the kind of bright yellow that makes you think of happy childhoods, whether you've had one or not. You can buy flowers like this in the stores, but something tells me Tom has made this one himself. He has signed a leaf.

Tom pops around the corner into my office. "Happy birthday," he says.

"This is gorgeous," I say, "thanks." I admire the flower and consider where to place it on my desk. "Want some cupcake?" I ask.

"Oh, no," Tom says, "that's yours."

We both stare at it. I notice it has no smell whatsoever.

"So, you know one of my authors, Josh," Tom says, not really a question.

"Yes," I say. "We used to be married for a while."

"Really?" Tom's surprised. "I didn't realize, I mean, I thought," he stops, nodding a bit. "I don't think he'll need to come by again," Tom says finally.

"It's okay," I tell him. "We get along now. We're kind of old friends now." I wave the flower in the air, tapping it against my lamp, my desk, my headset. Like a magic wand.

Tom seems stumped.

"I get to take tomorrow off," I say. When in doubt, state the obvious.

Monique comes by and drops some galleys in my in-box. She looks at Tom.

"Were you saying something?" she kids him. "The actual verbalization of thoughts?" Monique doesn't mind Tom's not speaking too much. She hired him. "It's a plus in a man," she once told me. "It's a plus in anyone."

"We were just saying how Holly gets tomorrow off," Tom says with a shrug. He's never seemed much intimidated by Monique. I think he likes her prodding.

"Only if she eats all that cupcake," Monique says.

"That might make it a sick day," Tom says, then bows out of the cubicle.

"Thirty-one," Nina says. At twenty-three, Nina must think I'm much, much older. "Thirty-one."

"Thirty was bad," I say, "I won't kid you."

"That's what I hear," Nina says. She has sat down on the new cow stool and has agreed to taste the blue sprinkles on my cupcake for me. I pick a few off for her and she crunches a moment.

"Flavorless," she says.

"Just carcinogenic food coloring?" I ask.

"Maybe," she says, "but at least they don't taste bad." I pick most of them off anyway.

"Now you can have two guests," Nina says, arranging my milking stools.

"They'd have to be very fond of one another." It's a small cubicle.

"Maybe you can get a bigger cubicle, if they remodel."

"Maybe."

"You must have some seniority."

"At my age," I say.

"Well," she says, rising, "have a great birthday. I can't wait till I'm in my thirties."

"That's what I used to think," I say. "Nothing wrong with being in your twenties."

"No one takes me seriously," Nina says.

"Nonsense, you're a very serious person."

She smiles and looks up. "Thanks." Nina walks off boldly. She sees Monique walking and makes a sharp left turn to avoid her. Monique drops off more galleys in my box. This isn't really her job, delivering things, so I eye her suspiciously.

She gestures back toward Nina. "You're not building her confidence, are you?" I think she's kidding, mostly.

I grab my galleys and refuse to answer.

"No one lets me have any fun anymore," she grumbles.

I'll be busy all day on my birthday, just in case those depressing thoughts about wrinkles try to sneak into my mind. I should also be occupied enough during the day to keep me from worrying about gray hairs, not to mention keep me from inspecting my freckles to make sure they don't resemble anything in my mole book. My idle mind, I know, leads to such pastimes. Instead, my mother has planned a restaurant lunch for me, with Ronny, Janie, and herself. "There will be singing," she's warned me. After that, Maria's taking the afternoon off so we can play.

I meet my family at a restaurant called The Great Catch, a fairly new place in a neighborhood uptown, the kind of area where people seem to dress up just to go out for some milk or butter. It's in the city code, I think. My mother and sister greet me with Happy Birthday exclamations, and Ronny takes my picture as I sit down at the table. My mother turns to him.

"Now, we've talked about this," she says, pointing to his camera.

"Just one of the birthday girl. Birthday Girl Seated, I call it," Ronny says, putting his camera under the table.

Ronny frequents this restaurant, we've learned, and as we reach for menus and look around the place, we figure out why.

"See all the fish?" Ronny asks. Large fish swim around in tanks that glow on each wall, giving that unearthly feeling you get from looking at blue and yellow glowing aquariums. The restaurant has dimmed its lights, and when only a few people talk, you can hear gurgling, bubbling sounds. It couldn't be more different from, say, The Jelly Deli.

"You get to pick your own," Ronny says. He's watching a large fish that keeps banging into the side of its aquarium.

"Do we have to?" Janie asks with a squirm.

"They can make you a nice selection," my mother says.

I watch the fish circling, wondering if I'd have the heart to condemn a fish to be my birthday lunch. They're beautiful, swimming in there. I have some real doubts about a restaurant where you're supposed to eat the decor. Especially when it breathes.

Janie and I decide on shrimp salads, since we won't ever see the shrimp alive, but Ronny picks out a bass. My mother asks him to select a nice perch, and the waiter leaves to go scoop up lunch with a net. Ronny follows to take a last picture of the swimming fish. Lunch never had a chance, I guess.

When he returns, my mother and Janie hand me gifts, which they insist I open in the middle of the restaurant. "On top of the table, too," my mother says. "No hiding it in your lap." Once a year, my family thoroughly enjoys embarrassing me in public, although I suspect they look for other opportunities during the year as well.

Janie gives me a thrillingly soft silk shirt, dangerous in its whiteness. I get it out of the way of potential spills as quickly as possible. Janie's an excellent gift-giver, I've come to realize, always presenting you with something sleek you'd consider too extravagant to buy for yourself. My mother's primary gift is in an envelope, a check.

"So you can buy yourself something you want, not just something I feel you ought to have," my mother says, not that she doesn't have a few suggestions. She's also given me a small box so I'll have something to unwrap, a gift from her and Ronny. Inside I find a silver, filigree picture frame, the kind of thing you might buy for someone's wedding gift, then feel bad you couldn't keep for yourself. I thank everyone.

Ronny snaps my picture again and my eyes fill with blobs of yellow and blue. I feel a little like the fish in the glass tanks, only less endangered.

"Now, what's new with you girls?" my mother asks.

Janie starts. "A woman came into the gallery yesterday," she says, in what sounds like the first line of a joke. "She told me that my high heels were an affront to feminism and the struggles of women across the globe."

"Wow," I say. I've always admired my sister's mastery of her high heels, although I've never wanted to wear them myself.

"Then she bought the ugliest sculpture in the place," Janie adds. "I made quite a nice commission."

"Now that's feminism," I say. Janie just shrugs.

"You know," Mom says, "only family has the right to criticize your shoes."

"Not to mention your social responsibility," I add, as someone places a shrimp salad in front of me.

"I'd love to take you girls fishing sometime," Ronny says when his bass arrives. Janie and I look at each other.

"I'm not sure about fishing," I say.

"I go," my mother says, which is news to me.

"You fish?" Janie asks.

"It's called compromise, dear," she answers. "I've caught a flounder! Ronny gets the job of pounding it in the head until it stops moving, though. I draw the line." Mom takes a bite of her fish, as if to prove something about eating your catch, I think. I feel a little dizzy again.

"You're modern women," Ronny says to us. "You should know how to handle a bass."

A waiter nearby scoops a long, pale fish from a case as a small group applauds him.

"Now there's a beaut," Ronny says.

Janie nods, watching the waiter carry off the squiggling fish. She looks down at her salad and pushes the shrimp around, then off to the side.

"I have news," Mom says.

I look up. Janie pushes her salad away, slightly.

"Ronny and I are moving in together." My mother and Ronny join hands and, for a moment, look almost guilty.

Janie picks up a shrimp with her fingers, then eats it.

"Well," I say, "that's great news." I'll actually stop to think about it later, I figure.

"I think so," Mom says.

"Yes," Janie says, "but, Mom, isn't your apartment kind of small?"

"We'll live at Ronny's."

"Oh," Janie says, "this is a surprise." I can tell Janie's

mind is working fast, but I can't begin to know what she's thinking. Now she's biting the heads of the shrimp and putting the rest of it back in her salad bowl distractedly.

I lift my wineglass to them. "This *is* a different birthday celebration," I say, toasting them with a smile. We all clink glasses. I catch Janie looking at me sideways, blinking slowly, kind of like a young, curious angelfish unsure of the waters around her.

"Wait till you see what they do with a flaming dessert," Ronny says.

After lunch I meet Maria at a movie theater, one of those newer triplexes on the East Side.

"Let's see the mushy movie first," Maria says, "then I want to sneak into the teen comedy."

"I haven't snuck into a movie in years," I say.

"It's illegal," Maria says, "but I want your birthday to be special. You can also have popcorn and Junior Mints."

"Good," I say, remembering the rolls of Tums my boss Monique always gives me. I have one in my purse.

We stand at the snack bar and look at the unappetizing food portraits. The colors seem one shade too dark, or as if everything's been overcooked. We can't bring ourselves to order anything.

"Let's just pretend we're ten years old all day," Maria says.

"Is this what ten-year-olds do on their birthdays now?" I ask.

"Nah," Maria says. "They probably sneak into much sexier movies."

After the movies we head for the ice-skating rink near Macy's. Maria rents us stiff skates and we make our way around the rink a few times.

"I think five laps justifies a hot chocolate," I tell her. "Don't you?"

"It's your birthday, you only have to go around three times." We watch as young girls skate through the center in graceful arcs, moving much faster than we are. Some spin around and around, then stop and spin the other way.

We each take a seat on the side and drink our frothy hot cocoas. "If we stay a little longer," Maria says, "the hockey boys will come in."

I notice a few tall high school boys slinking around the side of the rink, waiting.

"There's no harm in looking," Maria says. "You still can't touch, even though it is your birthday."

A couple of girls, maybe ten- or eleven-year-olds, ask if they can share our table, then sit in the extra chairs. We all watch the hockey boys take to the ice, speeding around each other and leaving deep lines behind them in the ice. Once in a while, one of us makes an oohing sound of approval.

After skating Maria and I head for the Pie diner to meet Henry. He's waiting for us at the last table.

"This is our table," Maria says, as Henry takes her hand.

"Happy birthday," Henry says, handing me a loosely wrapped package. Inside I find a burgundy scarf with a Transit Authority logo. It's kind of stylish, in its way.

"Thanks," I say.

"You don't have to wear it," Henry says. "They work amazingly well as dishcloths, too."

We're surprisingly hungry, after our cocoas an hour or so back, so we order banana pancakes. Adulthood, we know, gives us the right to eat breakfast food for dinner. And we can still follow it with cherry pie.

"My mother is shacking up," I tell them.

"Really," Maria says. "Good for Allison."

"It's kind of a surprise, when your mother tells you she's living with someone. Even someone sixty-five with memory loss."

"Especially someone sixty-five with memory loss," Maria says.

"I think Janie wanted to ground her for a week or something," I say.

"Mothers. The surprising thing is that they seem to have minds of their own," Maria says.

I nod. Our pancakes arrive with four kinds of syrup, so we all study the flavors carefully before choosing. Since it's my birthday, the waitress brings me a large, disc-like pin that shows a pie missing one slice, the diner's logo. Henry and Maria agree that if I put it on right away, they won't tell all the kitchen workers it's my birthday. Apparently, they keep an accordion or two back there for such occasions, but things can get out of hand. Accordion contests get started, ruling out any chance of quiet talk. I attach my pin and wear my pie proudly.

When I finally get home to my apartment, I feel a little dizzy again, a little dreamlike. It could be all the strange foods today, but I feel as if things are still moving around me, the way the fish swam round and round the tanks, or the hockey boys glided by on the ice. I take off my pie pin and hang it with a ladybug magnet on the fridge, my second decoration there now. I put the Transit Authority scarf on a stack of dishtowels, admiring its thickness. It might work well for washing the windows, too, which I tend to do once every two years or so, whether the place needs it or not. Then again, I may just wear the scarf.

In my mail I find a small package from my father. He's sent a traditional Hallmark, flowers on the front, rhyme inside, along with a scribbled "and many more, love, Dad and Sophie." They've also sent a blue-and-white toaster cover with a rooster coming out of the top. At least I think it's a toaster cover. It's loud and it screams Sophie, but still, I think it might look kind of cute, especially covering the juicer. I like the looks of my toaster as is.

Someone knocks on my door, which surprises me, because I feel like I've already seen everyone I know.

"Hiya, Holly."

It's Josh, hidden behind a huge bunch of red irises, which he hands to me.

"Thanks, Josh," I say. This bunch of flowers is even larger than the last group. I invite him in.

"What's with all the flowers?" I ask, putting them down. They're awfully heavy.

"Oh, you deserve them. Happy birthday."

"Well, thanks."

"I've known you now for ten birthdays, do you realize?" Josh asks. It's true, we met when I was twenty-one. He's got the math right, of course. "This is like a milestone for us," Josh says, settling into one of my wooden chairs. I hear a little snap when he sits down and wonder if he's broken part of the chair, but I let it pass.

"Well, we've had a few milestones, I guess."

"We have history together," Josh says.

"We'll always have Montauk," I say.

Josh starts scratching the left side of his neck. I've seen him do this while working out a mathematical theory, scratching large patches of ever-reddening skin. It seems to help him figure. As we sit there in my apartment, I feel a little tingly from my adventures today, if not from the overly stiff skates we rented. Still, it's a comfortable tingling, the kind I can imagine lasting all night. I'm not in the mood to determine why and how, or for how long, but I'm glad Josh is here.

"I've been wanting to talk to you," Josh says.

"I've noticed you hanging about recently."

"I'm getting married," Josh says.

I laugh. Then I notice the tingling has diminished, although now I feel a buzz in my left ear.

"No, really," Josh says. "Her name's Lauren. She's one of my research assistants. She's very detail minded but senses the broader picture, too. You'd like her."

I feel a little sick, sorry that I ate every bite of my cherry pie. I begin to think back, count how many bites I had altogether, which one might have been the place I should have stopped. I notice Josh is still here.

"I'm surprised, Josh. More than surprised," I say. "I thought, well, it's just that you've been stopping by recently. . . ." It seems all I can manage to say.

"I hope you'll get to know her," Josh says. I can't tell if he notices my sudden extreme discomfort or if he's just on another planet at the moment.

"It's just that I've been thinking, and we haven't really talked about anything, I mean, anything about the two of us," I start to say, then can't think how to continue.

"We should all be friends," he says. I can see that he means this by the intensity of his scratching, although I also recognize he may have sunk to new levels of oblivion, a new low in social skills.

"I'm not sure what to say. It's like my mind isn't working at all," I tell him. "This is all a little too much," I say. "So don't hold it against me if I don't congratulate you right away or say anything, well, anything particularly nice at the moment. I mean, it's not exactly why I thought you were here." I lean back on my couch. I love my couch. I'd like to be alone with it. I stroke one of its arms, certain that its feelings for me are reciprocal.

"Oh, well," Josh says, then seems to change the subject, not that he'd exactly started on one. "It's your birthday, you must be tired out from a long day."

Somehow, still, I'd been hoping he wouldn't notice this. I can imagine this new girl, Lauren, completely rested any time of day or night. Dressed in red. Wearing the kind of red lipstick my mother used to forbid Janie and me from wearing.

"Tired out," I repeat, patting my couch cushions gently.

"Well, we can talk about it more another time. It feels like there's so much to talk about," Josh says. And yet he looks a little at a loss for words. Not unlike me, actually.

"I hope you have a hundred more birthdays," Josh says.

"Well, I'm not sure I can take that, if they're like this one," I say. I get up and open the door, realizing that there's no point in, say, screaming into the space between his eyes right now, or telling him any of the things I've been thinking about him and the future. His mind is someplace else, with someone else, someone probably waiting for him right now. And although I can feel something that might be an unhealthy level of blood pressure rising, mostly I just want him out of here tonight. I'm not sure how much I've imagined about our relationship over the past few months. We've left so much unsaid that I've just filled in whatever I wanted to believe at the time. Or maybe I'm confusing myself with the heroine of the romantic comedy Maria and I saw today, the one who traveled all the way to France to get the guy in the end, although come to think of it, it wasn't the guy she expected to get. I find some kind of identification often happens to me at these movies—especially the romantic ones—where I'm certain I have taken on the looks, gestures, and vocal patterns of the girl on screen. But she got the guy, and Josh is leaving. I throw my hair back as she would anyway and lift my shoulders high. Such identification, I find, is often worth the $8.50, especially in times of need.

"Bye, Josh," I say. He hugs me. No kiss on the cheek this time, just a friendly, maybe much-needed hug, which I accept like an unexpected birthday gift that isn't quite my size, but that I know isn't returnable.

Chapter 11

Our Troubled Times

Over the last week, I've begged two new books from my boss, Monique, so that now I have four stacks of work surrounding me on my desk. I can tuck myself away from the world somewhere between the four stacks, where I feel safe and wanted. My books need me, or else they'll turn into stacks of mismatched tumor photos, lost conference symposia, and unloved splotches of skin cancer. Here I can focus on methodology and technology, ignoring things like my real life. At least, I think I can. Tom walked by once carrying a bag of something and glanced at me between two stacks, but he didn't say anything. Fortunately, I have enough work to take home some nights, even though we don't get paid extra, and no one encourages us to work overtime. My two new books feature calcium deposits (no pictures) and the gestation period of cows, a book Monique calls "Bessie" and that was pretty highly in demand around here.

"You got the cow book?" Nina whined to me. "My new book is on psoriasis."

"Not another one," I said.

"Monique thinks it's funny. I get all itchy looking at it, although Monique keeps taking the pictures away for hours at a time."

I've also started making lists for the new radio contest on the rock station. You need to write down every song they play from 9 to 5 that has the word "honey" in the refrain. It has to be the whole word—"hon" doesn't count. After three weeks, you send in your list for a drawing. The odds are high, and I'm not feeling especially lucky these days, but I honestly couldn't be busier.

Near five o'clock my phone rings—right as the next song starts—which means I'll have to consult Nina, who has got her own song list going. So do some of the art department guys. They'll usually trade us answers for chocolate kisses, which they line up around the department in wobbly pyramids. A few times a year they shoot them down with an air gun. It's a big event. I remove my headset to answer the phone.

"Hello, Holly, it's cousin Sophie." There's that silence you get when what you really want to say is "Who?" I'm not sure I've ever heard my father's girlfriend Sophie's voice over the phone, so it takes me a minute to figure out who she is. Not that I've ever really figured this out.

"Hi," I say. "We have a very clear connection." I think of Sophie and Dad living in Houston, several thousand fiber-optic miles away.

"No, silly, I'm here," Sophie answers.

I look around my office on impulse, nearly knocking over one of my stacks. The connection is that good.

"Where's here?"

"I'm in New York for a shopping spree," Sophie says. "A girl's just got to get away sometimes."

"I guess she does," I say.

"Let's get together," Sophie suggests.

"You know, I have so much work these days," I say. At least I'm not lying.

"Now, I won't hear of such a thing. I'm sure you girls work far too hard. A little break will make a world of difference."

Sophie's probably right here. A scary thought.

"You could ask Janie, too," Sophie says. "I just never get to see her. It would make your father so happy if I could tell him I took you girls to lunch."

"Okay," I say, thinking of my father. "But I can't say for sure about Janie. I'll ask her, though."

Sophie gives me her hotel number just in case, and we agree on where to meet. I pack up a couple chapters of my cow book to take home, then notice Tom walking by silently, carrying a plastic armadillo. I see him peek my way, but he pretends to look at the armadillo instead. Then he reappears.

"A new book on mammals?" I suggest, referring to the toy. "Burrowers?"

"No," Tom says. "I traded Nicola in the art department for it. She's collecting sawdust."

"Really?"

"She won't say why."

"A surprise," I say. The art department is filled with toy animals, although I'm not sure if this one roars. Many of them do.

Tom gestures to the plastic armadillo. "Protective armor," he says, knocking on the armadillo's shell.

I nod. "Practical."

Tom shrugs, looking back at the stacks of work I've surrounded myself with.

"Have a nice night," I say, packing up my bag.

"You too," Tom says, then walks his armadillo across the top of our partition, back over to his side. I watch it go, clunk-clunking along the divider.

Monique stops by on her way out and waves her hand at my bag of chapters.

"Wouldn't you like a good novel instead?" she asks.

I hold my chapters closer to me. "Leave us alone. 'Bessie' and I are bonding. Anything wrong with that?"

"Don't get me started," Monique says, then ducks out of the office.

Over the phone, Janie sounds firm and unsympathetic.

"You can lose her in the East Village by herself, for all I care," Janie says of Sophie. Janie rarely says much bad about anyone, but she can certainly hold a grudge.

"She's family," I say.

"That's what she thinks," Janie says. I don't believe Sophie's really a cousin either, and I don't much care to think about her relationship to us as my father's girlfriend, all of which leaves me with little ammunition against Janie.

"You're being naive," my little sister tells me.

"It's one lunch," I say.

"I'm busy," Janie says. "I have a gallery to maintain."

"Not to mention your sense of moral superiority."

"Sometimes, Holly," Janie says, "we just have different priorities."

"Fine," I say.

"Fine," Janie says. "Just don't you dare pay for her lunch."

"Beautiful women who carry too much are emblematic of our troubled times," says a voice greeting me on my way into the office the next morning. I'm carrying a big bag of my chapters, plus my usual tote bag full of crucial possessions, all of which causes me to walk at a tilt.

The voice belongs to Roy, our twenty-year-old messenger who delivers proofs from the type house we use. Roy's dressed in patched jeans—either he patched them himself or bought them from a used clothing store this way, it's hard to tell. He has long, thin, brown hair often tied back with a leather shoelace and pale, somewhat fragile-looking skin. Roy often greets me like a line from a depressed fortune cookie.

"Hi, Roy. How're the streets?" Roy rides around on a serious, no-frills black Moped. It looks like something the military might have stopped using years ago. A tough black basket at the back of his Moped holds the galleys.

"The streets are no place for those overcome by the minutia of life," Roy says.

I point to his Moped. "You can't tell me those things aren't dangerous," I say.

"No, no, riding in a taxi, now that's dangerous," Roy answers, taking my chapter bag from me and adding it to a stack of proofs he's carrying.

"I don't take taxis much. I usually walk to work."

"You should get a helmet," Roy says. "I know. I see."

Roy leaves me at the elevator on my floor. "Don't despair of the repetitive moments, now," he says with a wave. Roy is burned out from too many philosophy courses at a college upstate, he's told me. He finds his messenger job a relief, filled as it is with time for him to think. "It's a gift from the higher graces, to which I'm truly indebted," he said.

"He's on drugs," Monique claimed once.

"No," I said. "He's just young."

"Even worse," she said.

I'm thankful that my best friend and pharmacist, Maria, joins me at a fancy tearoom, where we'll be meeting Sophie for lunch. When I told Monique I was going out to lunch, she said only, "It's about time."

"I could run a little late," I said.

"I could pretend I care about it, if it makes you feel better," Monique said.

Maria and I find ourselves in a room with ladies who lunch. I don't see anyone I know from The Jelly Deli, which I feel a little homesick for.

"The Jelly Deli doesn't have cloth napkins," Maria says.

"They don't have any napkins," I say. "They just pull a few pieces off their roll of paper towel for you. It shows they care."

"This is so cool," says my closest friend, who's dying to meet Sophie. Maria has puffed out her hair special for the occasion, and she matches the other puffed hairdos around the room. If I didn't know better, I'd suspect she'd been here before.

"I'm not happy," I say.

"You haven't had any finger sandwiches, yet," Maria offers. "You'll come around."

"I want to go lie down in a big grassy forest," I say. "I want world peace and happiness."

"You want scones," Maria says.

"I do," I admit.

Sophie walks in the door, awash in pink silk, the color of strawberry Häagen-Dazs. A shiny gold pendant hangs down the front of her blouse. It could be one of those New Age God symbols, or it could be an acorn.

"That's her," I say.

"She's perfect," Maria says.

I do the introductions, and Sophie seems touched that I've brought my very best friend to meet her.

"You girls are so thin," she says, sort of a compliment.

"We haven't had scones with cream, yet," Maria tells her.

"Janie couldn't make it," I lie. "How's Dad?" I ask.

"Oh, your dad," Sophie says, with a wave of her hand. I take it this means he's healthy, thanks.

"Your dad's so funny," Maria says. I think about this, about how our friends always see our parents differently than we do, but yes, I guess he is funny, or was when friends were around.

"He's just a joy," Sophie says.

"I've never been to Texas," Maria says. "How're the pharmacies?"

Sophie answers without hesitation. "We've got the best, and the prettiest, in Houston."

I ask her what brings her to New York.

"Well," she starts, "I do love the stores, even though I don't know about your salesladies here. They seem to be lacking a touch of something we have in abundance back home."

"Manners?" I suggest.

"They have manners," Maria says. "They just don't believe in making a big display of them."

"But you do have The Latest fashion and decorating hints," Sophie says, taking a bite of a cucumber finger sandwich. It's the size you could stick entirely in your mouth, which is what I would have done. She's declined the scones, which Maria and I are breaking into happily, making the best of things.

Maria leads Sophie in a discussion of couch styles. Maria can talk to anyone, the five-year-old down the block or the eighty-year-old who needs company more than she needs a refill of her prescription. Sophie's no problem for her at all. I'm so grateful, I offer Maria the last scone.

"You know," Sophie says, "your father misses you and Janie terribly. Your visit meant the world to him."

"Oh, good," I say, not really sure how to answer. Maria plays with her scone, waiting, I think.

"If only we could get our Janie out for a visit!" Sophie says, as if it were a good idea.

"I don't think that's likely," I say.

"But surely you must have great influence over her,"

Sophie says. "She must trust and listen to her big sis. Your dad would be so pleased."

"I've found Janie's usually pretty stubborn," I say. "Very independent."

"We'll just have to see what we can do, then. As long as you know how your dad feels," Sophie says, reaching over for a piece of Maria's scone, whispering, "Maybe just a teense."

I'm not sure what to make of her little hint to me, whether Dad really misses Janie (and me) or whether she wants me to believe this, not to mention why she wants me to believe this. I do believe he misses us, but I'm not sure there's that much I can do about it. I'm pretty sure there's nothing Sophie can do about it.

We finish our lunch and Sophie hugs both Maria and me good-bye. She has more shopping to do. Maria lets her in on some sales she's heard about around town, and Sophie asks if we're sure we don't want to join her and an old high school friend to see *Cats* tonight. I hadn't realized *Cats* was still playing. We decline, and head back downtown.

Alone with Maria, I say, "What was she thinking?"

Maria shakes her head. "Other people's families are always so interesting."

"We could have gone to see *Cats*," I joke with her.

"*Cats* will always be with us," Maria says. "Kind of like the common cold."

"Thanks for coming," I say. I feel a little weighed down, as if I were suddenly wearing arm or leg weights, or maybe full body weights. It could be the scones, but I don't think so.

"Oh, I wouldn't have missed it," Maria says. "That Sophie, she might be okay. Her eyebrows are overbleached, but you have to admire a woman who can wear pink ankle socks like that."

I look at Maria skeptically. She puts an arm around my shoulder.

"Okay," she says. "You don't have to admire her."

* * *

I return to my office, patting the stacks of books on my desk, greeting each stack personally. I couldn't be happier, what with people milling around the production editor area, the voices of my coworkers lightly muffled around me. I put on my headset, and an hour or so passes as I put together my cow book.

I can hear a louder murmur around me even through my headset, so I take it off to see what's up. Carl walks by.

"There's a disaster on a train upstate," Carl says boisterously. I hear someone laugh. Carl always has rumors and jokes ready. He doesn't usually announce them to the whole room, though. Tom rises in the cubicle next door.

"No, really," Carl says, "there's been a shooting on a train. Like a hundred people dead."

We all just stand there a moment, looking around. Then people start to drift toward the center of the room. Tom takes a radio out from his bookcase—it's a tough little transistor radio, not a headset, the kind of radio I'd want to have in my emergency kit, if I had an emergency kit.

People gravitate toward the transistor. Tom turns it to the news station and balances the radio at the corner of our modular wall. I find Nina beside me, and Monique lurking not far behind. She seems to have one eyebrow permanently raised, as if at attention.

The announcer sounds rushed, but tells us that yes, Carl's right, there's been a shooting on a train headed for one of those wealthier areas upstate, the kind of place where diet doctors always seem to live, I think, although the newscaster doesn't say this. The details are sketchy. Thirty or forty people seem to have been shot, but they don't know how many are dead or only wounded. I don't think that any of us moves during the broadcast. The news guy knows so little that he begins to repeat himself, not hiding a sense of hysteria in his voice all that well.

"This is terrible," Nina whispers to me. She sits down on one of my milking stools and stares at the floor.

"Somebody upstairs has a TV," Jan suggests. "One of the vice-presidents."

But none of us leaves. We just listen to the transistor repeat itself. They believe that the shootist—they use the word "shootist," which sounds to me like an old Wild West term—the shootist has been killed in turn by local police on the scene. It was a young woman, about sixteen, according to sources.

"A girl," Monique says.

The report keeps changing as they repeat. Now they say a high school–age girl has killed up to thirty-five people on a commuter train upstate. If anything, the details just get worse and worse. We stand there listening for maybe ten minutes—we've heard the story now eight or nine times, with increasing numbers of dead each time. Thirty-eight dead and ten wounded. Up to forty-five dead. An automatic weapon removed from the girl. Blood. Commuters. People trapped in their seats. Toddlers. The newscasters are about to get a live hookup from the scene. It strikes me that the words "live hookup" never indicate good news. Then we hear warbling, crying, the sounds of confusion, traumatic sounds behind the newscaster's repeated list of numbers. As the announcer begins to repeat once again, Tom turns off the radio, lowers the antenna, and puts it back on his shelf firmly. The sudden quiet stuns the room. We stare at one another, the walls, the floor. Monique slaps her hand against a modular wall, then walks away, silently. Eventually, the group breaks up, but no one leaves the room.

I sit down behind my desk and push my headset and radio contest list away. Nina's still on my cow stool, lightly tapping her right arm with her left hand. She looks at me, takes a deep breath, then goes back to her own desk. I stare at my large yellow sunflower that's stapled to my wall. I wish it were real, I think at first, but then I disagree with myself. I wish something, but not that. My phone rings, startling me. I answer it quickly.

"Hello, dear." I can barely recognize my mother's voice after listening to the frantic boom of the newscaster for so long.

"Hi, Mom," I say. "How are you?"

"Fine, fine. I'm just checking up on you."

"I'm right here," I say, patting my book.

"Good. I knew you wouldn't be off anywhere too unusual, like taking a trip upstate," she says.

"I heard the news," I say. "Awful."

"Yes," my mother says. "Well, as long as you're fine, I'll let you go. I'll make sure Janie's at the gallery, which of course she is."

"Okay, thanks for calling," I say. I imagine mothers all over the city, all over the tri-state area, making calls like this. Some mothers will get no answer.

I think about the day when there'll be another call, a different call. Something about my mother or father, something tragic but far closer to home, something I'm not nearly ready for. Something like the call my mother and father received when my brother had been hurt, only to die the next day. Maybe that was some kind of final straw for their marriage, as they'd been arguing for years, then had started to become quieter around one another and the rest of us. It's not just the phone call that's the scary part of all this, of course; it's what might happen after you hang up.

I feel as if I've just watched a sickly violent movie—every little noise makes me jump and check behind me, watching for the villain, the loaded gun, the shining knife. The guy in the hood. The high-school girl with the automatic weapon. Our filing cabinet closes with a thud, making me stand up and look around. Several of us stare at the photo department guy who slammed the drawer. He notices and slinks off. I lean way over my desk to peek into Tom's cubicle. He's staring straight ahead but looks up to see me. I wave. He waves back, and I sit down again.

A group gathers at a desk somewhere behind me, and I can make out their whispers.

"Someone got stabbed outside that new bakery on Amsterdam last month," one says, "but it was late at night."

"My hairdresser was mugged on Eighteenth."

"Eighteenth," another says.

"Somebody tried to follow my mother home, but she lost him at the police station."

I put on my headset and find the calmest, sweetest music I can, something with violins and what may well be oboes playing. I don't think I'd know an oboe if I saw one, but I turn the music up and go back to my cow book, "Bessie."

Leaving the office after work, I find our messenger Roy sitting on the steps outside the building, his chin resting on his helmet in his lap. I sit down beside him.

"Tough day," I say.

"The world is often no place to be," Roy says, stroking his helmet slightly, the way a pregnant woman touches her stomach.

"I don't know," I say. "It beats other options."

Roy sits up straight. "Envision the possibilities for hope and the true nature of meaningfulness," Roy says, bucking up I think. I try to envision the possibilities. Somehow, my mind flashes on Sophie, who has probably been in Bloomingdale's all day, obsessed with pink silk, happily oblivious to the unnatural workings of mankind.

"I'm trying," I say to Roy.

"You have a tenacious spirit," Roy says, patting me on the arm and rising. He walks me to the street.

"Are you sure you wouldn't like to borrow my helmet for

your walk home?" Roy asks. He places it over my head for me to try on. It feels soft and padded. Everything sounds lighter and safer, although I probably look pretty stupid standing there. I laugh and hear it echo in my ears, then I remove the helmet and hand it back to Roy.

"Thanks anyway," I say. "It's not far."

"A true friend keeps an eye out," Roy says.

I start to walk off toward my little apartment, where my buzzing refrigerator and my sofa bed await me. I notice as I walk that Roy rides behind me a ways on his Moped. He's maintaining a healthy distance, but he's back there just the same, like a guardian angel, or a parent secretly watching a child walk to school for the first time. I turn my head, but Roy pretends not to see me, pretends he's just riding that way. When I reach my apartment door, he rides back off the other way, his motorbike bucking and dipping through the New York City potholes. He doesn't bother to go around them, I notice, but bravely rides right through.

Chapter 12

The Game of Life

It's the kind of day that makes you wonder what we've done to the environment, what kinds of sprays, powders, solutions, and gases we've used to give us an artificial and yet spectacular spring day before we have any right to one. Our fake spring melts the mountains of sludge along the sidewalks and allows us to chuck our rain boots and bounce to work in our tennies. It's the kind of day that could make you throw that old, unraveling muffler to the wind, if there were any wind. Mostly though, it's deceptive.

Maria calls me at work.

"She's in the hospital, again," she says, simply.

What most people don't sense about Maria, I think, is that underneath the big hair and that professional yet personal pharmacist's tone lies a woman whose mother has been steadily dying for the last ten months. This would be hard for any of us to handle, a challenge to any of our mother-daughterhoods. But Maria has it a little worse, I think, as she and her mother have never gotten along. Impending death has not brought them closer.

"We can't sit around now and remember the good ol'

times," Maria tells me. "We didn't have any good ol' times. We didn't even have that many 'times.' "

I've come to keep her company in the hospital waiting room, which looks a little like a modern art gallery. The pictures on the wall are covered with Plexiglas boxes. I point this out to Maria.

"They're sealed for your protection," she says.

The room has a damp coolness and the faint smell of air conditioning. It has a purplish swirly carpet you could easily stare at for five days, then realize, Hey, it's purple. Or you could just stare into those swirls, losing yourself deeper inside yourself. Nothing in the room really calls out for your attention, nothing interrupts, nothing aggravates. The room assumes you have enough on your mind.

Maria's mother has suffered her second stroke. "She's still there, you know?" Maria says. "I can still feel her watching me, waiting. Waiting for me to do something she can disapprove of. Although she could just be longing for a cigarette."

In our modern health-conscious age, Maria's mother remains a throwback to now-unacceptable times: She's a woman who has refused to take good care of herself. Even after her first stroke, after a tendency toward diabetes, Angela (Mrs. Bruno to most of us) still smoked, drank her several glasses of wine with dinner, and snuck sweets. Eventually her husband (known to all of us as Frank) gave up on asking her to stop. Maria just waits now for the next hospital stay, feeling frustrated that so many of her women clients at the pharmacy accept her advice, but her mother stubbornly ignores it. Or worse, belittles her for it.

"What can you know?" I've heard Maria's mother say to Maria. "When you have children, then maybe you'll learn something." Classic Mrs. Bruno, whose idea of women's roles excludes most of the things Maria and I do each day. Maria and her mother have never been able to approve of one another.

Despite Maria's and my tendency to order rich yummy foods at restaurants now and then, we—and especially Maria—know our limit. Maria swims twice a week at the pool of an elderly client, plus she works out a few days at the gym. Fat doesn't have much of a chance with Maria, who only eats elaborate desserts when I'm around, I suspect. She's not a dieter, she's just nutritionally practical. She's also the only person I know who's comfortable with her body. "So I've got hips," Maria has said. "I'm used to them." Body weight has never much been an issue for me, either, since I come from a line of skinny women. Weight tends to drop off me if I get too stressed, thus Maria's attention to fluffy treats when I'm around. She tries to tempt me, and often succeeds.

"This time's bad," Maria says about her mother.

"Can she still talk?" I ask.

"Barely," Maria says. "I think she asked for a Coke."

"Maybe she asked for cocaine," I say, hitting her lightly on the arm.

"I like that," Maria says. " 'My mom, the junkie.' It sounds funnier than 'My mom, the fat woman down the street with a cupcake in her hand.' "

Maria looks out the window.

"Sorry," she says. "That's terrible."

"It's just a nervous reaction," I say.

"It's just the truth, unfortunately."

"You're exhausted," I say.

"It's true. I'm so tired by it all, the illness, her anger," Maria says. "My anger."

I nod.

"Still, I guess I hope it goes on," Maria says. "Or maybe I don't."

Maria's dad comes into the waiting room carrying a yellow plastic cup. He's a friendly but quiet sort and bends over to give us each a hug. He's always just loved doing that. He refuses our offers of food and coffee, just waves them away as if there's nothing in the world he could want. Maria watches as he leaves the room.

"There's someone who needs a cupcake," Maria whispers to me.

I'm going through my closet, looking for something funereal.

"I'd loan you one of my spare black dresses," Maria says, "but they're way too sexy." She's lying across my couch, watching me pull clothes from my closet. I've got her covered with a blanket and I've fed her freshly squeezed orange juice, which she sips from every ten minutes or so. She's been pretty subdued up till now.

"That might be interesting," I say. "A sexy funeral."

"That's what I want," Maria says. "I'll leave instructions in my will. All the women must wear low-cut dresses and big rhinestone earrings. Champagne at four. Male strippers at five."

I pull out something mysterious covered in plastic from my closet. Somehow, my mother's blue-and-white sailor suit, last seen on Janie, has landed in my wardrobe. Somebody's idea of a joke. I show it to Maria.

"I'm always worried I'll see someone wearing the same dress I'm wearing," Maria says. "There's your solution."

"A real woman could pull this off even at a funeral," I say.

"A real brave woman."

I decide on a navy suit my mother bought me a while back. I join Maria on the couch, sitting near her feet.

"You know," she says, "it's like the Game of Life. Did you play that as a kid?"

"Yeah," I say. "I always adopted twins, then lost my life insurance."

"I always had to turn around three spaces, or go back

over the bridge. That's what this is. I have to go back over the damn bridge again."

"Or lose your turn," I say.

"Or lose my turn," Maria agrees.

The funeral falls on another of our mock-spring gorgeous days, a Sunday that would bring everybody outdoors anyway, bumping into one another happily on the street. It's one of those New York days when couples say to one another, "See how wonderful it is here? How could we consider leaving the city?" Even though two weeks ago they'd longed for a Caribbean island and a few mosquito bites. The sky has turned a color that makes you think, Now that's blue—clear and strong, like a paint swatch. A fearless New York blue sky.

"I thought it was always dreary for funerals," Janie whispers to me. Both Janie and my mom have come to the funeral out on Staten Island, a show of support for Maria.

I shrug. "Maria has influence," I say, but Janie just gives me a look. She's wearing a navy blue linen dress that matches my suit perfectly, in fact, a little too well. We're not the only ones in navy, but I feel a little funny about it. My mother looks at us approvingly.

"You two could be sisters," she says.

"Thanks," Janie says.

I join Maria next to Henry, who never met Maria's mother. "I refused to subject him to the interrogation," Maria has said, "not to mention to so much secondary cigarette smoke." Henry looks the best I've ever seen him, in a pressed gray suit.

"This is nice," I say, pulling at Henry's suit coat.

"My dad's idea of a suit," Henry says with a shrug. I find it funny that our parents still choose our dress-up clothes for us.

"Henry cleans up nice," Maria says, "but I still say dirt is underrated." Maria likes Henry with a layer of Transit Authority grime. "It's no secret," she has admitted.

"How are you really?" I ask her.

"Okay enough," she says. "So far, this isn't as bad as the senior prom, but it has the potential."

Maria sits in front with Henry and her father, along with her five brothers, assorted wives, and grandchildren. Each grandchild has a different stuffed bear, and one child—a little girl in a dress with a star over her heart—seems to be trying to pull the ears off her bear. The brief service may be in honor of these children, who should really be somewhere else on a day like this. I sit with my mother and Janie behind Maria. My mother sighs several times, I notice. Janie sits very straight. The bear loses one ear.

When it's over, Maria quietly announces to the children, "Lots of cake back home." They scream and run around. I return to Maria as several older women with pinkish-gray hair hug her.

"Clients from the pharmacy," she says to me after they disperse. "They love to ride the ferry, so this is sort of an occasion for them."

"You love to ride the ferry, too," Henry says to Maria, surrounding her with an arm.

"It's true," she says. "Let's get some of the cake from the house and feed it to the birds on the way back."

"Sort of a memorial of our own," I say.

"Yeah," Maria agrees. "But I still think my mom would say we're just wasting good cake."

Maria spends the afternoon in a daze. At her parents' home, various people I've never met continue to hug her in an almost dancelike pattern.

"It's getting more and more like the prom," Maria says sitting down, a little dizzy.

My mother sits with us for a while. "You'll still have me to kick you around," my mom tells Maria. Maria seems to appreciate the thought.

We spend the hours surrounded by cakes and cookies with a sweet, heavy smell.

"There's too much food," Maria says, exhausted by the array of pastry that stretches across one wall. The place is lined like a bake sale, only with more Jell-O than usual.

"These are the scents that lured Hansel and Gretel," Henry says quietly.

Finally, after a series of aunts insist on washing up, Maria's father tells her to go home. "Maybe others will take the hint," he tells her.

One of the brothers and his wife have moved in for a while, to take care of Maria's dad, despite his insistence he'd be okay. "They were afraid he'd eat batter mix right from the box," Maria told me. "As if they haven't done it themselves."

"The big city needs you," Maria's dad says, hugging Maria once again. I picture all those older women at Maria's pharmacy who do need her, and I wonder how much Maria's dad imagines about her daily life, how much of it is close to being true.

Maria and Henry follow me back to my apartment, where we raid my refrigerator in search of liquids that aren't too sweet. We settle for bottled water and recline in my living room, removing what pieces of dress clothing we can, while still remaining semiclothed. We throw our shoes into a pile across the room, listening to the loud clunks they make.

We sit quietly, admiring our shoes. Maria speaks first.

"It could have been worse," she says.

"They could have made us eat the Jell-O," I say.

"They could have made us make the Jell-O," Maria says.

"I kind of liked when that bumblebee flew right for the minister during the service," Henry says.

"Yeah," Maria agrees. "You just can't plan things like that."

We sip our drinks, listening to the birds outside my window. They chirp loudly, no doubt confused by the unseasonable sunshine. I can never see them, but I hear them. They sound a little like a couple trying to redecorate, arguing over what to keep and what to throw out. We let their sounds fill the apartment.

"You have to admit," Maria says, "male strippers would have made all the difference."

We nod.

I've fallen asleep in my chair, which I only notice when the doorbell awakens me. Maria and Henry both have been asleep on the couch. For a minute, I wonder if I've imagined the doorbell in my dreams, where it sounded like my mother's voice, as she told a small bird the best way to make a nest. "Now cross the branches like this," she said to the sailor-suited robin who looked on with an impatient gaze. The doorbell rings again.

"I hear ringing," Maria says. "It that a sign?"

I find a familiar person at my door, but in my sleepiness, I don't quite know what to say. I stare at him.

"Hello, Holly," he says. "It's Jackson?"

My sister's ex-fiancé, the last one at least, stands outside my door. He seems to be questioning why he's here, too.

"Of course," I say. "Jackson." I still stand there, feeling creases of sleep on my face. I look down at my clothes, and see that I'm creased all over.

"Sorry to be so creased," I say.

"Oh, no problem," Jackson says. "I didn't call first." Jackson wears more casual, Sunday gear, khaki shorts and a green shirt, even though I don't think it's time for shorts yet. They're relatively uncreased, it seems to me, but they might be the no-wrinkle kind. I invite him in.

Maria and Henry greet him from the couch.

"Hello," Jackson says happily. "It's so nice to see you."

"You all remember Jackson," I say.

"We just woke up," Henry says.

"We've just come from a funeral," Maria says.

"That's a shame. I've been walking through the park," Jackson says.

"You're not very sweaty," Maria says.

"I was earlier," he says, then turns to me. "I've changed in the past weeks. I've grown."

"Really?" Henry asks, perking up.

"Well, not physically," Jackson says, settling on my hardest chair. "Emotionally. Psychologically. You know, it used to be I'd get up early on a Sunday, work a little, jog, then go play tennis or soccer with guys from work, some activity organized way in advance."

"Squash," I say, proud of myself. "Right?"

"Right," Jackson says.

"What's squash?" Maria asks, looking at Henry. He just shakes his head no.

"Anyway, no more," Jackson continues. I've settled back into my comfy chair. We're all reclined, except Jackson, as if we're listening to a bedtime story. Awaiting that happy ending.

"Today I slept in, then strolled through the park, come what may. No plan at all! And, I'm looking for a new job."

"Aren't you a lawyer anymore?" Maria asks.

"Well, yes," Jackson says. "But I'm looking for something more meaningful than corporate work."

"Meaningful's hard to find," I say.

"Especially in the classifieds," Maria says.

"But it's out there, waiting," Jackson says. "I know I can help."

"Well, the Transit Authority's always looking for people. Especially the F line," Henry says.

"It would be a challenge," Maria says.

"Maybe that's just the thing," Jackson says, considering. Maria and Henry look at each other and shrug.

"Why the desperate changes?" I ask. "Is it Janie?"

"No, no," Jackson says. "I know that's over. But I did want to talk to you, I guess some other time, in private."

"You can talk in front of us," Maria says, with Henry nodding. "I plan on blocking today from my memory anyway."

"Your secrets are safe here," I tell Jackson.

"But you have to take off your shoes," Henry says, pointing to the pile. "It's a pact."

Jackson starts to unlace his sneakers, then daringly pulls them off unlaced.

"This is a little embarrassing," Jackson says to me.

"Why?" Henry asks. "Your socks don't have holes or anything."

"Embarrassment is good for you," Maria says. "Cleans your pores."

"She's a pharmacist—she knows these things," Henry says.

"It's just," Jackson starts, "I've been thinking about us."

"Us?" I ask. I look around the room at all of us. Maria points a finger back at me.

"Yes, you and me," Jackson says.

"Is it you and me, or you and I?" Maria asks Henry quietly.

"I thought maybe we could have dinner, something casual, it'd be just the two of us, see what we think, how it might go," Jackson says, falling back into his questionable grammar.

"But you were engaged to Janie," I say.

"Who wasn't?" Maria says. "No offense," she tells Jackson. He waves the notion away with his hand.

"I'm still not sure," I say. "I still think there's a conflict of interest."

"But you seem to understand me," Jackson says, then adds, "God, that sounds so eighties, I'm sorry."

"It's okay," I say.

"Sometimes the eighties slip out of me, too," Maria says.

"I'm sort of not seeing anyone on purpose right now," I say, and immediately think about Josh, who I know I'm not seeing, and then Tom, who I guess I'm not really dating, although I can't be sure. I don't think it's a good idea to add Jackson to the mix, though.

"Holly's ex-husband is remarrying," Maria says.

"That's very eighties right there," Henry says.

"I thought it was more nineties," Maria says, "but you may be right."

"I'm sorry to hear that," Jackson says. "It must be upsetting news."

"I'm still refusing to deal with it," I say. "I feel that's the most mature approach at this time."

"She's a pro at fooling herself," Maria says enviously.

"It's nice to have something you're good at," I say.

"But you must move on, develop, experience, embrace," Jackson says.

"I thought mostly I'd try sleeping it off," I say.

"Oh," Jackson says. "Well, you'll always have me as a big fan, for what it's worth, if you want to keep it in mind."

"Fans are highly underrated," Maria says, "and those little nightlights that attach to your books. They're underrated, too."

"It's been kind of a tough day," Henry explains to Jackson. Jackson nods at us, three people in crumpled dark clothing.

"Thanks, though," I tell Jackson. "I think I'm best on my own for now."

Jackson gets ready to leave. He grabs his shoes and tries to slip them on without untying them, a practice he looks unfamiliar with, judging by his struggle.

"I still may try again," he says to me. "We can't just give up on our lives. Maybe I'll just keep in touch."

"Okay," I say. "But things don't change drastically around here."

"You never know," Jackson says.

"No, you never know," Maria agrees.

"I never know, anyway," I say. We all nod. Jackson says his good-byes and I see him out. He shakes my hand at the door. When I return to the living room, Henry and Maria have snuggled back down into the couch, so I plop back into my chair and reshape the pillows more comfortably. I close my eyes.

"I just had the strangest dream," I say.

Chapter 13

Hurricane Holly

Last year brought us Hurricane Gabrielle, down by the Carolinas, which effortlessly toppled houses for miles. The year before that we had Hurricane Felicia, which managed to miss us way to the north. This time, they're keeping an eye on Hurricane Hollis, just off the Atlantic coast. Of course everyone around me insists on calling it Hurricane Holly. She's headed right for us.

I walk to work this morning guided by a cool wind that makes me feel almost weightless. There's also an energetic crispness that for some reason makes me think about hopscotch. Another person might skip to work in such a delirious breeze, but I manage to keep one foot in front of the next in a fairly normal pace. Still, something tempting lurks in the distance—possibilities hide somewhere beyond the buildings, just off to the left, just where you can't quite see.

"Such a fuss," my boss Monique says, as we haul out the masking tape and prepare our office for Hollis. We have beautiful large windows that allow us to keep an eye on New York City, letting us note every possible form of snowflake or raindrop from above. We treasure our windows, marking them with big Xs of masking tape that supposedly strengthen them, the newscasters always say.

"Ridiculous," Monique says, refusing to involve herself with the masking tape. "Besides, they're always wrong about the hurricanes."

"They're often wrong," I tell her. "I wouldn't say always."

"Please," Monique says. "The weathermen don't know anything. I saw one of them caught uptown in a downpour without an umbrella. Everyone was laughing."

We tape the windows anyway, despite Monique's grumbles, mostly because it's such fun to stand on the desks in the middle of the day in our socks, stretching masking tape across the room, listening to the pleasing squawk it makes as you pull it from the roll. All around the city, people in offices run around on their desks, grab masking tape, and wrap it around their coworkers when no one in charge is looking.

"Let's tape up Monique," Carl has suggested more than once. We all ignore him.

"Let's tape Carl to Monique," Nina whispers to me.

"Maybe for her birthday," I say. We go on with the windows.

Returning to my desk, I find that someone—the art department, no doubt—has made a new nameplate for my outside partition, renaming me "Hurricane Holly." I'm official.

I get back to work late in the morning, getting ready for my appointment with the head of our proofreading department. Sondra, a tall chic woman who wraps herself in purple fabrics—I know there's a dress in there somewhere—has intimidated her share of production editors. But I've always found her fascinating. She has that rare ability to create and re-create a new set of rules every six or seven months, I suspect whether they're needed or not. It's always difficult to see where she's made any changes. Still, she insists upon meeting with each of us regularly, I guess to reinforce the importance of her revolving set of proofreading rules.

I don't mind saying that I pride myself on how well I get along with my coworkers. It's part of the job, dealing with everyone, and I hate tension. I know that as a child I got plenty of comments on report cards indicating that I didn't always get along with others, and I guess I took this personally. I even get along with the proofreaders, who can be touchy because they have to read everybody's scrawly writing all day. I try to print neatly. I also thank them for their work, which one of them confided to me that no one else ever does, not even Sondra.

Still, there's something luxurious about these trips to Sondra's purple majesty. Her office combines shades of lavender, grape, and plum, what seem to me like all the relatives of the purple family I can think of. I head upstairs and knock at her door, watching Sondra turn, swishing her ruffly fabric around her. I enter the kingdom and inhale her scent (of lavender, naturally), as Sondra is an experience for all of the senses. The strong breeze from her open window forces her door shut behind me with a bang.

We examine her revised instructions for how to send galleys to proofreading. They look suspiciously like rules I've seen before.

"Have you been careful to label your galleys correctly on the top left-hand reverse side?" she asks me.

"Yes," I say. "I try to be careful."

"In nonrepro blue ink?" she asks.

"Whenever possible," I say.

"No, Holly," Sondra replies harshly, "always."

"Always," I repeat.

Sondra makes a note of something, then swishes back in my direction. I make a mental note that her fabrics seem synthetic to me. I wonder if they itch.

"Please take the new set of instructions with you and destroy the old ones," she says, after we've examined every inch of the new rules.

I start to leave, but something in the air, no doubt a gale wind, stops me.

"These look a little like the rules before the last rules," I say. "I'm sure I have them somewhere."

"Never," Sondra says, her voice creeping higher, "keep an outdated set of instructions. They are to be destroyed per my request. To do otherwise is to violate the principles I've worked so hard to enforce. That is why I bother with these time-consuming meetings. So that you'll know the correct way to proceed, and follow it."

"Well, thank you," I say, trying to smooth away any rumples in purple fabric I may have caused. "I just meant I feel familiar with these rules, and I'm sure I'll be able to proceed correctly."

She glares at me. Now feels like a good time to leave, so I thank her again. Then I sort of bow my way out of the kingdom. Once outside her office, I get as far as the stairs before I have to stop and sneeze a few times. This always happens—I blame her scent, which seems harmless enough at first. But these things can be deceiving.

I return to my cubicle, where someone has taped across the entrance with a huge **X**.

In the late afternoon, I suddenly have an urge for a cup of lemon tea. I keep tea bags in my drawer for such occasions—I think there are also some in my tote bag, although I haven't actually gone through my bag in ages. I take my tea bag and mug to the frost room, our tiny kitchen, where we have an electric kettle that works sometimes. I'm also hoping to find sugar, the real craving, I suspect, behind my sudden interest in tea.

As an extra treat, I find Monique in the frost room, standing before the open refrigerator wearing electric-yellow rubber gloves.

"No one ever cleans this out," she says, removing something brown from the fridge.

"Maybe you should get a picture of that," I say. It would fit perfectly into Monique's collection of disgusting pictures.

She pulls out a Baggie of green mush. "This isn't a scientific experiment," she says, "this is what's wrong with people today."

"I think it was just something from Carl's lunch."

"Same thing," Monique says, slamming the fridge and leaving the room, still in her yellow gloves. She could walk around the whole place like that, and I know no one would dare ask about them.

I make my tea and turn to find Tom lurking behind me.

"Hello," I say. "We're out of sugar."

"We had sugar?"

"I remember finding a cube once. I don't remember what year that was."

"I have honey," Tom says, a little suggestively, I notice.

"I didn't realize that," I say. Tom's hair has grown some since our one and only dinner date some months back. It gives him a more attractive, more relaxed look. I ask about the honey. "Is it in one of those bear-shaped bottles?"

Tom reaches around me for a coffee stirrer. We have lots of those, although I don't see him holding any coffee. He smiles.

"Oh, yes," he says, then gestures for me to go through the door first. I decide to take him up on his offer, partially because I'm intrigued by the idea of a man who keeps a honey bear stashed in his desk. When I squeeze some into my tea, I feel a little as if I've entered a dangerous but exciting fairy tale, something with bears and temptations in it. Tom offers me the stirrer, holding it just out of my reach.

That evening I tape my own small apartment windows, preparing for the storm as best I can. I spend the rest of the evening watching an unpleasant documentary on TV about how cats mate, which seems a little voyeuristic even for a nature special. The wind blows against the windows, making creaking noises that make me look up every minute and a half, distracting me from the cats. I pull out some mail I took home from work, and find one piece includes the missing photo from my mole book. The mole's shape resembles an old-fashioned wall phone, the kind you'd have to ring the operator on, back in the days before computerized voices. I pick up the mole photo and compare it to the moles on my own body, two on my legs, one on my abdomen. My moles don't have any special shapes, which disappoints me a little, even though I realize this is probably a good thing.

I turn off the cat show and fall asleep listening to the whistling sounds of increasing winds, the threatening but still soft tapping of Hurricane Holly.

At the office's front steps the next morning I find our messenger Roy again, this time seated and talking away to the usually quiet Tom, who answers enthusiastically, waving his hands. The wind swirls their hair and scarves around. Something about them strikes me as an odd pair. Monique passes behind me and points in their direction.

"Boys," she says, then keeps walking. I join Roy and Tom.

"Don't let me interrupt," I say, interrupting.

Roy hands me a large box of doughnuts. There must be thirty or so in there.

"One of the other offices I deliver to gave me these," Roy explains. "They said they were all on diets."

"How ridiculous," I say.

"They're uptown," Roy explains. Tom and I nod.

"No one here ever diets," I say. "We get enough exercise walking up and down the stairs, since the elevator doesn't usually work."

"It's the key to the cracking foundation of our generation," Roy says. "Calorie counting."

"Not to mention broken elevators," I say.

"Someday we'll learn," Roy says.

"So what were you guys talking about? Rotting environment? Malnutrition? The younger generation's malaise?"

"Basketball," they both answer.

"Ah, basketball. I think it's at the heart of the cracking foundation between men and women," I say.

"You're only pretending you don't like basketball because you're a girl. Social pressure toward femininity," Roy says.

"We know that in secret you go home and indulge your masculine side," Tom says. "Drinking beer, yelling at your TV, and burping loudly."

"I thought that was my feminine side," I say.

"It's what men really want from women," Tom says.

"Good to know," I say, heading off. I turn to see they've resumed their active conversation, gesturing wildly with their crullers.

Inside, I nearly crash into Carl, who looks at me as if he's very afraid, then whispers "Sorry," getting out of my way quickly. Everyone's going nuts, I think, with storm fever.

I settle into work as the wind pushes against our X-marked windows, making sounds like a slow heartbeat pounding. The lights flash a few times quickly, giving the office a Halloween-like eeriness. Something electric is in the air, and there's more activity, more chattering than usual all around me.

My friend Nina comes into my cubicle and sits down. "I've heard a rumor," she says.

"It's true. I really do like basketball."

"What?"

"Nothing," I say. "What have you heard this time? I'll dispel it for you." Our rumor mill works so badly.

"I heard you had a bad time with Sondra yesterday," Nina says. "Carl heard it."

I'd forgotten about Sondra after filing away her new set of rules. I never did destroy the old ones. I just don't like throwing things away.

"It went okay," I say. "You know how those meetings go. I might have said a little something, I guess."

"I never say anything to Sondra, except yes and thank you, of course."

"What else did you hear?" I ask.

"It gets a little fuzzy after that."

"There's more?"

"I think so, you better check," Nina says, then starts to leave.

"Sorry," she says on her way out.

I'm not a great one for gossip, and I dislike being talked about, so I'm both worried and angered by Nina's hearsay. I storm over to Monique's cubicle and sit down next to her.

"Want to see something putrid?" Monique asks, holding a slide up to the light.

"People are talking about me," I say. "Something about Sondra."

"Oh, the memo," Monique says, turning her slide one hundred and eighty degrees.

"What memo?"

Monique puts down her slide. "She wrote a memo, something about your meeting. I put it away." Monique looks through her trash. She finds the paper beneath a pile of torn galleys, damp from something.

The memo, from Sondra to all the vice-presidents and supervisors, insists that I have "failed to grasp the basic tenets of the editor-proofreader relationship," that I have "not followed the standardized rules set forth by the head of proofreading," and that I have "challenged her authority by minimalizing the importance of crucial standards."

"I've challenged her authority by minimalizing the importance of crucial standards?"

"I like that one, too," Monique says.

I suddenly feel like everyone's watching me, even though I'm fairly hidden in Monique's cubicle. Still, I'm beginning to feel blustery, unreasonable, panicky, as if some uncontrollable force inside me desperately wants out.

"It's nothing," Monique says.

"But this memo went to everyone," I say.

"So now it's gone in everyone's trash." Monique rolls it into a ball and throws it, banking it off my shoulder and into the trash can.

"Go take a walk," Monique says. "Enjoy the hurricane."

I rush outside still angry and stand on the front steps, winds circling around me. The wind brushes my hair against my face, which tickles my cheeks. This may be as bad as the storm plans to get, just wind that lifts your hair, rattles your windows and slaps at your knees, teasing you, taunting you. But it's still a forceful wind, and it may be about to play harder.

Roy comes back up the steps with more galleys. He stops and looks at me, then stands next to me, waiting. I hold my hair off my face and we watch the wind push a large silver-studded leather collar down the street, the kind of thing I guess punk rockers wear, if there are still punk rockers.

"There is much to learn from a hurricane with a good sense of humor," Roy says. He goes inside, and I follow. I answer the ringing phone at my desk.

"Hello, dear," my mother says. "Would you like an armoire?"

"Mom," I greet her. "I just couldn't say right now."

"Well, I have all this furniture to deal with," she says. "We don't need it all at Ronny's, and I hate it to sit in storage somewhere in New Jersey."

"I'm having a little trouble here at work," I say. "Can we talk later?"

"Problem? You know you can always tell your mother."

"Just something I have to work out," I say.

"I'm sure it will all blow over, dear," my mother says. After I hang up, a secretary from upstairs, Lily, comes by. "You're wanted in Cheryl's office," she says.

Cheryl, our vice-president in charge of production, always says hello to us when she passes by in the hall. Not all the VP's do this. She's a little older than Monique and sometimes brings a small collie to work with her. You can hear its nails clicking on the floor as it walks. Although I'm always happy to see Cheryl, I can't say I'm happy to be called upstairs. I try to smooth my hair back down and follow Lily, although I get a shock when I rub against the hallway wall.

It turns out Monique's in Cheryl's office waiting for me, too. Monique closes the door behind me.

"Hi, Holly, good to see you," Cheryl says. "Have a seat." I sit next to Monique, who has crossed her legs and swings the top one a little too wildly.

"I've learned that you've seen the memo from Sondra," Cheryl says.

"Yes," I start to babble, "I'm sorry if my meeting with Sondra didn't go well this time. I didn't mean to be disrespectful."

"Well, you certainly set her off," Cheryl says.

"She was fairly insulting," I say. "And I did ask some questions. But I didn't mean to set her off."

"Well, that's the difference between you and Monique, I guess," Cheryl says. Monique just swings her leg.

"Sorry?" I say.

"The difference," Monique says, "is that I always go in there *intending* to disturb Sondra. It's a quest of mine."

"Right," Cheryl says. "Although between us, Sondra's a little disturbed to begin with."

"A little," Monique says.

"She is?" I ask. "I mean, you know she is?"

They laugh. "She's cracked," Cheryl says. "Oh, look," Cheryl goes through her desk, pulling out some files. "Here's a pile of Sondra's memos about Monique. And here are the memos she wrote about me, when I was a production editor." She and Monique grab at them and read, laughing all the while.

" 'A snooty and uppity attitude not conducive to the responsibilities of a production editor,' " Monique reads. "Uppity, that's you all right," she says to Cheryl.

Cheryl picks up another. "Yeah, here's one about Monique: 'Blatant refusal to appreciate the seriousness of the editor's role in the handling of proofreader's rules. Her tendency to trivialize and her disgruntled approach add to her incompetence.' " Cheryl shakes her head. "Can you imagine anyone trying to insult Monique by calling her disgruntled?" They both laugh.

"It's my best feature," Monique says. They spread the memos out all over Cheryl's desk, and keep pointing and laughing.

"Anyway," Cheryl says, "welcome to the club, as it were. You certainly have nothing to worry about with this memo. I'd be more worried if she didn't write one about you."

"It's your first," Monique says, "you know, the first time's a little painful. It gets better."

"Why do you keep her working here?" I ask.

"She's good at some of her job, and it's a hard post to fill. She's been here years. I think the higher-ups feel a little sorry for her," Cheryl says.

"Once you get used to the idea," Monique says, "she's really very entertaining." They start laughing again.

"Go take a long lunch or something," Monique says. "Go minimalize someone's crucial standards with a drink."

I leave them laughing, shuffling through papers, Cheryl saying something like, "Where's that one that called me pernicious?"

I return to the production editor floor below, where Jan and Nina lift open the windows a crack. The winds seem to have died down. When I get to my cubicle, I see someone has made me a little basketball net and attached it to the modular wall in front of my desk. I pick up an eraser and dunk it. A crumpled piece of paper comes flying from Tom's side of the wall, falling smoothly through the center of the net. We play this way for a while, invisible to one another, paper balls and erasers sailing through the air. The breeze from the open windows gives me a sense of having escaped, having beaten something even, taken control. People begin to peel the Xs of masking tape off the windows, dancing around on the desks, and sticking balls of used tape to one another's backs, as we all revel in the aftereffects of Hurricane Holly.

Chapter 14

Lucky Number Seven

I'm back at work, finishing up my whale manuscript, which goes to the printer today. I examine each page for completeness, wishing it bon voyage, watching whales jump and glide. I won't see the project again until it's thickly bound, when I can hold it in my hands as I do all of my finished books, admiring its weight, smelling its freshly cut pages. As I look through it one last time, some of the other production editors mill around my desk, floating in and out of my vision, making those crooning whale noises, whale songs. One of them—I think it's Carl—starts singing "New York, New York," Sinatra style, and the others croon the harmony like lovesick whales.

When it's quieter, an origami basketball comes sailing over my wall, sinking through my net and landing on my desk. The orange paper has printed on it, "You're invited," but it doesn't say to what. For a minute, I enjoy just being included in something, and toss the light paper ball in the air. Then I get up to find out what the something might be. I go into Tom's cubicle.

"You're setting the whales free today, I hear," Tom says.

"Yes, I've done all I can for them," I say. "What's this about?" I hold up the paper ball.

"Someone gave Roy three tickets to a basketball game. He asked us along."

"Three tickets?" I say. "Isn't that a little odd?"

"It's Roy," Tom reminds me.

Our messenger Roy attracts all sorts of gifts: doughnuts, ties, basketball tickets. Someone once gave him cufflinks that say "Ray" on them, but unless you look closely, it looks like "Roy." Roy's still not sure what to do with them, though.

"People like to see Roy happy," Tom says.

I look back at the origami basketball.

"You're not still trying to make a point about men and women and basketball?"

"No, it's not really a gender-specific invitation," Tom says. "They're very good seats." Tom raises his eyebrows, as if he were offering me candy I'm far too young to accept.

"So is this a date?"

Tom thinks a moment. "You could decide that afterward," Tom says. "Depending on how the home team does."

I meet my mother for lunch in a restaurant she likes that has sawdust on both the floors and the tables, which seems a little excessive to me. I always end up taking home sawdust in my shoes and sleeves.

"This is like eating in a barn," I tell her.

"It's pastoral," she says, relaxing.

"It's a health hazard," I say.

My mother waves away my worries. We're waiting for Janie, who's uncharacteristically late.

"Janie, late," I say, shaking my head.

"Yes, Holly, I guess your little sister has finally grown up." I admit I'm relieved for once not to walk into a restaurant and see the always-early Janie scribbling away in her notebook, one eye checking her watch. Still, the idea of Janie changing makes me feel unsteady, vulnerable to a world where maybe anything really can happen.

"Janie, late," I say again.

"Two daughters," Mom says. "It's harder than you'd think. Not that I don't recommend it."

"Well, we're a little easier to handle now that we feed ourselves most of the time," I say.

"Oh, I don't know. You single girls. There's plenty to worry about."

"We're very careful," I say.

"Oh, not just those things," Mom says. "I've lived alone. I know you don't only worry about who's lurking outside your door and what disease they might carry. You worry about just living alone, how long you'll be alone, how you'll deal with it."

"I'm pretty good at it, I think," I say.

"But is it a long-term commitment?"

"Who can tell?" I say. I wonder about people reminding me about how I live alone. I think about it plenty, but I still think it's something I manage fairly well. I just hate thinking about the future, and whether I should actually do something about it. We sip our country-style lemonades for a moment, which come in huge mason jars, and think about our lives, mine in my little apartment, my mother's in her newly shared life with Ronny.

"Josh is remarrying," I tell her.

"Ah," she says, then sips again.

" 'Ah' is your final comment?"

"Is this good news?" she asks.

"I have no idea," I say. "It may be, in a masochistic kind of way."

I kick some sawdust around, and my mother doesn't even tell me to stop.

"How's the living together arrangement?" I ask bravely.

My mother and I don't talk about sex per se, not that we're talking about it now. But we're definitely in a gray area where the word—not to mention unwanted images—could arise. Too much sawdust will do that to you.

"I like it," she says with finality.

Janie rushes in and sinks into a chair, smoothing sawdust off her place mat with a fussy look on her face. Then she looks up at us.

"Guess what?" she says.

My mother and I look at each other as anticipation, dread, curiosity, and a sense of déjà vu hit us all at once. You could call it psychic, or you could call it experience, but we know what comes next.

"I'm engaged!" Janie says, grabbing the lemonade we've ordered her and lifting it in a toast.

My mother lifts up her jar, so I follow her lead. The jar's pretty heavy. The clinking is deep and serious, kind of like a cowbell.

"Congratulations. I hope you're going to live together first," says my modern mother.

"You'll love him," Janie says, ignoring her. This would be Janie's seventh engagement, unless I've lost count. Lucky number seven.

"Congratulations," I say. "Where's the ring?"

"No ring yet," Janie says proudly. "We're picking one out together."

"A first," my mom says. "Anyone we know?"

"Is it Jackson again?" I ask.

"No, no," Janie says. "That was over ages ago. Why would you think that?"

"I don't know," I say defensively. "How do you meet men so quickly?" My mother and I both lean in for Janie's technique. She ought to market it.

"I meet men everywhere," Janie says. "Mostly at the gallery, but also at the symphony, with friends, at artists' shows." I admire Janie's social life, although I doubt it leaves much time for lying around on the couch. "You have to be open, yet critical," she says.

"Are you taking notes?" my mother teases me.

"I'm memorizing," I say. Open yet critical.

"Oh, Holly meets men," Janie says. "They just don't register." I try to think what this could mean. Does Tom register? Sure, he worked in the office for nearly a year before actually saying hello out loud, but that's not so unusual at our office.

"Okay," I say, "but why do you get engaged so fast?" It's the unasked question, the line that perhaps we're not supposed to go beyond. But Janie answers unembarrassed.

"Why waste time?" Janie says succinctly. My mother and I shrug, since we don't have a good reply, even though there must be several, given how many engagements Janie has broken so far.

"All right," Mom says, "let's have the basics on this guy."

"Well," Janie starts. "I did meet him at the gallery. His name is Bucky Newbury. He plays hockey."

"For fun, you mean?" I ask.

"Of course for fun," Janie says, "and for a large sum of money it would be indiscreet to discuss."

"Hockey," my mother says. "That's where they hit each other with sticks, right?"

"No," Janie says. "They don't hit each other with sticks, although there is a certain amount of battle to the sport."

"They cream each other," I say.

"Interesting," my mother says. "A physical type."

"Hockey has its intellectual side," Janie insists.

"Is it like tennis," my mother asks, "where the players get too old after thirty and sit around the house complaining about sore joints?"

"After retiring," Janie says, "Bucky intends to go back to finish college and open a sports center for children. He's very practical."

"A practical hockey player," I say. "Wow." It's all so fascinating.

"With a personal fortune," Mom adds.

"Of course," Janie says, opening a menu. "What did you think?"

I think Bucky Newbury is one of the cutest men I've ever seen—that's what I think.

We're at Ronny's apartment, my mother's newfound home. I notice a few old pieces of my mother's furniture that have made their way into Ronny's collection, and I have to admit they fit nicely. The room has an easy-goingness to it, not too bachelorlike, not too feminine. Flowers and plaids. Ferns and cacti. Our old piano in one corner and husky ceramic pots in another tell me two people live here, two people share. I could do without the huge fish over the fireplace, though. Tonight, Mom and Ronny host an extended family dinner, another in a long line of engagement parties. Janie has invited Maria and Henry to join us for Ronny's home-cooked festivities.

"Good, more eaters. Why make potatoes for two when you can make potatoes for ten?" Ronny asks. My mother admits she doesn't see the logic here, as she doesn't like cooking for groups. But it seems to be Ronny's specialty. He serves us fried clams with homemade cole slaw and French fries, which he even cut himself. I can tell they're not the frozen kind, which is all I've ever made. Ronny serves the kind of food that deserves a little sawdust on the floor, which of course there isn't a chance of in my mother's home.

"I just caught these clams myself," says Ronny the fisherman.

"From the Hudson?" Maria and I say, almost in unison, definitely in fear.

"Just kidding, you girls," Ronny says, patting us on the back.

The guest of honor, Bucky Newbury, is twenty-six years old, like Janie, with slightly curly brown hair, freckles, and dimples. Maria and I sit across the table from him and kick each other in the shins.

"Freckles and dimples," I whisper to Maria in awe.

"Usually it's an either/or situation," Maria whispers back. "It's the combination that's making your hands sweat."

I nod. "Not to mention the clam sauce."

"Zesty," she says, spearing a French fry.

Bucky offers a toast. "I just want to say how happy I am, how happy I hope Janie is. She's changed my life. I'm just so happy to be here. I'm sorry—I'm just babbling, now," Bucky says. His face turns red, which only brings out the freckles more. My mother has not stopped smiling all night, even when Ronny dropped a fried clam in her lap.

"Why, he's just like something out of a Charlie Brown cartoon," my mother whispered to me earlier. She meant it as a compliment.

Bucky and Ronny have made a date to go fishing in a couple of weeks, and Ronny gives Bucky instructions on how to bake a swordfish.

"Don't smother the thing," Ronny says. "Let the fish be in control." It sounds like he's talking about catching it, or maybe letting it go.

"I want to cook all of our fish," Bucky says to Janie.

"I'll make the salads," Janie says.

"You'll never go wrong with romaine," Ronny says, and Janie pulls out her little notebook to mark something down.

She shares her notebook with Bucky, I notice, who glances at it over her shoulder and whispers in her ear. I've never seen Janie let anyone look in that book before. It must be love.

Even Henry, Maria's boyfriend, has been chattering away with Bucky about, of course, hockey.

"Henry's made a friend," Maria says sweetly.

"When's the wedding?" Ronny asks.

"Very soon," Bucky says. He pages through Janie's notebook and they point to dates, nodding.

"A summer wedding," my mother says.

"Salmon season!" Ronny adds. "You can't beat salmon."

"Everyone likes salmon," I say to Janie, who says "Oh" and writes it down.

"Be careful," Maria says to me quietly, "or you'll end up wearing a salmon-colored dress."

"One step above flesh-colored," I say.

"But not a very big step," Maria whispers.

"A toast to the happy couple," Ronny says, standing. "May they find every joy awaiting them in the ocean of life."

"So to speak," my mother adds.

The happy couple grip each other with real affection as they toast. Janie shows us her old-fashioned engagement ring with an alluring jewel, and we all snuggle in for dessert. Ronny has baked us a rhubarb pie.

"He baked it?" Maria asks my mother while Ronny's in the kitchen. My mother nods.

"Hang on to him, Allison," Maria instructs my mother, who winks.

Janie and Bucky talk happily about wedding cakes. Bucky wants the little groom figure on top to wear a hockey suit. My formerly traditional-minded sister seems to like the idea.

"Maybe the whole wedding party can wear hockey suits," Maria whispers to me. "You look good in jersey," she says.

"Shoulder pads make me itch," I say.

"But you might get your own number."

"True."

"You know," Maria says, "I think your little sister's really getting married this time." I have to look down, because this makes my eyes tear up, which catches me off-guard. I've always felt a little responsible for Janie, and I guess I've always felt that my role as big sister was to make sure little Janie was happy. That she is now just gets me, somehow.

Maria grabs a can of whipped cream and applies some to my pie. We pass the can around the table.

"It's an old Italian tradition," Maria says. "The passing of the pre-wedding whipped cream can. It means all the women at the table will find great happiness before the fluorocarbons reach the ozone layer."

"Have you noticed," I ask, "that we're always eating pie?"

"It's our way," Maria says, digging in.

That night I go through my office tote bag, looking for some scientific reading to make me sleepy. Something with long, hypnotic words. Seems I've had too much pie. I find an unexpected package in my bag, mysteriously labeled "To Holly. Not a Bomb. Monique," and wrapped with that curly ribbon you get to zip the ends of with your scissors. She's wrapped it really tight, so I can't slide off the ribbon without breaking it and can't untie it, either, so I have to cut it. These kinds of decisions throw me, sometimes.

Monique has apparently had the art department make me copies of the whale pictures from my book. Whales look my way through the eight-by-ten glossy waters. She's also gotten me a tape of whale songs, *The Whales of Prince William Sound*, and I run to my cassette deck to play track number one, called simply "Evening." One whale begins crooning, singing in that clear, echoing way, until another joins it.

They sing a slow, unhurried duet as I sink back into my couchbed and look at their pictures. I know it's probably not the same whales, but that's okay. I listen to them float forward, into the evening, until one seems to leave and the original one (I think) sings by itself. It's not that sad a song, although their calling always strikes me as a little sad. The lone whale sings evenly, moving off into the distance, off into the dark waters of the Pacific. The ocean in the photos looks freezing and dark, but then I remember, this is their home, it must be familiar, comforting, somehow warm enough in its way. I place the photos on the side table, propping up one of a whale springing from the water, so it will be the first thing I see in the morning. I'm hoping for inspiration. Then I settle back to fall asleep to the music of the whales.

Chapter 15

The Playoffs

"Lucky you," Maria tells me. "It's a playoff game."

"I think Tom would like it to be a date, even though there will be three of us," I say.

Maria lies across my hardwood floor, her feet on a pillow, resting after standing all day at the pharmacy. She calls my floors "too soft" sometimes, which always makes me think of her as Goldilocks.

"Which bear's bed would you have ended up in?" I've asked her.

"Oh, I'm the Daddy bear type," Maria answered, "no doubt about it."

But for now we're discussing me, my officemate Tom, and the appropriate thing to wear to a basketball playoff that may or may not be a date.

"You'd want to dress up a little for the playoffs," Maria says. "But you still want to wear rubber-soled shoes, or you'll seem snooty. Plus, everyone will hear you when you get up to walk to the bathroom."

"You know," I say, "this isn't really worth thinking about."

"I don't know," Maria says. "It distracts us from our real worries, so it seems worthwhile."

"True. But feel free to distract me with your real worries."

"I'm worrying about my feet," Maria says. "Do you know they've grown a half size in the last year? You'd think after thirty, at least your feet would stop growing."

"It's one of those things they don't tell you," I say. "Like that you'll have gray hair *and* pimples at the same time."

Maria closes her eyes. "Tell me more about Tom," she says, uncrossing her feet on the pillow.

"I think he's gotten more attractive in the last few months," I tell her. "Something about his hair."

"Could be a perm," Maria says.

"No, something natural."

"So you're attracted to him?" Maria asks.

"I didn't say that. He just seems generically more attractive."

"Generic attractiveness is underrated," Maria says.

"But is it enough?"

"That depends. Do you find him attractive enough, generically speaking, to become more attached to him as time goes on?" Maria rolls her back a few times against the floor, making creaking sounds. It hurts me just to think of lying on the hard ground. I have a bony back.

"I'm not sure," I say. Am I more attracted to Tom now than I was at first? More fond of him? Will I find myself slowly more and more attracted to him? Does it work that way? "Doesn't there have to be some sort of big bang when you first meet a guy? Isn't that where we get the big bang theory from?" I ask.

"There are no scientific theories when it comes to love," Maria says. "Look at it this way: You're sitting here thinking about him now."

"I'm worrying, not thinking," I say. "There's a difference."

"You're agitating," Maria says, "not worrying."

"Yes, but I don't know if that's such a good sign for Tom," I say.

"Obsessing would be better than agitating," Maria says, "at least for the person you're obsessing over."

"I'm not sure any one of them makes for a good relationship, though."

"Maybe," Maria suggests, "he's the type to settle for agitation."

"Maybe."

"But you're not," Maria says.

"Agitation's normal for me," I say. "I want something even more stomach-wrenching, like love."

It's the most uneventful playoff game in the history of basketball. Neither team plays especially well, and sometimes it seems as though hardly anyone can make a basket. Both coaches sit calmly at the sides until they can stand it no longer, then they jump up and scream in their expensive suits, wrinkling themselves aimlessly. The crowd jeers even its favorite players. No one seems safe.

"Basketball is representative of the realities of life," Roy says in his way. "Today, they're holding up a mirror to all our insecurities and doubts."

"They're just not passing enough," Tom says.

"Maybe we should cheer harder, or cheer for different reasons, like neatly tied shoelaces or something," I suggest. I somehow feel responsible for the home team's problems. I can't speak for the other side, though.

"Even the beer tastes weaker, as though it has lost its enthusiasm for the sport," Roy says.

Just then two players crash into each other.

"A large number of personal fouls," Roy says. "They're indicative of people's inability to connect on a responsive level."

"I think that guy's unconscious," I say.

The crowd is on its feet until the guy rises. Then they start booing again. A man in a suit behind us reads the paper. I show Tom.

"Not even the sports section," Tom says, shaking his head.

"At least we've got good seats," I say.

They agree, but their hearts aren't in it. The men in the audience seem especially subdued, hurt, as if they're taking it personally. I see a lot of women patting boyfriends on the back, in sympathy. Clearly, there's more at stake in the play-offs than I thought.

Our team loses badly, and slinks from the room. The winners don't much hang around, either. The crowd, exhausted by inaction, slithers out of the place with a low, grumbling sound.

"There'll be trouble on the subway tonight," Tom says.

"The murmur of animosity," Roy says, agreeing, I guess.

Oddly enough, I've had a pretty good time, but I seem to be in the minority. We avoid the subway for a while, just in case. I've offered to buy them pizza, so we hop on a downtown bus that looks slightly dimmed inside. The passengers seem sedated, or maybe they're just tired. They don't look like they've sat through a frustrating evening though, at least not one that was nationally televised.

We chew slices of pizza over a tiny round table. The cheese seems to bring us all back to life, although it could be the grease.

"We wanted your first basketball game to be special," Tom says to me in apology.

"How can you say that wasn't special? I've never seen a fan grab the coach by his tie before and play tug-of-war with him like that," I say.

"It happens," Tom admits.

"But of course, this wasn't my first basketball game."

They look surprised.

"I went to college. I was true to my school," I say.

"What other secrets have you been keeping?" Tom wants to know.

"Holly conducts the life of a modern woman," Roy says. "Hers is a world strewn with confusing trails and lined with secrets she's tucked away from years of social combustion. She's experienced in the wherewithal of basketball's intricacies."

"Tell us more," Tom says.

"I never spilled beer all over myself, if that's what you want to hear," I say.

"Just as I thought," Tom says.

We leave Roy off at the corner, but Tom walks this modern woman to her door. He reaches for my hand as if to shake it, and we join hands, but I feel as if I'm standing back and watching him hold my hand, watching for signs. I'm afraid I'll miss something, the moment when he first leans in to kiss me. But I don't miss it—I'm right here—and there it is, our first real kiss. He's still holding onto my hand when the kiss ends. It seems like time to say something, but I can't think of anything. I'd like to say something lightly humorous but not too funny. My mind whirls, but I just stand there.

Tom lifts up my hand and looks at it.

"You get so quiet," he says.

"I do?" Tom's the one we all think of as quiet.

"I sit right next to you," Tom says. "You can go for hours without a sound, not a clearing of the throat, not a sigh, just this silence." I smile, a little embarrassed that someone has been listening for my sighs, but pleased, too.

"I don't think I ever know what to say, really," I tell him.

"It's okay, it's nice," Tom says. "Your silences, I mean. I

can still tell that you're there. Oh, no, I'm sounding like Roy."

"No, no," I say. "Not at all." Tom has not let go of my hand, but he plays with it, turning it over and over in his gentle grasp. This may be what I want, I think, someone who will find one of my hands fascinating. Maybe to distract me from watching our hands, or maybe for reasons of his own, Tom kisses me again.

"Good night," he finally says, after the kiss. He walks away slowly without releasing my hand until his arm straightens out completely. Then he lets go.

I head inside and think about the kiss. Normally, let's say if Maria were here, we might try to evaluate it on a scale of one to ten. But somehow this doesn't seem appropriate. I try to think of other kisses I've known, but my mind goes blank. Then a few come back to me. This one does well in comparison, certainly in terms of technique, plus a slight element of surprise (I thought we were both going to watch the hands a little more). Surprise, of course, can be bad news in a kiss, or it can be a plus, as in this case. It occurs to me that I may be overanalyzing, but it's either that or the TV news.

All in all, I feel the evening has been a success, and I celebrate by getting into my oldest sweat clothes, the thin ones I sometimes sleep in. I open up the couchbed and put on my softest little socks—one pink, one red. I'd put one of those cold cream masks on my face, if I had anything like that, although it sounds like it might itch. Instead, I fluff up my pillows and sink into my bed.

There's a knock at my door, a knock I recognize, and I wonder for a moment if I shouldn't just ignore it, just lie here enjoying my socks. Why not stay in bed and let sleep overcome me, then wonder in the morning if I'd dreamed the knock? But no, creature of habit that I am, I get up to answer, even though I know better.

"Hiya, Holly," says my ex-husband, Josh. I realize I don't really want to see him now, that I should have stayed in bed. I must look a little sad, as though my home team lost big tonight or something. Josh looks just fine, as does the woman standing on his right.

"Holly, this is Lauren, my fiancée," Josh says.

She shakes my hand politely and has that little look on her face that says, *This wasn't my idea.* She's a bit younger than I am, with hair that has that no-fuss curliness and goes all the way down her back. She's wearing one of those long, all-purpose black jumpers that are just loose enough to show you're a carefree woman but fit just tight enough to show you're a thin and well-exercised carefree woman. Plus, her socks match. I consider closing the door and hiding in the bathroom till they leave, but instead I exchange muttered "Nice to meet yous" with Lauren, and both of them somehow end up inside my apartment.

A silence drags on for what seems like five minutes but is probably only fifteen painful seconds. Okay, maybe twenty.

"It's pretty late," I say.

"I wanted you two to meet," Josh says. "We came by earlier but you were out." If he were someone else, I might wonder if he were being spiteful and vindictive. Since it's Josh, I realize he's just oblivious to socially uncomfortable situations, not that I find this character flaw of his at all endearing at the moment.

"Well, I was out, but now you've found me," I say. Maybe if I'd had a second slice of pizza or walked more slowly, they would have given up and I'd be happily dreaming by now. And alone, which would have its advantages, especially if I started snoring.

"Josh talks about you so fondly," Lauren says, clearly sensing my discomfort. "It's nice that you've stayed friends."

"It is," I say. I think about offering them something to

drink, then decide to forget it. I notice Lauren looking at my socks.

"Lauren's working on her master's," Josh says. Lauren nods, smiling, trying hard not to be noticed picking at her thumbnail, which I notice. I have to say it makes me feel better about her.

"And she's been a great help in my research, of course," Josh doesn't forget to add.

"How's the book coming?" I ask, hoping I can add something harmless to the conversation before asking them to go.

"It should be published any day now. Your friend Tom was a big help. He caught a lot of mistakes just in time."

I nod. I don't want to talk to Josh about Tom. I feel my privacy a little invaded just by Josh's mention of him, but I'm pretty sure Josh isn't aware of this.

"And you're doing well?" Josh asks.

"Busy," I say. "Busy and well."

"It is late," Lauren says in Josh's direction. I already realize this, of course.

"Oh, right," Josh says.

"Thanks for coming by," I say, trying to get them out of here.

"I'm so glad you two got to meet," Josh says sincerely.

I shake hands with Lauren again and trade good-byes. I wonder where they'll go next, whether Josh will drag her somewhere else, insist on meeting her ex-boyfriend, perhaps. But they'll probably just go home. I realize this is something I don't want to think about. Josh hugs me good-bye absentmindedly, like you might hug someone you're dropping at the airport, someone you might not see for a while, someone you might not think about all that much.

* * *

As I fall asleep, I try not to dwell on any of the men from tonight, yet they all run through my thoughts. They're beyond my control. I see them all sitting around Madison Square Garden, each cheering for his special team. I suddenly imagine the coaches in their wrinkled suits, jumping up and down doing cheers with the crowd, instead of their usual screaming at the players. I imagine them suddenly wearing short cheerleader skirts, with pom-poms. If I were awake, I'd probably realize I'm dreaming. I do sense this as the crowd stomps its feet on the floor in a cheer, then wake to realize it's really someone tapping at my door. Again.

"Hiya, Holly."

"Josh, no, it's really late."

"I know." He stands there not saying anything, and I try to picture him as a basketball coach. How frustrating he'd be. He comes in, although not entirely invited. He sits down back in the same chair he chose earlier, not that there's much seating space to choose from around here.

"She's nice, don't you think?" Josh asks me. "Lauren," he adds, in case I've forgotten he's remarrying someone named Lauren.

"Yes, nice," I say. "Too nice to object to being dragged over here, I guess."

"Oh, no," Josh says. "She did want to meet you. She knows I think the world of you."

"Josh, I wish you well, I think, although less tonight than usual," I say, feeling a little riled up from the cheerleading dream. "I think that's very big of me, given what's gone on between us in the last few months, which I really don't even want to ask you about at this particular moment, or probably ever."

"Oh," Josh replies, then turns silent. It's a good thing I didn't ask an actual question, as this isn't much of an actual response.

"So given our relationship and where it may have been going, or as it turns out wasn't really going at all, I think I'm behaving pretty well, pretty nicely, don't you?"

"Of course," Josh says, hesitating about whether to continue, which I've decided not to let him do.

"Good. Then, let me just say that I'd really like you to stop dropping by, because these surprises are just more than I really want anymore. Just go get married. Move to another city even. So I can sleep. Not to mention so my waking hours can be improved."

"It's just—" Josh starts.

"You know," I say, as I start waving my arms and moving around my room, the room I really love right now, "I'm not sure I'm incredibly happy these days, but I'm not too unhappy. I'm relatively happy. I'm okay. I have my little apartment and soft clothes. I have a kitty postcard on my fridge." I point toward my kitchen, the kitchen I also really love right now. "And I like that about myself. I feel good about it. But if I have to hear one more thing from you about either how great your new about-to-be wife is or how happy you are—"

I don't finish. I notice that Josh is looking strangely at me, or at a space just above me, actually.

"Well, what?" I finally demand.

"There's a huge moth on your wall," Josh says.

I turn. There's a huge moth on my wall. Josh goes over and gently catches it between two fingers, like you do when you're a kid. He walks over to the window, opens it, and lets the moth out almost lovingly, then returns to his chair, all in a smooth, dreamlike gesture. In this minute or so, my anger has evaporated, as if it has gone out the window with the moth. I feel as if I'm under a spell.

"So you think I should marry her?" Josh asks. The spell is broken.

"Earth to Josh," I say, a little more exhausted than angry

anymore. "Don't ask me this. We're done with this. We're pretty much done with everything."

"But you have better judgment than I do," he says.

If it were earlier in the evening, I might like to consider what this means. We married one another. We divorced, my doing, when I couldn't take Josh's inability or unwillingness to think ahead or in less abstract terms, or maybe I just wanted him to think more about me. Does Josh consider my divorcing him as good judgment, in some masochistic kind of way? Or is he thinking of something smaller, like my better judgment than his in picking out a set of dishes, for example? I'll probably never figure out what he means.

"Did you ask someone's advice before you married me?" I ask.

"No," he says.

"And look what happened, right?"

"No, I'm still glad I married you," Josh says. "I didn't like being divorced from you, but I think of it more now as just a stage of our progression."

"Sounds scientific," I say. He shrugs.

I take a deep breath and sit down on my couchbed. Josh looks somewhat forlorn, a look I know from having argued with him before, and it's not that I fall for the look at this point, it's just that I don't hate this person. Not at all, for whatever reason, for many reasons over many years. He's just who he is. And he's not mine to worry about any longer.

"Marry her if you want to, if she'll let you," I say. "But please, don't even think about inviting me."

Josh looks down at his well-worn shoes. One of the laces looks like something has been chewing on it.

"It won't be a wedding without you," Josh says, smiling.

"Oh, it will," I say. "A wedding I don't really want to know anything more about. You're on your own. We both are. I really mean it, Josh."

He nods. "Okay," Josh says, rising. "But I'm not sure I like thinking of you as all on your own."

"Get used to it, please," I say. "Besides, I kind of like it, which is lucky, because I am officially, for the record, on my own." I move my arms over my head then out to the side, as if to say, "Ta-da!" As if I'd just performed a very difficult gymnastic feat, one for which I'm about to get a very high score, if not a perfect mark.

Josh nods. I wave at him from my couch as he leaves—there's no move to kiss or hug here. I've had my kisses for one night. After he leaves, I go over and double-lock the door, and I can hear him walking down the stairs. I walk by the kitchen and straighten the ladybug magnets on my softly buzzing refrigerator. I grab the playoff ticket from my purse on the counter and put the torn ticket on the fridge, under its own ladybug, then return to bed to try, once more, to fall asleep.

Chapter 16

Love in the Time of Recession

The office fills with a kind of underwater quiet that makes me nervous, makes me wish for a playgroundful of screaming children, or at least a barking dog in the vicinity. It's the kind of quiet you sense when you wake from a bad dream and don't know where you are, even though you're in your own darkened bedroom, the place you felt so safe only hours ago. It's the kind of quiet you feel when you find a memo on your desk like we all find this morning.

Our office, Science Press, Inc., has been purchased by one of the larger publishing houses in town, MacWhitton Publishing, which previously had only a small line of science books known as Whatsit Press. Several of our company's departments will be "overhauled," the memo says, and some employees will be "released to find new areas of interest." Further memos will be forthcoming, this memo claims. A memo that promises further memos is never a good sign.

"'We sincerely regret the inconvenience this may cause our employees,'" Tom reads to me from his memo, although the memo on my desk in front of me says the same thing. Hearing it out loud makes it sound even more frightening, as if something unrecognizable, something shadowy hides from us just beyond the memo. We in the production room have started to cluster, hovering over one another's desks. I notice Carl across the room consoling several young women with great compassion, not to mention enjoyment.

" 'Employees not included in the reorganization will be redirected in regard to their career path objectives,' " Tom reads further.

"Meaning?" Nina asks.

"They're firing our asses and kicking us out into the real world," Monique says. "In translation."

"Still," Tom says to Monique, "it sounds better when you say it."

I feel a little sick to my stomach and dizzy, as if I've just taken too much allergy medication. Now would not be a good time to operate heavy machinery, I believe.

Monique has come over to my cubicle, where Nina's also sitting on my cow stool, staring at her memo.

"I suggest we all work on our résumés today," Monique says quietly.

"Did you know about this?" I ask her.

She shrugs. "You hear things. Some of them you choose to ignore, either out of arrogance or stupidity, take your pick."

"Redirected," Tom says.

"We'll all be out on the street," Nina says woefully, if not with some exaggeration.

"Go get yourself a muffin," Monique tells her.

The memo says the sale and move to the Whatsit offices will occur in the next two months. Anyone laid off in the "restructuring" will get two weeks' notice and "ample severance pay." Still, this doesn't seem to me to cover the bigger picture. I've worked here for years, since college. Since I was married to Josh, since Janie's first-ever engagement. I've had the same chair for over eight years. Will it be "restructured," too? My parents were still a couple when I first started here. I like it here, I like the rut I may or may not be in, I like my job that may not exist in two months' time. I keep running these thoughts through my mind. I'll have to take my milking stools home, where they'll end up in a corner, or hidden under the little kitchen table. Purposeless. Abandoned. I'll have to find a new job.

"I don't have a résumé," I say. "I've only worked here." I realize that I sound pathetic, but I don't care.

"Oh, get her a muffin, too," Monique tells Nina, who is swaying back and forth on the black-and-white milking stool.

I also suddenly remember the memo that Sondra, the head of proofreading, wrote about me, the accusation that I took my responsibilities less than seriously. Maybe the new people will get hold of the memo and not realize that we all consider Sondra as a frightening example of a proofreader gone over the edge. Perhaps if they see her memos about everyone, they'll take the hint. Still, in my slightly paranoid state, I feel certain that they'd see only the memo about me. And redirect.

Tom has begun to fold his memo into an intricate object I can't quite recognize. I stare back at my own sheet and see it in a hallucinatory blur, probably because tears have begun to fall down my cheeks. I seem to have no control over this.

"Oh, no," Monique says somewhere behind me.

"Oh, don't cry," Tom says.

They all start to shuffle about, but I just put my head down on my arms, the way they have you do in kindergarten at rest time. I need my nap. I need one of those brown mats they spread out for you, and the fig cookies you get when you wake up. And chocolate milk. I'm not out-and-out sobbing or anything, I've just got these streams for eyes. Everyone has disappeared from around me. Whether they've actually left or I just can't see them anymore, I don't know. I don't much care. I long for a soft-voiced adult to read me something kind-hearted, with pastel-colored illustrations that will lull me into a light sleep.

As I open my eyes, a box of tissues appears before me, I think from Monique. Nina places in front of me a large chocolate-chip muffin that looks like it has no nutritional value, but also looks like she has picked it out especially for me. Tom brings me a plastic bottle of juice, along with something that looks like an origami crab—it must be the memo in its new life-form. You can move its little claws in a slow crablike motion. I've stopped crying, or watering, or whatever it was. I sip my juice and make my crab pick the chocolate chips off the muffin with its claws. After what may be an hour or so of relocating the chocolate pieces into a little pile with my crab claws, I notice it's lunchtime.

"Come along now," Monique tells me. "I'll buy you a hamburger."

"I don't like to eat meat," I tell her.

"You don't have any fun," Monique says.

I grab my purse and follow her. We go to a small, classy Japanese restaurant in the neighborhood, where Monique orders us sake.

"Whatsit Press?" I ask her. "Is this a respectable name for a company?"

"As long as they don't make us wear T-shirts with the company name, who'll know?" Monique says.

"Don't you have an inside line to the top? Don't you know who's going to be fired? Can't you get more details?"

"No," Monique says.

"Oh," I say, looking at my sake. I'm not sure drinking it is a good idea right now. Monique pushes it toward me.

"Think of it as chicken soup," she says, so I take a sip.

"Very sweet chicken soup," I tell her.

"You want to know what I did find out?" Monique asks, after ordering us plates of sushi. She raises her eyebrows. "Hmmm?"

I raise my eyebrows in response.

"Three of our production editors resigned this morning."

"Without severance pay?"

"I think there were some arrangements made," Monique says.

"Details."

"Rachel is going on tour with her band."

"Wow," I say. "She's finally doing it." Rachel, one of the senior production editors—like me, part of the just-over-thirty gang—has long been a drummer with a rock band called The Translators. They play at all the Christmas parties. Each band member speaks at least four languages, and they take requests.

"Reggie is going to work uptown for one of those men's fashion magazines," Monique says. I nod. Reggie, always perfectly dressed, is the only one who wears cologne in the office.

"He always smells like cream soda," I say.

"Probably costs him a fortune," she says. "Carl's leaving also, for Discoveries United." Discoveries, one of our biggest competitors in science books, mostly publishes basic science, like *Your Friendly Universe* and *Making Friends with Ants*.

"How did they know to go out and get new jobs? Or is it just a coincidence?" I ask.

"I don't believe in coincidence," Monique says. "It's not a malevolent enough concept."

"So Carl knew?"

"So he got one rumor right in five years," Monique says. The waitress brings us our sushi lunches with an impressive silence, as if she knows to be gentle with people facing possible unemployment.

"What'll we do?" I ask Monique.

Monique takes her chopsticks and dips a California Roll in its sauce.

"We'll be good scouts. We'll be prepared."

"I guess," I say.

"We'll order more sake," Monique says. "And count up our unused vacation time."

As I leave the office after work, I find Roy, our messenger, sitting on the building's front steps.

"The reality of it all overwhelms me," Roy says.

I sit down next to him. He seems bereft.

"You'll never all be in the same place again," Roy says. "You'll be spread across the publishing world, some people falling into the crevices of PR and advertising. The expansion of the vista upsets me."

"That might happen, things might change, but it might be okay," I say. Somehow his near state of panic calms me, puts it all in perspective, for a minute, anyway.

"I have trouble adjusting to new circumstances," Roy says. "I thrive on monotony. It's all too much."

I pat him on the shoulder. "Monotony might be the enemy," I say, trying to speak to Roy in his own language. "You'll see, it'll all work out." I try to sound convincing, hoping he hasn't heard about my crying jag this morning.

"Where will I find you? What if our office doesn't deliver to your office? I feel trapped in the thick fog of the future, strangled, choked."

"Poor Roy," I say. "The fog will lift, though."

"Holly, I feel a strong connection between us," Roy says. "A bond of great human proportions, maybe greater."

"I like you too, Roy."

"I feel as if I have a purpose, my role here has been predetermined."

"Really?"

"I'd never interfere with you and Tom, of course."

"Oh. I'm not sure there's much to interfere with."

"I see you two as my guiding spirits."

"I'm not sure what Tom and I are, Roy."

"Guiding spirits," he repeats. "My role is to ease your way."

"Well," I say. "Thanks. Roy, have you thought about going back to school yet? Not that your efforts aren't appreciated here."

"I think about it. I'm not sure I fit in there. University life is so stressful. And the trees on my campus make everyone sneeze in the fall."

"Ah."

"Stress," Roy says. "It's torn away at the heart of endeavor at the end of the twentieth century."

"I think you're right, Roy."

"I know. It's in the air between us."

I put my arm around his thin shoulders.

"I hope I haven't failed you," Roy says.

"Couldn't happen," I tell him. "You always give me so much to think about."

Roy smiles.

"You have such a good sense of purpose, Holly," Roy says, then goes to his Moped, puts on his black helmet, and rides away.

Tom joins me on the steps.

"Roy, riding off into the sunset," Tom says.

"The masked man."

"Are you feeling better?" Tom asks.

I'm not sure I ever properly thanked him for bringing me juice earlier. "Yes, thanks. I've decided to try to think of this as a bad dream, try to pretend it really has no meaning, that it's just something I made up."

"Virtual reality."

"Along those lines."

"And when reality comes crashing in?" Tom asks.

"Maybe it'll ease its way through the window," I say. "Or

maybe I'll have a much bigger problem by then, so this will seem like nothing."

"It's a plan," Tom admits. "Could we go somewhere and talk?"

I think what I'd most like is to be alone with a quiet bottle of wine, but I realize this isn't good for me, so I walk a ways with Tom. We sit at a park bench, apart from a crowd of people hurrying home after work.

"This probably isn't a good time for this," Tom says, and at first I think he means a time for sitting in the park, then I realize he doesn't.

"It's okay."

"Okay," Tom repeats. "Let's see. Sometimes I wonder if it's turning out as I'd hoped. You and I."

"Oh," I say. I don't know what to say.

"And maybe it's just fine as it is. Maybe it's progressing slowly, but progressing."

I nod.

"Do you think it's progressing?" Tom asks. I look over at him, and he seems so sincere and well meaning that I realize how really fond I am of him. And I know that it isn't progressing, not really. That even if we tried to make it progress, we'd always have this feeling that maybe something's wrong.

"I'm sorry," I say. "I'm not sure what it is."

Tom jumps in. "I probably haven't done the right things. I wanted to ask you out again after dinner at my apartment, but then I just didn't. I thought I'd wait, but then I seemed to wait too long. Then I didn't know what to say, exactly. But I've been fond of you."

"I'm glad about that, actually," I say. "I've thought about it, I mean, a relationship. Maybe you're not supposed to think about it, it's just supposed to happen."

"No," Tom says, "that's just idealistic. But then, I liked thinking about it."

"It wasn't bad, thinking about it, wondering," I say.

"Oh, well, no, wondering's okay," Tom says.

"So we've both wondered."

"The curiosity is getting to me," Tom admits.

"Yeah, me too. But I don't feel we'd be right, somehow. Not that you're not, well, fascinating, really."

"Thanks," Tom says. "It feels like the timing is off, though. I keep thinking that. I hate thinking that, but I do."

"You know," I start, "I always think that nothing much ever happens to me, but there's really so much going on. My work life is falling to pieces. My sister and ex-husband are both getting married, although not to one another. Then there's you, and this whole area of possibility. And now that's ending, I guess." I feel my shoulders start to slip forward as I fall into a sadness like this morning's again. If I start to cry, I'm going to squeeze my cheeks to distract myself. I don't want to be that pathetic.

"There are new possibilities," Tom says, "think of it that way. Although I can't think what they are yet."

"We need fortune cookies," I say.

"I'm not sure I like thinking somewhere there's a fortune cookie that knows more than I do," Tom says.

"That's funny, I find it a little comforting," I say.

Tom puts his arm around me on the bench, not a romantic gesture, but a friendly, protective one. There have been times in my life when I might shrug off such a gesture, might have felt offended and asked him what he thought he was doing, might have felt I had to explain away his arm. But right now, it's purely a gesture of acceptance. Some kind of resolution. It's the one thing I don't have to worry about right now.

Instead we sit and listen to the sounds of traffic, people running for the subway stop, the guy selling incense on the corner. A siren off to my right in the distance. Somewhere behind all that noise, I pick out the slow roar of a small motorcycle. I listen to the low roar, to its dipping left and right to avoid pedestrians who know these streets are theirs and are determined to prove it. The Moped's hum seems to circle the park, and I can just picture Roy riding round and round us, as if trying to set some kind of spell. I wonder if he has given up on his guiding spirits, or if he feels we've led him to the place where we're all supposed to be. The bike picks up speed, and I can't help but find its zooming buzz a little bit hopeful.

Chapter 17

While You Were Out

It's Chop Your Own night here in my living room. Sometimes, when Maria and I get together for dinner, and we're too lazy to cook or hunt down a cheap restaurant, we grab some large vegetables and a knife. Tonight, we've got broccoli, cauliflower, somebody's prize-winning carrot, and a bowl of dressing, all splayed out on my chopping board on top of the coffee table. It's chop as you eat. We have magazines around us that we've been paging through without paying them too much attention, since they're not fashion magazines. Women's fashion magazines are the best for sharing—there's so much pointing and laughing at you can do. I sometimes think how sad it is to sit home alone with a *Vogue*, with no one to share your laughter.

"*Harper's* has something about pie," Maria says. The mention of pie, one of our favorite treats, gets my attention. "It says the smell of pumpkin pie arouses men the most, forty percent," Maria says.

"Is that forty percent more than usual, or forty percent more than blackberry pie, or forty percent more than *Playboy*?" I have a problem with statistics.

"It's unclear, you have to admit," Maria says. "But it beats the smell of roasting meat by five percent, if you combine the pie with lavender."

"Why would you do that?"

"Not to mention how," Maria says. "Still, it's the only pie on the list."

"*New York* magazine says that fifty percent of us between twenty-five and forty-nine stay up past midnight."

"I must be a statistical error," Maria says.

"I often feel that way," I say. "It also says we worry about finding a bigger apartment and AIDS, but I'm not sure in which order." We both toss our magazines into a pile and get started with the evening's real entertainment, discussing our problems, which I notice isn't listed at all as the usual night's activity in the *New York* magazine poll. Clearly an oversight.

"My problems first," I say grabbing the knife. We find the chopping part of our meal therapeutic.

"Good," Maria says. "We'll build up to mine."

"Okay," I start. "I'm about to lose my job."

"Maybe," Maria adds.

"Probably."

"You could think of it as a life experience," she says.

"I'm not up for a life experience right now. I'm more in the mood for moo shoo chicken."

"You just need to eat more broccoli," Maria says, handing me a piece.

"You're just belittling my problems."

"Nonsense. I'm adding to your supply of vitamin C so you'll be a strong enough woman to handle them."

"Oh. Thank you."

"Have a carrot."

"I'll have to find a new job, and times are hard. There's a recession now, or a post-recession, or maybe we're on the brink of one. I get confused watching the news."

"That's because ABC said we're in a recession, but CBS

insists it's over. None of them seems to realize CNN is in charge. Have you checked the classifieds?" Maria asks.

"Yes."

"And?"

"There are some editorial jobs. But all new people work there."

"It's true. So you were hoping to die at this job?"

"Well, something like that, although not right away. I guess I can imagine all of the production editors growing old together, all of us listening to our headsets tuned to the oldies stations, editing books on gray hair, hip replacements, arthritis, that sort of thing."

"It's nice to dream," Maria says.

I chop some pieces of carrot and chew on one awhile. "You know, carrots seem more like a lunchtime food. We shouldn't have to eat them for dinner. Things are bad enough."

"I didn't know you felt that way." Maria takes what's left of the huge carrot and puts it on her side of the table. "Let's do my problems now."

"But I didn't get to talk about the toe cramps I've been having."

"Your shoes are too small," Maria says.

"But it's still a problem."

"It is, it's true."

"Okay," I say. "Your turn."

"It's Henry," Maria says.

"No! Nothing can go wrong with you and Henry. They're passing a law that forbids it."

"Please," Maria says, "I'm not very good with authority."

"Okay, go on then."

Maria takes a deep breath and starts pulling the flowerets off part of the cauliflower and arranging them on her plate. No two flowerets are exactly the same, I notice. This still doesn't make them particularly appetizing, though.

"We started fighting. I don't even know what about."

"Dirty and/or missing socks?" I suggest.

"Something on that level of significance," Maria says. "It's always something like that, your schedules or your laundry, something you promised on the phone and forgot about entirely because it meant nothing to you at the time, something small. But it's always an indication of something larger, an imbalance in the relationship. Something potentially unresolvable. Even if it's just one sock."

I nod. Maria considers one of her flowerets, then beheads it.

"Then Henry had to leave, to go to work," she continues. "So I was left all alone. Fine. Okay. I started to think about life without him. I mean, I wasn't looking for anyone when Henry came along. I wasn't advertising in the personals when I met Henry."

I make one of those clearing-your-throat noises that always mean you're not really clearing your throat.

"I didn't say I hadn't advertised in the personals, just that I wasn't doing it right then."

"Okay."

"So I started to think what I'd do at night, what I'd eat for dinner. How I'd get organized. And that night, I felt readjusted to Henry not being around, to it all being over, you know?"

"All over?" I repeat like a little, unhappy child.

"Yeah," Maria says. "It seemed like it wouldn't be a big deal. That it was simply a matter of moving on."

We look at each other. Maria begins shredding some broccoli, and hands me a stalk to shred. None of this food has any smell to it at all, I notice. We might as well be eating sponges. Still, Maria concentrates on her shredding. I want to ask her what happens next with her and Henry, but I can see by how intently she's dismantling her vegetables that she's thinking it through. I know how that goes. I wait, arranging broccoli stalks from smallest to largest.

"The thing is," Maria says, "when Henry came over after his shift? I knew it was all baloney. I knew when I looked at his hands that I didn't want him to leave again. Hands amaze me that way. I didn't want to start over. I can't believe this has happened to me."

"Of all people," I say.

"It's a threatening feeling, caring about someone's hands."

"Not to mention the rest of him."

Maria scoops up all of her shredded food and dumps it back onto the board. I have the feeling we'll need to go out for dessert.

"I've always been so independent," Maria says. "It's always been my first priority. That's what I told Henry. He says we can work around it."

"Wait a minute, this is your bad news? This is your problem? That you've discovered you're actually in love with Henry?"

"Yeah," Maria says. "Don't tell anyone."

"My problems are much bigger," I say.

"Size isn't everything."

"You know, according to the magazine, we're supposed to be sitting here worrying about getting bigger apartments and AIDS."

"We worry about those things on the weekends," Maria says.

"I guess we should be worrying about where to buy pumpkin pies this time of year," I say.

"You have to make them with the canned stuff," Maria says.

"Oh." I wouldn't have thought of that. "Love is so complicated these days."

"It might be worse than I think," Maria says. "It might

be true love. Is this a concept that still exists? Or is it completely meaningless and outdated?"

"I think it's fairly meaningless and outdated," I say, "but I like the sound of it anyway."

"True love," Maria says. "Tell me that's not the biggest problem of all."

We consider this for a while. I see Maria's point, but I'm not at all convinced that she's right.

At lunch the next day, Nina and I take a walk around the Village. We've decided we need to get more exercise so we don't get what's known in our trade as "editor's butt." The words "editor's butt" sound funny coming out of Nina's mouth. She's the type of woman who laughs when she says "butt," the type who makes you laugh when she says it. We admire shops and storefronts we've been working near for ages, knowing that if we move into the new office, or worse, get redirected in our career paths, we won't see these familiar spots anymore. We become more and more attached, with each block we cover, to the fabrics in windows, the faded awnings, the smell of greasy falafel. Other neighborhoods might have similar sights and smells, but they'll still never be the same.

When I return to my desk, I find someone has left me one of those pink While You Were Out slips. It says "Call your dad," with a local number. I turn the message slip over, as if expecting it to say on the back "Just kidding." It doesn't.

Talking to my father on the phone is always a brief experience. Although he sounds happy enough to hear me, we talk just long enough to decide when and where to meet, almost as if there were something clandestine to the arrangement, or as if I'd just caught him coming out of the shower, and he's dripping onto the good rug. It's generally one of those single-syllabic things:

"Hi, Dad, how are you?"

"Good! You?"

"Fine. Thanks. So, are you in town?"

"Sure am."

I find the apartment where my father's staying in a red-brick apartment house on a sunny street on the Upper East Side—the only street where I've actually noticed sunlight easing its way into apartment windows, a slowly fading light before sundown. The other streets all seem to be covered in a gray haze. My dad gives me a quick hug at the front door.

"Holly, Holly," he greets me in his way. He doesn't seem to have changed much since my visit to Houston, at the home he shares with Sophie. Dad's wearing a blue-green shirt that's the kind of color that makes you wonder whether it was once blue or green, but got washed with the other by accident. He's also got a pair of Levi's Dockers pants—I've seen advertisements for them but have never seen them in person. They look a lot like the kind of pants Dad has always worn, but, like so many brands, they have a little label in back for identification. I don't remember Dad wearing labels before.

He invites me in to this oddly cozy apartment, done in shades of red mixed with shades of beige. I hadn't realized there was more than one shade of beige before. The place has a warm feel to it, partially from the sun that comes in the front windows and despite a wall full of masks of different sizes and facial expressions, some a little too judgmental for my taste. A dark brown mask grimaces as if it's just tasted something sour, or as if it disapproves of your hairstyle. A gray mask sticks its tongue out and crosses its eyes. I also notice that in every corner of the living room sits a new-fangled exercise machine, so the apartment looks like a Sharper Image store combined with a crafts museum. Somehow, the combination works.

"Don't the masks make you a little nervous?" I ask my father.

"Oh, maybe at first," he answers, bringing me a glass of something sparkly. "Now they seem like pals."

"You've been here that long?"

"I'm just settling in the last couple days," Dad says. "Some old friends sublet the place to me. They're traveling, seeing the world. Probably picking up more masks."

My father and I sit in red armchairs, watching the sun's imprint on the carpet. "Dad, does this mean you've left Houston?" And Sophie, I want to ask, but feel like this crosses some father-daughter boundary I haven't figured out yet. My father sips from his sparkly drink, so I taste mine. It's not mineral water, and it's not lemon-limey like a regular soda. I'd ask what it is, but I've got bigger questions right now.

"I'm thinking I'd like to settle back here, Holly. What would you think of that?"

"I'm surprised. Where's Sophie?" Asking this feels a little like sticking my foot into the really cold part of a river.

"Houston was great," Dad says, "and Sophie," he stops here, maybe trying to figure out what part of the river he wants to jump into. How does a father talk to his daughter about his girlfriend anyway? Such things are new to me.

"Sophie had us very comfortable. She's a sweet person. I don't know that you two hit it off, or that you even could have, given the circumstances."

"You seemed happy," I say, then change it to "comfortable."

"I did talk to her about moving here. I think she came to check it out, but I also think she agreed it wouldn't be that good of an idea. I'd have tried if she wanted, I didn't just abandon her," Dad says, and I wonder if he's referring just to Sophie or also to his history with my mother.

My father laughs at a thought. "The domesticated cowboy," he says. "That was me in Houston. I read that in a book, the domesticated cowboy. I'm not sure I liked that role. Of course, I may just miss it."

"So you've come back, to stay?"

"I think so. I've contacted some old friends about some consulting I might do. They're involved in some youth projects, need some help with the engineering end of things. Sounds worthwhile. And of course, there's you girls."

My dad cuts off here for a moment, then adds, "Not that I expect any special treatment. But just so you know I'm around."

I feel tears starting to tickle my eyes, but I don't want to free them, because I want to talk. Or at least listen.

"I'm glad you're back," I say. We smile at each other and sip the unknown soda. "And not just because I've always wanted to try one of those skiing machines," I say, pointing to a shiny piece of exercise equipment behind the sofa.

"That contraption is not for the faint-hearted," Dad says. My father and I are most comfortable when joking, I realize. I used to think this a problem, but now it feels like a treat, a gift that's been wrapped in thick golden paper.

"You'll miss all your ducks," I say, thinking of Dad's old decoy-lined study.

"Ducks, masks, everyone's got something, it seems." He points to the wall at a face with ducklike lips. I can't imagine where it's from, or whether it's held as an example of great beauty or ugliness.

"Should I mention to Mom that you're back?"

"Oh, Allison knows."

"You've talked to her?"

"Allison and I talk. We've talked over the years I've been away. Not much at first, but more so lately."

This is also news to me.

"We talk about you girls, how you're doing."

"Wow," I say. It's all I can think.

"How are you doing?" Dad asks. "Firsthand."

"I'm okay," I say. "Everything seems to be in flux at the moment, though."

"Disconcerting, change." Dad nods. "But not always such a bad thing."

"I'm starting to agree," I say. "Since I don't have much choice."

"Then there's Janie," Dad says. "She tries to be so tough, especially about me. Not that she doesn't have reason."

"I think she may be glad you're back, too, though."

"In her way. I hope she'll be."

I look up to the wall of faces as I listen to my drink continually effervesce. On the left side of the wall, a fat cherub face laughs hysterically, its round cheeks reddened, as if someone has just pinched it. I laugh just looking at it, then point it out to my dad, who laughs with me. I wish I could carry that fat cherub face with me everywhere.

That night, I dream that Maria and I rearrange the broccoli and cauliflower heads I seem to have lined up on my living room wall as decorations. They're shiny and shellacked, hanging in an abstract pattern here and there above the couch. The vegetables seem to change during the dream like little Mr. Potato Heads, taking on the faces of people I know. My boss, Monique, forms out of a smirking broccoli face. A perky cabbage turns into a shy Nina. Tom pops out of a surprised-looking carrot. I can't recognize the other faces but feel certain I know them—they may be people I work with, or people I see on the street every day. The woman who rushes out of the newsstand with her glove in her mouth, the man at the salad bar who puts out the fresh croutons without dumping any on the floor. One of the vegetables has a laughing face, but I don't know whose. Maria and I give it the place of honor in the center of the wall, and nod our heads at it in approval.

"I knew it," Maria says, and before I can ask her, the dream mistily changes into something else.

Chapter 18

Janie's Dream Wedding

I was hoping for a black silk dress, a dress that would know to drape itself around me and make me either more curvy or less curvy, somehow curvy in the right areas. A dress I'd be able to wear to any special occasion, not that I've ever had an occasion for such a dress, or even for such curves. But no, Janie believes wearing black at weddings brings bad luck. She thinks these trendy black-and-white weddings you hear about are just one more reason for the increasing divorce rate. I consider telling her that no one at my wedding wore black, and I still ended up divorced, but I'm afraid this might prove some other theory of hers I'm not up to hearing right now.

My dress, then, is a deep blue—as dark a blue as you can get before dropping off the color charts into black. Wearing this satisfying, rich color makes me feel like I've just taken a couple bites of the best blueberry cheesecake imaginable. I feel sated.

This is Janie's dream wedding, the one she's planned continually in her twenty-six years. She knows this wedding, after seven engagements. It seems to me that someone from *Brides* magazine ought to be covering it, writing an article titled "Longest Subscriber Takes the Plunge." I wonder if Janie will keep her subscription running just as a tradition, or maybe out of habit.

I'm sitting in the Bridesmaids' Room, allowing Janie's bridesmaid friends, Renée and Beverly, to have their way with me and about a pound of blusher. Janie directs them to my cheekbones, then disappears. She seems less nervous than I am, or maybe she just hides it well. Maria stands off to my side, brush in hand for last-minute hair fixes, and just for support. Maria's own dress, in a majestic maroon color you might imagine on a throne, has a cross between ruffles and layers. I would look and feel about twelve years old in ruffled layers. Maria just looks elegant.

"Are you the maid of honor or the matron of honor?" Maria asks me. "I'm never sure of these things."

"I think it's matron," I say, trying not to sneeze at the blusher powder. It's heavily scented, probably expensive, in a fancy black case it took me a while to open. I always buy the unscented hypoallergenic makeup, although most often I can't be bothered to use it.

"But she's divorced," Beverly says about me. "Doesn't matron mean married?"

"Maid sounds bad, though," Maria says. "Can you be an Old Maid of Honor? Would that really be honorable?"

"I thought there were no more old maids anymore, except in that children's card game," I say.

"It's probably been renamed something more socially correct," Maria says. "Like instead of 'Old Maid,' you say 'Executive Vice President.' "

"Still, 'matron' implies 'matronly,' " I say.

" 'Bosomy,' as my grandma used to say."

"Bosomy, please," I say. "I've seen sumo wrestlers with bigger breasts than mine."

"But theirs sag," Maria says.

"True. Still, I don't think you can go back to being a

maid when you've been a matron, even for honorary titles,"
I say. "Besides, I'm over thirty."

"Over thirty you get to choose," Maria says, brushing my
hair, trying to get the ends to go under right.

"I choose to wear less blusher," I say, grabbing a tissue
and wiping some off. Beverly and Renée make groaning
sounds at their pointless efforts.

"Makeup," Maria says. "It's fun to play with when you're
a kid, but the charm wears off when you're older and have
to pay for it yourself."

I see Beverly coming at me with a container of blue eye
shadow, but I have to draw the line somewhere.

"Blue eye shadow went out with Barbie dolls," I insist.

"Barbies are a valuable collectors item," Maria says.

"I gave all of mine shag haircuts," I say. "I think I imagined it might still grow back. I had a little trouble with the
reality thing."

"The reality thing is pretty troubling, especially when it
comes to Barbies," Maria agrees, "especially if you had the
ones where the legs didn't bend."

"Mine used to bend, but their legs made cracking noises
in the joints. Barbie goes arthritic."

"If they'd only make them more practical. Prematurely
gray Barbie. Cold sore Barbie. PMS Barbie, with optional
accessorized bottles of vitamin B and Motrin."

"Some things you just can't learn from a doll," I say.

"It's true," Maria says with a nod, finishing off my hair.
"But everything you *did* learn from a Barbie, you can un-
learn through self-help books."

"Not to mention life," I say.

I stand up and look at my midnight blue–dressed self.

"Barbie's big sister grows up," Maria says.

I crack a knuckle for her, to get the full effect.

*   *   *

There's a moment when I find myself alone with Janie and about fifteen different shades of pink roses. Janie inspects each one, looking closely, as if she were nearsighted, which I don't think she is. Maybe she's looking for bugs.

She's got a kimono-type robe over her wedding dress—tufts of white silky fabric stick out here and there. I find I want to tell her something, some prewedding, big-sister secret, but I can't think what. It can't be about sex—she's got all the manuals, some of them illustrated. Can I talk to her about commitment? I'm not sure I know that much about it, and I suspect Janie would agree.

"The flowers look nice," I say, stumped.

Janie makes a sighing sound, a doubt-filled one, I think. Now is my chance to come to her aid, honorable matron that I am.

"What's up? Are you having second thoughts, cold feet? Concerns? Questions?"

"Oh, Holly, you worry too much. I'm just trying to slow it all down. I want to remember everything."

"Just take lots of wedding pictures," I say. I saw about six people with video cameras milling around outside. I'm pretty sure I ducked at least four of them.

"You know," Janie says, "I wanted this all to be exactly right. 'My Wedding.' Yesterday Bucky suggested we just run away, and I almost went for it."

"But I thought this was what you wanted. Big." I gesture.

"Yes," says Janie with a returned confidence. She sniffs at a rose in somebody's bouquet, maybe mine. "It's all going my way. Everybody's doing the things I tell them to. Look at you, you've even got all this makeup on." Janie takes out a tissue and wipes off a little more of my blusher. I can't tell her how much I appreciate this.

"Only for you," I say.

Janie smiles. "It's a little odd, you know, everybody being so agreeable, bringing me juice all morning."

"You're the boss today."

"Not entirely a bad feeling," Janie says.

"So you asked Dad to walk you down the aisle," I say. "I was surprised, even though he came back." Janie and I haven't gotten a chance to discuss Dad's reemergence. I know that she's been mad at him for a long time, not just for the divorce, but for the way he left. Janie can hold a grudge.

Janie makes another deep sigh. "The thing you have to remember about Dad," she starts, "is that he isn't perfect. Dad makes so many mistakes. So you can't put him on a pedestal. It's like, he's Man, not Art."

"Pithy," I say, impressed.

"I've started on the champagne," Janie admits.

"Do you think Dad will stay?"

Janie hesitates. "I don't know."

We take a few deep breaths, inhaling the prewedding scent of roses.

"I've been thinking," Janie says, refreshed. "There are twenty-two uninjured hockey players out there. Lots of them single. A good selection, do you know what I mean?"

"Oh, no, please, I don't think I want to pick up anyone at your wedding."

"I don't see why not. It's an exclusive guest list."

"Still," I say.

"It's not something you have to plan," Janie says. "It's a perk that comes with your position. The matron of honor can take certain liberties, with dance partners, you know?"

I wonder why it is that my little sister, in her last-minute jitters, ends up trying to reassure me. But this seems to be her way, part of her process of being. And it's really okay with me.

"Some of them can really dance," Janie says. "And besides, blue is your color." I hadn't realized this, I think. Janie straightens my shoulders and hands me a heavy but tasteful bouquet. I secretly thrill to the idea of holding a bouquet, having such vibrant colors so close to me. It makes me wonder at the things we women carry for special occasions, what they mean, and I'd like to talk with Janie about this. But we've run out of time.

My father walks Janie down the aisle, smiling in a blue suit, which doesn't quite fit him right around the middle, although I can't tell if it's really too small or too short. Then he sits down next to Maria and Henry in the front row as planned, not next to my mother, but within shouting distance. Not that there will be any shouting. My mother sits beside Ronny, nicely clad in his deep charcoal suit with a blue hankie that matches my mother's dress. I think it's cute that my mother and her boyfriend color-coordinate, although I do notice that Ronny's gray tie has bluish circles on it that are slightly fish shaped. Ronny's consistency must be reassuring for my mother, as Ronny seems to prize both fish and her, though hopefully not in that order.

As I stand to Janie's left during the ceremony, I'm struck by the language that booms out at Janie and Bucky, words of love and commitment that reach over our heads to the hockey team and the rest of the crowd. The serious words seem to bounce right off of my stomach with a burning sensation. Words of sharing, concern, words of challenge, continuation, collaboration. Words of love, the word love itself, private words pronounced clearly by a deep-voiced woman in long black robes. Janie's judge, it turns out, is a woman named Jocelyn Hand, which would be a funny name if the woman had any less of a no-nonsense voice. These words seem to require a softer voice, though, a whisper even. I look at the bridesmaids who stare straight ahead of them with giant smiles, unscathed by the words, and wonder if I'm making the whole speech up. Then I look to Janie, who has come undone, I think at first, tears flowing freely down her face and into a lace handkerchief with a big J on it. Of course, how could anyone stand up to such words being spoken in your direction?

But Janie does stand up to them—they aren't hurting her a bit, I realize, but seem to be adding to the essence of Janie, although I've yet to determine exactly what that is. She looks at me and smiles, still in control, or at least more or less in the state she wants to be. Her look tells me, A bride's allowed to cry, after all, so why not? I hear more of the judge's words of permanence, lifetime, fulfillment, eternity, words I'm not sure I believe in anymore, but that scare me anyway. Words Janie's looking right in the eye.

I glance back to the front row. Maria and Henry hold hands, their fingers interwoven and moving slightly. I can barely tell from here whose fingers are whose, but I can almost feel them touching.

Janie glides through the "I, Janie" speech smoothly, without a misstep, as if on ice skates. She's the kind of girl you see at the skating rink who goes round and round the ice and doesn't ever look cold. Or who looks good looking cold. I feel myself sitting off to the side, sipping hot chocolate by the snack bar and rubbing my hands together, admiring her graceful arcs and painless pivots. I want to know how she does it, whether it's an inborn talent or whether, with lots of practice, any of us can learn.

A reporter from *Puck!* magazine, a woman our age named Deidre, a name I've always had trouble saying, stands around talking to Maria and Henry. It seems Deidre and Maria have been to the same hairdresser downtown and have even left him for the same reason. Something to do with too much red.

Deidre's telling us about the world of sports magazines. "We compete with two other brand-new magazines now, *Hockey Today* and *Goaltenders Weekly*, but they didn't get invitations. I have an exclusive," she says proudly. *"Puck!* covers the human interest."

"Goaltenders Weekly goes in more for the blood and gut shots," Henry says, and Deidre nods.

"They like the close-ups," Maria says, surprising me with her knowledge of hockey magazines. I've never seen one. Maybe it's a potential new career avenue for me, sports weeklies. Especially if the photos show things like torn ligaments and laser surgeries, things a science book editor has lots of experience with.

Hockey players take to the dance floor, one of them tangoing with a toddler girl he holds sideways, not unlike a hockey stick. Deidre takes notes. I watch my mother and Ronny moving slowly back and forth in a romantic rocking all their own, and I sense that they could take over the dance floor if they wanted to show off. But they don't. Janie and Bucky dance while talking constantly and excitedly, but in a hush the rest of us aren't invited into. As Maria and Henry abandon me for their own close moment, my father comes up to me and asks me to dance. We are less practiced than the others, which hurts me. Somehow, I think, it should be an old-time feeling, something remembered that you fall into easily, dancing with your dad. Which doesn't mean I'm not happy to.

"It looks like she's finally gone through with it," I tell him.

"I'm just thrilled to be here," Dad says. "You girls, the both of you," my dad says a little cryptically, then stops in what seems midsentence. But I know what he means. We watch the crowd move slowly around, each pair making a little circle around themselves, the tangoer with the sideways kid cutting through the middle, a small chamber orchestra playing what I think is a song from a recent Disney movie.

My father and I smile at one another and at the pairs

floating by us. At the end of the Disney tune, the band takes up a classical rendition of a Bette Midler piece. It's not really my taste—I haven't heard any rock oldies yet—but still a hockey player approaches and asks me to dance. He introduces himself as Beau, and I agree to dance with him even though he has a huge gash across his left eyebrow and hands so large they look like he's wearing baseball gloves. Maybe I dance with him because of these things.

We finally assemble for the cake cutting, watching as Janie and Bucky lift wedding cake gently from face to face. Deidre takes a picture of it for *Puck!* Then all the hockey players—or hockey boys, as Maria likes to call them—present Janie with her own jersey and number. Janie slides the red-and-blue shirt over her dress for another picture, giving her an athletic yet still bridal look. I can hear in the back of my mind *Brides* magazine making her a Fashion Don't, if they do such things, and yet on Janie, it looks just fine. Still I'm surprised by her trying on the shirt, and not just because she did it without mussing her hair.

"You have to admit," Maria says, "it's a whole new look for evening."

The players then hand Janie her very own hockey stick, which they say is to keep Bucky in line. Janie holds it up proudly, and we all applaud.

Back in the Bride's Room, my mother and I hoard second pieces of cake while Janie changes into an ivory suit. It's not lost on me that you could write a book about the three of us, our experiences of marriage, pre- and post-. My mom, who's been enjoying her role today—she's danced with no fewer than ten hockey boys—says she supposes some advice is in order. Janie listens attentively.

"My best advice is that I don't much have any. I absolve myself of all meddling."

"Oh, sure," I say.

"Really," my mom says, "there's nothing I could say that hasn't already been written in a best-selling pop-psychology book. Even though they're all wrong, especially the ones that put all the blame on the mother."

"Oh, those," Janie says, pinning a small bouquet to her waist. Janie grabs her hockey stick and her larger bridal bouquet.

"All any bride really needs," my mother says, admiring the two.

Janie starts to hand me the bridal bouquet—that meaningful object to single women everywhere—but I shake my head no in a somewhat violent manner that gives me a pain over my right ear. It goes away instantly.

"Don't make me throw this at you," Janie warns me, so I take it and inhale deeply.

"I hope everyone in this room will be very happy," my mother says.

"Of course we will," Janie says with her usual authority, and for now I feel she must be correct. She leads us out of the room, holding her hockey stick in a drum major style. We do not hesitate to follow.

Chapter 19

The Body in Motion

It may be thoughts of Janie that make me keep hearing marching music, the kind of trumpet-led sounds you hear at a football game or parade, with heavy downbeats punctuated by crashing cymbals. Even at times when I'm not thinking of anything special, I find the music floating through my mind, and I find my thumb beating against my desk with the bass drum. The music's propelling me, I sometimes think, as if I'm marching down Main Street, not exactly following the rest of the band, but interested in the forward movement just the same. It's a little distracting, these imagined sounds, but at least I haven't started humming yet.

It's perhaps with all this in mind that I find myself climbing the stairs at our offices at Science Press headed for the oblivion we call the sixth floor. There sit those with actual—and no doubt some extra imagined—power, those who control our future. The hallway looks surprisingly just like our own one floor down. Most of us production editor types don't much venture up here, except to use the restroom occasionally or to sneak extra paper cups when we run out, although I admit we tend to do this at the end of the day when the higher-ups are gone. I slip past one office and hear a stream of classical music played low—it seems they don't bother to wear headsets up here, although I do notice they keep their doors nearly shut. The Chopin has to creep through the crack under the door.

Behind the half-opened door I'm most interested in sits a man at his desk, a man somewhere in his forties, I'd guess, although I'm not that good at guessing. The sides of his curly hair are gray. He's a handsome man hiding behind candy-apple red glasses, although I'm not sure hiding is the right word for it, considering how bright and delicious looking the red is. I'm not sure if I've ever really seen him before, although I know his name from the plaque on the door. It's Patrick McCorkle, and I believe his title is Senior VP, Books, or maybe Books, Senior VP. I know there's a comma in there somewhere.

He's staring at his computer screen with a serene expression I don't think I've seen on anyone in this building. Not that I haven't enjoyed my work, but whatever it is he's feeling, it's a state of being or two above. I knock but he doesn't hear me, so I approach and watch. I like to think he's looking at one of our newly acquired books, a book so exquisite it will put beatific expressions on the faces of all who see it, a book I myself will get to work on, if I get to continue working here. It's possible, of course, that he's just playing computer games, but I try to erase this thought as soon as possible.

I move my feet around in a sort of fake tap dance shuffle, just for the noise really, and Patrick looks upon me with his religious kind of expression in tact.

"Hello, Holly Philips," he says, and I feel stunned, as if I've just bumped into a highly ranking public official and he knew my name, or maybe something even more personal, like my weight.

"Mr. McCorkle, hello," I say, then run on, encouraged a little by his half-smile. "I came up here to see about the new move, the, well, the new company." It suddenly pretty much occurs to me that I don't have a plan, but I still hear a cymbal crashing in my ears, not to mention something coming from my stomach that sounds a little like a tuba.

Patrick McCorkle nods. "I understand. You all must be wondering. Perfectly natural, of course."

"Of course," I say. "Plus, I just wanted to say how happy I've been in my position—"

"Production editor, yes," Patrick says, his mind seeming to veer off into a space I can't quite follow. Then he comes back. "You work under Monique. We were production editors together."

"Really?"

"Oh, years ago. That was quite a time." He goes back to looking at the screen, then touches a key with what seems to me like true fondness. I'm not sure I can picture him working closely with Monique, but then again, I can imagine her tormenting him mercilessly. Perhaps that's added to his sense of calm. Maybe it's really relief.

"You and Monique get along well, I've heard," he says.

"Sure," I say, although I think afterward that it doesn't sound very professional.

"Your work's been quite good," he says, "generally speaking."

Despite his little smile, the words "generally speaking" alarm me, as I don't think they're usually indicative of good things to come. But the words also seem to give me a certain push, as if someone had slipped behind me and aimed a blow-dryer's worth of air at my back, which is actually something Monique has done to me in the ladies' room more than once.

"If you mean the memo—" I say, thinking about that memo Sondra the proofreading head sent around about me, the one that said I didn't respect my elders, or whatever. I can't exactly remember her wording.

"Memo?" he asks, clasping his hands together on his desk.

"From Sondra, about the meeting I had with her, about new proofreading-editor rules. You know, the rules that get changed needlessly from year to year?"

He looks at me as if not quite understanding, or maybe he's just pretending not to, I can't be sure. He rests one hand against his computer and rubs his finger against it. I feel fairly certain I'd be really curious to see what's on the screen if I weren't starting to sweat so heavily.

"You know, Sondra?" I seem to say again, emphasizing the name. He nods slowly, and the smile hasn't much left his face, which worries me a little. He could be a friend of hers, for all I know. Perhaps he's been drugged by her lavender perfume. You just can't know these things the first time you walk into someone's office.

"Memos," he says. "We get so many, of course." He rises and walks over to a very impressive file cabinet that might be mahogany, although I'm not certain. It's definitely not one of the gray metal ones we use downstairs. He stops before it and puts his hands against it as if taking its temperature, or perhaps reading its contents psychically. I notice bits of the Chopin reaching us from the other office, the tempting sounds of lightly touched piano keys.

Patrick pulls out a set of files. I catch a glimpse of my name on the top file as he sets the rest of the bunch face down on the desk. He shuffles through my file, starting from the back, I notice.

"Hmm," he says, then peeks at me.

"I'd like to continue on here, or at the new office, I mean," I say. "If you ask anyone, well, anyone else, they'll tell you how responsible I've been for the last nine years. The memo is—" I'm at a loss for a second. "I'd like to defend myself against that. The memo is just wrong," I say, taking one step forward firmly.

Patrick smiles again. "I'm not certain I see that particular memo," he says.

"Oh," I say, surprised. "Well, that's good, I guess." I think I feel my thumbs throbbing, but maybe this is a good thing. Maybe it means blood is flowing back into my hands again. I can't be sure.

"Of course," he says again, "we're always happy to see our production editors up here. I'm glad you came by to visit."

"Thanks, it's been nice," I say, and start to back out of the room.

Patrick gives a slow little wave, the kind where you move your hand back and forth without wiggling your fingers, the kind beauty queens and politicians seem so good at. Then I see him turn on a machine and place a sheet of paper into it. The paper comes out in evenly cut shreds. He picks up the next file, takes out another sheet, smiles in my direction, and keeps shredding.

I leave the sixth floor and descend back to the fifth, with its earthy smell of burnt coffee coming from the kitchen, its crash of mail carts against the file cabinets (those guys never quite make the turns), and the sound of two production editors tugging at the window that always gets stuck, then the deep screech of the window frame freed from its sill.

A few weeks later, I'm sitting in my new cubicle at Whatsit Press, a slightly plusher version of my old office. My still-modular walls are lined with a cool blue fabric that's soft and thick—I've found myself rubbing it more than once. My milking stools line one of my walls, but I also have a visitor's chair, in bright, welcoming yellow. Rather than losing my job at Science Press, as I'd feared, I've been promoted to co-supervisor of the production editing team, a post I share with my former boss, Monique. I hope that my visit to Patrick McCorkle played some role in all this. I mentioned it to Monique later that day, but all she said was, "Ah, Patrick," in her cryptic way, then she raised both eyebrows and sighed deeply. It could be that they had some sort of inter-office romance, or it could be that she locked him in the freight elevator overnight. Either way, I'm not sure what it has to do with my new position, although I know which of the two scenarios I like to think happened.

We've smoothed our way into a rhythm of production editing around here that suits us. Many of my coworkers in production and art have made the big jump twenty blocks uptown from our old Village office, and several newcomers have joined us. A few of us still wonder if Whatsit Press is a respectable name for a company, but we keep this to ourselves.

Nina and Tom and some of the others still report to Monique, but she has a few new young production editors who're just getting used to her.

"I like them young," Monique says. "Frightened. Trembling. If they're bad, I'm going to make them sit in the corner on one of your stools."

I have a newer squad myself, nine new production editors I can call my very own. My job is to help them learn the production steps, watch over each project. I still get to work on books myself, too.

"You get first pick, now," Monique has told me.

"I'll have to try to be fair," I told her, "and not give myself all the best books."

"You still have so much to learn," Monique said, shaking her head and spinning my yellow chair before she left. Her own cubicle is lined in a deep green, not a yucky green, but the kind that inspires respect. On a small corner of her wall, she's begun a collage of photos that looks like a work of abstract art from far away, but as you approach, you realize they're internal snapshots of the unhealthiest kind. You realize you don't want to get too close, which I think is Monique's whole idea.

This managing of people is all new to me. Maria's boyfriend, Henry, has also recently been promoted at the Transit Authority, so, as Maria puts it, "He's now in charge of other people in orange jumpsuits." The three of us get together often to discuss how to get along well with others, as my mother might put it. Or, how to get others to do what you want, as Janie might put it. Maria, junior pharmacist that she is, already works well with others, since she always considers her clients—those elderly women who bring Maria homemade cookies and homegrown spices—as her coworkers. She insists they take an equal role in their own health, if not a greater one.

"You have to work with them," she says of her devoted clientele, "make them take an active role. You have to listen." Henry and I nod when Maria speaks. We listen, and prepare to listen more. Her advice makes sense to me, and it occurs to me that I'll be wearing my Walkman less and less in the office, but I'll be hearing more, in a way.

Our streamlined production room—we're still all on one large open floor, still all neighbors—has a homey feel, with its arched windows (one of them right in front of my desk). Gone are some of our old sources of entertainment, though. Carl, our chief gossipmonger and keeper of the grapevine, left for a competing publishing house. It seems Carl—and we were all just shocked to hear this—was sleeping with Sondra, that purple wonder, head of the proofreaders and the woman who wrote the poisonous memo about me. Sondra, finally, was asked to move on in an after-hours session none of us was in on. Rumor has it she ripped some of the purple fabric from her walls. The proofreaders celebrated for weeks when they found out, and can still be heard cheering every now and then. Just reminding themselves how happy they are.

But still, Carl and Sondra? Even putting aside the difference in age and Carl's unexplainable way with women, it seems odd.

"Disgusting," Monique says.

"Because she was so much older?" I ask.

"Because it was Carl. Some things are better left unimagined," Monique says, pinning a new photo to her wall collection.

"I wonder if she had all purple sheets," I say to Nina.

"She scared me," Nina says, "but maybe men feel differently."

"No," Tom says. "She scared me, too. I don't think it's gender-related. More of an all-encompassing creepiness."

"You'd think," Monique says, "given the relationship, at least Carl would have gotten more of his rumors right."

"He must have been sneaking a look at outdated memos," Tom says.

But Carl and Sondra have gone, as has our vice-president of production, Cheryl, a personal hero of mine. Whatsit Press cut a whole layer of vice-presidential management, including some VP's I'd never met, but it hurt to see Cheryl go. Still, her leave-taking was a classic. On her last day, she stepped over to the old production room's stairway and sang "So Long, Farewell, Auf Wiedersehen, Good-bye" from *The Sound of Music.* Several of the production editors helped her do all the hand movements. We gave her a standing ovation, and not only because she hit the high notes at the end.

The new management encourages us to take full advantage of our lunch hours, which is a lucky thing right now. We're in the midst of a lunchtime party, courtesy of our favorite rock station. It seems Nina won one of the call-in contests for "lunch for thirty or so of your colleagues," and the station has catered an enormous buffet for us. A DJ out on location haunts a corner of the room, chatting with some of our more aggressive, or at least friendly, editors. Monique's not one of them.

We stand by the food table, which stretches an entire wall's length—a real wall, not a modular one. We've got equal-opportunity food here, food from all over the world (although most of it comes from our old haunt, The Jelly Deli). Bagels and cream cheese, dim sum, noodles, pizza, little meatballs, falafel, you name it. No one need feel left out.

"We'll all be sick," Monique says behind me, as rock oldies play in the room, the phrase "People are strange" echoing around us.

"Management insists you at least have a bagel," I say.

"No one told me I'd have to go to parties here," she says, still in her grudging, half-joking way I've grown to rely on.

"Check your employee handbook, chapter four," I say.

Monique examines the spread. "This looks like someone couldn't decide what to serve."

"Someone with a lot of cash," I say. "Besides, it's basic party food. If you were throwing a party, what would you serve?"

Monique raises an eyebrow. "Things not recommended by your employee handbook," she whispers. She takes a bagel and some lox.

"I'm going to frighten that DJ now," Monique says, armed with smoked fish.

The DJ, whom we all listen to daily and know as Ron Ronson—although we suspect it's an alias—is much cleaner cut than we'd been expecting from someone who plays so much old rock and roll. He has that habit of throwing his head way back when he laughs, then leaving it there a moment, which looks like it hurts a little.

"I think Monique's going to try to pick him up," Nina says.

"In her way," I say. I like the idea.

Nina has placed her "Rock N' Roll Never 4-Gets" T-shirt—part of her prize-winning package—over her clothes, since Ron Ronson insisted. She seems a little embarrassed by all the attention but has admitted to me that dim sum is her favorite treat. Nina uses the word "treat," then takes a little plate of dim sum over to her desk, where someone has put a large sign that says "You Are Already A Winner!" It's from the art department; I can just tell. No one appreciates free food quite like the art department.

Some of the editors start to dance in one open area of the room, beneath the streamers Jan found in her desk left over from someone's birthday party. The streamers have little bunnies all over them, but no one seems to mind. I see Tom ask Nina to dance, and I wonder if I shouldn't be seeing this, or if I should have some sort of reaction. I'm certainly not surprised. I've noticed a pretty origami swan that holds a place of honor on Nina's desk, and the thought of it makes me smile. No one's really said anything, but let's face it, a swan is a swan.

"What a pair," Monique says to me, looking at Tom and Nina. I didn't realize she was back.

"I think it's nice," I say. "I think it's perfectly nice."

"Ech, nice," Monique says, the way someone else might say Ech, lice. "It's nice like a Disney film."

"What'd you say to the DJ?"

"You don't want to know."

"Come on. Educate me."

"I think he's a little old to be playing records in a room with bunny streamers," Monique says.

"Maybe," I say.

"Then again, that may be what I like about him," she says.

I make an attempt at raising my eyebrows. I can't quite get the gesture down, but I'm learning.

"Why don't you ask Matt to dance?" Monique says.

"Since when do you arrange dances?"

"It's in my new job description."

"You're not my boss anymore, remember?"

"I'll always be your boss," she says, then points to Matt. I try to hide her hand so no one will see.

One of the new production editors on my team, Matt has been finishing up another book in the Tummy series for me. I was in on his hiring—my first hiring session—where we kind of hit it off, which I felt was important for a supervisor and her new hiree. I also felt he had one of those great casual ways about him, as if he'd known me all his life, but I didn't say this in the hiring review.

"If I ask him to dance," I tell Monique, "it's sexual harassment."

"You read too much."

"And, if he asks me to dance, that's sexual harassment, too." I've placed myself in an interesting, if sad, double bind.

Monique gestures toward Tom and Nina dancing away on our hardwood floors. "You'll notice, Disney characters don't feel such social-political pressures."

"It must be nice to be animated," I say.

Just then, Matt walks over.

"Remember, new guy in town. Be nice," Monique says to me, then turns to him and says, "You have egg roll on your shirt." It's true, he does, but it's only a small spot. Matt wipes at it with a thumb, then shrugs.

"Come dance," he says to me simply.

"I can't dance, I'm a supervisor now," I say.

"That just means you can't slow dance," Monique says.

"Or maybe that I never could," I say.

"It's a sixties party," Matt says. "Come on, you need to rebel."

"Oh." I look at the smiling Matt. "Okay, then."

Matt and I dance to three in a row by Creedence Clear-water, at a pace that seems not conducive to digestion, but such occasions come up so infrequently that they're worth a little tummy trouble, it seems to me. It's my first dance as a production supervisor, and I think it goes pretty well. I'm reminded of the junior high school auditorium, noontime dances on rainy days, impromptu sessions where the floor got all sticky and slippery from the rain, where the windows got all steamy, and where you never got to dance with the one you really wanted to dance with. Even with the bunny streamers, this is a vast improvement over those days, in every way.

"**S**ummer is the time for true confidence to overtake all of life's insecurities and direct the body in motion." Roy, our former messenger, greets me as I leave the office.

"Hi, Roy," I respond. "Would you care to simplify?"

"You have a bounce in your walk," Roy says.

This is news to me. I look behind me where I've just come out of the building, as if to see what I might have tripped over. "Thanks," I say.

Roy has come to meet Tom and Matt and some of the others, who all go to play basketball at some playground or other. Because they're all aware, sensitive men they've invited me to play, but I don't like asphalt, and not just because I'm a woman, I like to think.

"How's life, Roy?"

Roy's heading back to school after all, undoubtedly to confuse academic minds everywhere. He says he'll still drop by for "spiritual and emotional contact," and he seems to mean it, too.

"Life is one of the funny things. It's the unsolvable riddle, but it's that way for a reason."

"Should I know the reason?"

"You can only know it through understanding it, live it through living it. We're meant to wonder."

I wonder all the way home.

When I get home, the phone is ringing, so I have to drop my bag in the little hallway and jump for the phone. Answering machines have never much changed my behavior in such matters, I'm afraid. I guess I like the challenge of beating the machine to the phone, although I'm not usually such a competitive person.

"Hello, dear." It's my mother.

"Hi, Mom," I say, falling onto the couch and glancing at my beaten answering machine glowering in the corner with its angry red light.

"I'm just calling to remind you about Ronny's little expedition this weekend." Ronny has planned and planned, apparently, to get us all together for a fishing trip. I'm not much looking forward to the actual fish part, and I know Janie isn't, either.

"We've ordered you and your sister some of those clunky boots from L. L. Bean," Mom says. "Not very attractive, I'm afraid."

"That's okay," I say. "I'm hoping the fish won't be too judgmental." Maria and Henry are coming along, too, but it seems Maria already has a pair of clunky fishing shoes. This is something I hadn't realized about my best friend. Either she's borrowed them from one of her five brothers, or she has a secret life as a crab catcher. Either way, I feel the need to know.

"Well," my mother says, "nothing wrong with a little family bonding, as long as I don't have to hit any fish over the head."

"Or sing. We aren't going to sit around a fire and sing, are we Mom?"

"I'm afraid Ronny knows some fish songs," she says with a sigh. "Actually, some of them are pretty raunchy," she says enthusiastically. I have to admit my curiosity about this, about our extended family sitting around singing sexually explicit songs about fish. I can't really picture it, but it does have a peculiar allure to it. Then again, maybe I'm just tired.

"Well, you'd better go eat dinner, dear," my mother says. "Don't scrimp on the vegetables, not that I'm meddling, of course."

"Of course not."

"Just simple dietary advice you could get from anyone, any book even. Any book who cared about you, of course."

I throw together a large bowl of stir-fried veggies and bits of chicken, which tastes just fine but looks soggy and stringy. It's the kind of food you wouldn't really serve to guests.

I've bought some new fabric for drapes, since the ones I started months and months ago never quite got finished. I suppose I could have ripped out those crooked seams and washed and ironed the old fabric, but for some reason, I felt like starting fresh. Besides, I don't like ironing.

The new fabric reminds me of a perfect blue sky on an autumn day, the kind of day you only get two or three of each year. It's the kind of blue sky that drags you outside even if you have no clean clothes to wear, because you know you'll feel better once you're in the midst of it. It's the kind of blue that works every time.

I lug out the old Singer and get started, careful not to get any of my low-salt soy sauce dinner on the fabric. I sew listening to a special oldies show put together by Ron Ronson, who usually only does the daytime radio show. Tonight he's playing songs that start and end with the same word, so that if the first song ends with "Baby," the second song picks up that way, too. I wonder how long it took him to put this together, especially once he got past the "Baby" songs, and I wonder just what kind of person does this sort of thing anyway. Although I have to admit that I'm the kind of person who'd like a little project like this.

As we pass a long stretch of songs with the word "yeah," which I think is cheating somehow, because I'm not really sure "yeah" qualifies as a real word, I come to the end of my sewing, for this set of drapes at least. I hold up the two panels—all the seams are more or less straight, and the drapes aren't sewn to themselves or to anything I'm wearing. I run a wooden dowel through the top and see that the drapes fall into nice folds here and there—clearly, they know what I've had in mind, they know how to arrange themselves. They're just long enough, just wide enough. True, there's still the second window to get to, a window just to my left that waits patiently, a little nakedly, expectantly. But that seems like a minor thing right now. I like having this one set of drapes, seeing the other window yet to go, knowing that its turn will come, although not tonight, and probably not next week, but sometime, eventually. I'll get to it.

ABOUT THE AUTHOR

Linda Lenhoff has worked in publishing as a writer and editor for several years, having edited nearly everything from makeup techniques (apply blush up and over the "apples" of your cheeks) to migraine studies (cut back on that chocolate). In between this series of jobs, she earned an MFA in Creative Writing. Linda grew up in Los Angeles and has lived in New York, San Francisco, San Diego, and Switzerland. She now lives in California's Bay Area with her husband and magical little daughter. She is currently at work on her second novel, which explores the themes of best friends, mothers who pay your cable bills so you'll have something to talk about, and the appropriateness of looking for eligible men door-to-door.

For more about Linda and *Life à la Mode*, visit her website at http://www.informativity.com/linda-lenhoff.htm.